Hi Jasmine,
Hope You d
B

About the Author

B. J. Rowling, a native of England, is an author, screenwriter, producer and cousin of Harry Potter author J. K. Rowling.

D. G. Lloyd is an American-Australian author, screenwriter, producer, actor and script coverage analyst.

Hi Jasmine!
Thanks for stopping by!
Hope you enjoy the book
Keep on dreamin'!
BJ Row

The Misfit Tribe and the Secret of Mystery Island

B. J. Rowling and D. G. Lloyd

The Misfit Tribe and the Secret of Mystery Island

Olympia Publishers
London

www.olympiapublishers.com
OLYMPIA PAPERBACK EDITION

A CIP catalogue record for this title is
available from the British Library.

ISBN: 978-1-78830-218-0

This is a work of fiction.
Names, characters, places and incidents originate from the writers'
imaginations. Any resemblance to actual persons, living or dead, is purely
coincidental.

First Published in 2018

Olympia Publishers
60 Cannon Street
London
EC4N 6NP

Printed in Great Britain

Dedication

"We're all misfits in one way or another. Our lives are an adventurous unfolding story, just like the lives of the main characters in *The Misfit Tribe*. Characters who D. G. Lloyd and I are hoping readers are able to relate to in some form or fashion, and with a bit of luck, are also inspired by. So, with that said, take a break, sit back, open the book and prepare yourselves for a thrilling ride of mystical and magical misadventures." - B. J. Rowling

Chapter One

The helicopter's blades cut through the humid July night as it soared over the treetops of a quiet Michigan neighbourhood. When it neared its target, a digital voice stated, "Silent Mode engaged." The regular thump-thump-thump quieted to a bare whisper and the machine dipped below the treeline. It momentarily hovered at the Shelby Court Estates' gates, then slipped, unseen, over the wall.

Slightly smaller than the crows that *cawed* at it, the delicately crafted drone wove between the houses before stopping at a spacious two-storey colonial at the end of a cul-de-sac. In the glow of the streetlights, the house's coffee-brown exterior appeared almost black, the cream-coloured trim nearly white. A nice house in a nice neighbourhood, carefully conformed to match the others around it. The drone's controller wasn't interested in the house, however, but in its inhabitants. The helicopter carefully approached one of the second-storey windows and hovered next to it.

The drone's built-in video camera peered into the room, the open screened window allowing its external microphone to pick up the conversation going on inside.

***

"She's got boobs, Mom. Full grown, woman-sized boobs." Karli Franklin plopped down on the edge of her mother's bed. With her slim build and splash of freckles across her heart-shaped face, she looked much younger than her fifteen years and she hated it. She hated it almost as much as she hated her mop of red-orange hair, no matter how much her mother told her it was the colour of the sunset. She didn't want sunset hair and light grey eyes. She wanted the type of figure that made boys look at her as someone other than the bookworm artist with a penchant for making her own jewellery.

Beverly Franklin turned toward her daughter, a pastel pink tracksuit in hand. Karli hadn't gotten her red hair from her mother, a natural blonde.

"I like this one." Beverly held the outfit up against her body. "What do you think?" In her late thirties, she still looked more like Karli's older sister than a mother.

Karli shrugged. She didn't care about the stupid tracksuit. She crossed her arms over her chest.

Beverly tossed the tracksuit into the open suitcase on the bed next to Karli. "Not all boys are interested in boobs, Karli."

"Yeah, right." Karli scowled. "I haven't come across one yet that isn't."

A smile played around Beverly's cotton candy lips. "They do exist. Take your father, for instance. He's a self-proclaimed, bona fide ass man."

Karli groaned. "Gross, Mom. I didn't want to know that."

Beverly just grinned and threw a hot pink hoodie into the suitcase. With her perfectly coifed golden-yellow hair and expertly applied make-up, Karli had often thought that her mother looked like a Barbie doll come to life. The excessive amount of pink clothing she owned just supported that image.

Karli decided to change the subject before she suffered any more permanent scarring from her mother's lack of tact. "So, remind me again why we're going on this geo-thingamabob trip anyway."

"'Geo-cache'," Beverly said. "It's kinda like a treasure hunt."

"Ooh, a *treasure* hunt." Karli knew her voice dripped with sarcasm, but she didn't care. Wandering in the wilderness was not something she wanted to do... ever. "Would you tell Dad that I'm not six years old anymore?"

Beverly gave Karli a look that said she didn't entirely approve of Karli's tone. "It's a 'family building exercise.'" After a moment's hesitation, she added, "Your father thinks it'll be fun."

Even though Beverly tried to hide it, Karli sensed her mother's doubts. "We'll be picking burrs out of our clothes for the next year. That'll be *so much* fun."

"Karli, you know how competitive your father and his friends can be. It wasn't his idea to involve the families, but he couldn't say no."

Karli flopped onto her back and stared up at the ceiling. "Why don't you and your friends ever involve the families... in a weekend spa treatment?" That's the type of thing she needed to get her creative juices flowing, seeing as how she'd been struggling with the artist's equivalent of writer's block.

Beverly shifted tactics. "The winning family gets a spot on some sports channel–"

"Great! I hear TV adds ten freckles."

"That's ten pounds."

"Right, just what every teenage girl wants – to look chubby."

"There's also a huge trophy, and–"

Karli interrupted again. "If that's the 'treasure', this treasure hunt is even lamer than I thought."

"You didn't let me finish." Beverly paused for dramatic flair, then said, "And a cheque for ten thousand dollars."

Karli sat up, grinning. "Cha-ching!"

A sudden, deafening boom made the pictures on the wall rattle. Karli rolled her eyes. Brothers. Beverly sighed and crossed the room. She smacked her palm against the wall and yelled over the music.

"Michael! You'd better be packing!"

***

The helicopter turned toward the noise, then flew to the next window over. As with the previous room, the curtains were drawn back, the screened window open, allowing for easy audio-visual access.

Fourteen-year-old Michael 'Digger' Franklin sat in front of a giant LCD screen, enraptured by the animated video game carnage it displayed. His light brown hair was cut into a military crew cut and he wore camouflage T-shirt and shorts. His dark blue eyes were fixed on the screen, the reflections of the game turning them almost purple. The gunfire and explosions blaring from his surround-sound speakers drowned out his mother's shouts.

To his chagrin, Digger's narrow face favoured his mother's looks, causing friends and relatives to remark that he was such a pretty boy. Which just made him work all the harder to always prove that he was the toughest guy in the room.

An empty suitcase lay open on his bed.

A light came on from below and the helicopter soundlessly dropped to investigate. It flew alongside the house, careful to avoid the pools of light created by security lights, and found the source of the new illumination. One of the garage windows was open to let in the non-existent summer breeze, providing the chopper's front-mounted camera a clear sightline between a gap in the curtains.

Inside the garage, George Franklin stood in front of a wall covered with military schematics. Like his son, George sported a crew cut, though his hair colour was a greying version of his daughter's shade. In his mid-forties, George still had the bearing of a military man, even with his muscle mass slowly softening. His eyes had the same intensity as his son's, but their resemblance stopped at the eyes and hair. George was not Ken to his wife's Barbie, but rather was the embodiment of G I Joe, his ruggedly handsome face lined from years of combat.

His attention was focused on a field map of Mackinac Island, Michigan, complete with a military-style grid reference system and an aerial photograph overlay. Then, as if he had a sixth sense, George whirled around and looked right at the helicopter.

The helicopter jerked up. The drone's remote operator got over their surprise quickly and descended again, slowly. They figured there was no way George could have seen them since it was brighter inside the garage than outside, which would cause George to just see his own reflection in the window.

But what the spy forgot was that the window was *open*. And unlike the bedroom windows, there wasn't even a screen to obscure George's vision.

As the helicopter lined back up with the window, there was movement by the windowsill. The mini chopper's nose dipped and its camera lenses whirred as it refocused. A shiny black pipe came into view, sliding toward the drone. A bright red flash overwhelmed the video feed and the sound of a shotgun blast rang out across the neighbourhood. The helicopter exploded, raining bits of plastic and wires onto the suburban lawn.

***

Digger stared at his computer screen lost in thought.

"Well, don't keep me in suspense, son," George said, staring down over Digger's shoulder. "Is that our culprit?"

"The motor is Japanese," Digger said, a serious expression on his face. While he sometimes struggled with conventional school, when it came to mechanical technology, he was brilliant. His computer screen displayed a three-dimensional schematic of the aircraft motor they'd found among the wreckage, which was now spread out on Digger's bed.

George had picked up every bit and piece he could find and had smuggled it all up to his son's room in a camouflaged rain poncho. The poncho now protected Digger's bedspread from any damage. Beverly would not be happy if she found stains or burn marks on the expensive comforter. It had taken Digger and George over twenty minutes to get some semblance of organization out of the fractured remains of the helicopter, but with the computer's help they were now getting some answers.

"The manufacturer?" George asked. The intent look he gave his son said that he was treating the teenager's findings as he would have an adult's.

Digger clicked on a link. "The Tahama Corporation." He looked up at his father as he continued. "All of the serial numbers have been removed, but I suspect an ultraviolet scan will reveal holographic imprints from the internal components."

George nodded. "Keep at it. I want a point of origin on this bird by oh nine hundred."

Digger's voice instantly shifted from professional technician to fourteen-year-old boy. "But Dad, I still have to pack."

George was already on his way towards the door. "Oh nine

hundred, soldier!"

"Dad, wait!"

George stopped just short of the doorway. He turned, but did not walk back to Digger's side. He just waited, expectantly, his expression making it clear that he would not argue the point further.

Digger grinned cockily. "How about oh nine seconds... from now?

"What?"

Digger pointed at his screen, where he'd pulled up purchasing information. "This bird's not available for purchase in the U. S. of A., not even through third party importers."

"And who do we know that's been to Japan recently?"

"Exactly."

***

A few streets over, a telephone rang.

Hiroto Kumai looked at the call display and chose not to answer.

On the outside, the Kumai house was very similar to the Franklins', the paint just a shade lighter, one or two different plants lining the pavement that led to the front door. Inside the garage, however, was another story. Hiroto had transformed his garage into an office that better resembled a laboratory than a war room. Each wall was lined with humming, high-tech equipment and, at the centre on a massive glass and metal desk, was a state-of-the-art computer system.

Hiroto sat behind his desk, his right eye twitching as he stared at the ringing phone. In his late forties, Hiroto's hair still didn't have a trace of grey and his face was unlined, but his normally stern expression generally made him look much older. That expression deepened into a frown when, after going quiet, the phone began ringing again. The number on the call display was the same.

His hand shook in trepidation as he reached for his cordless phone, but he knew he had to answer.

"Hello?"

The voice of George Franklin came over the line. "Hey, Hiroto, whatcha up to?"

Hiroto tensed. His friend's casual tone didn't give anything away. Did he know? Best to play it casual, too. "Just finishing packing. How about you – are you ready for tomorrow?"

"You bet! We're going to be getting an early start tomorrow. How about you?"

"We will be there an hour before you, of course," Hiroto said, a friendly challenge underlying his words.

"By the way... I have some top of the line model copter parts if you're interested. I'll sell 'em to you real cheap."

Hiroto could almost hear the mocking laughter in George's voice before the dial tone buzzed in his ear. Hiroto cringed, thankful that it was over. Before he could put down the receiver, the door to his office crashed open, sending his heart galloping.

"Hey, Pop!" Thirteen-year-old Takumi 'Genius' Kumai was all energy and excitement as he strode into his father's office. As usual, Takumi's jet-black hair was a mess, his clothes rumpled as if he'd just picked them up off of the floor. While he'd inherited his father's brains, his unkempt nature was all his own. And being influenced more by American than Japanese culture, he did not understand or adhere to his father's inexplicable aversion to smiling, as evidenced by the carefree grin he wore.

"Takumi," Hiroto said, internally trying to calm his rapidly beating heart, "what have I said about knocking?"

"Sorry," Genius said, "I was just wondering if you'd seen my remote control chopper? I want to take it on our trip."

Hiroto sighed.

Genius stared at him expectantly.

Hiroto sighed again, then forced an unnatural smile. "Would you believe Godzilla stepped on it?"

***

"Would you believe I have superpowers?" Thirteen-year-old Jonathan 'J. J.' Hanks Jr smiled at his web camera in a way he hoped was charming, not "constipated" as his older brother, Aaron, had commented when he'd caught J. J. practicing the look in front of a mirror.

J. J.'s bedroom walls were plastered with posters of pretty girls, mostly from the swimsuit edition of *Sports Illustrated*, yet the only picture his eyes had burned holes through sat on his dresser. It showed his best friends Digger and Genius splashing each other at a neighbourhood pool party, but his friends' humorous antics were not what had gotten the photo a place of honour in his room – it was what was in the background: a curvy blonde teenager in a bikini, standing on the diving board.

That same girl's smiling face now filled his computer screen. But not as his background wallpaper; she was live on video. "Nope," she said in answer to his question.

"Then would you believe a little birdy told me?"

"Depends who that birdy is." Fifteen-year-old Sandra Collins appeared to be more interested in examining her recently manicured nails than listening to the sandy-haired boy staring at her, but her baby blue eyes contained a playful sparkle when she glanced up at him through her webcam. "And if you say, 'Hedwig', I'm gonna kick your scrawny butt."

J. J.'s cheeks flushed red as a pleased smile crossed his face. "You've looked at my butt?"

"What? No! But I'm serious about kicking it if you don't stop wasting my time. I still have to pack, you know."

"Right. Uh... okay, here it is. But I'm trusting you to keep this between us. This is top secret military stuff. Digger's dad hacked into Mackinac Island's Geocaching database last night."

"Are you serious?" Sandra's shoulder-length dirty blonde hair shimmered in the glow cast from her computer screen.

J. J. couldn't suppress his grin. *Finally.* He'd wanted Sandra's attention like this for a long time. "Digger got me a complete inventory list of the containers."

Sandra's face fell, her interest in J. J. obviously waning. "That's it? Big deal." She leaned back in her chair. "Is that big, strong, handsome brother of yours around?"

J. J. scrambled for something to say that would bring her interest back to him. Sometimes he really hated Aaron. "You don't understand, some of these containers have 'Signature Items.'"

Sandra rolled her eyes and didn't even bother to try to suppress a yawn. "Yeah, little tokens and pins, I know. Digger's sister is my best friend, you know." Before J. J. could say anything else, she kept going. "Look, J. J., I gotta go... I think my cell phone's about to ring–"

J. J. had promised Digger he'd keep the really good stuff to himself, but he blurted it out before he could filter himself. "I also got a navigational chart! It has 'spoilers' and provides details on *all* of the cache locations throughout the island." He saw Sandra's eyes light up and continued. "With this, I know my family's going to win the Grand Prize!"

Sandra gave him that slow, sultry smile that had made her head cheerleader. "Is there any way I could get a look at this chart of yours?"

Uh-oh. J. J. backpedalled. "Um... I don't think that's a good idea. My dad would kill me if I divulged the info that gives us the winning edge."

"Digger and Karli's family has that edge, too, don't forget. Why not one more family? A one in three shot at ten grand is still pretty good odds, don't you think? You know you *want* to tell me..."

He did, of course, want to. But he knew he shouldn't. "Uh, I don't know."

He breathed a sigh of relief when Sandra didn't seem to be upset. In fact she smiled. But there was something strange about the way she looked at him. "Hold on a sec, J. J.," she said as she started to get up, "I gotta close my door."

J. J. sat back and waited. He picked up a liquorice stick from a bag next to his computer and took a bite as he wondered what was going on. Why would Sandra need to close the door? He was sure that whatever he told her was going to go straight to her parents, so it wasn't like she needed the privacy for that.

Wait a minute. J. J. leaned forward as Sandra walked back toward her computer. She looked different. He'd been ogling her for the past forty-five minutes so he knew every little detail of what she was wearing and something had changed. It wasn't until she slid back into her seat that he realized what it was.

Half of the buttons on her blouse were undone. The remaining half of J. J.'s liquorice stick fell from his limp fingers. As Sandra deliberately leaned toward the monitor, he saw a thin strip of pale flesh, the flash of white cotton.

Sandra's voice took on a new, deeper tone. "J. J., this is an *uplifting* development."

J. J. coughed and a piece of liquorice flew from his mouth and landed on his keyboard. He barely noticed. He felt his cheeks burning, but he didn't know if it was from his coughing fit or what was happening on his computer screen.

He took a swig of water from a bottle he had nearby.

"You know how I love to be kept *abreast* of your work." Sandra stressed specific words, all the while making sure her assets were perfectly displayed. "You certainly have a *firm* grasp for *bountiful* information."

J. J.'s heart was hammering so hard he could barely hear what Sandra was saying. He turned up the volume on his headset, immensely grateful that he hadn't decided to use his speakers.

"So, what do you say?" Sandra licked her lips. "A quick peek..." She glanced down. "For a quick peek?"

A strangled sound came out of J. J.'s mouth and he flushed even darker red. How was he supposed to respond to this? The hottest girl in school, the head cheerleader, was offering him a glimpse of what every guy dreamed about for information on some stupid competition?

Sandra's full lips twisted into a pout. "Pretty please?" She shifted so that the folds of her blouse parted further.

"Okay!" J. J. nearly shouted. "Okay! Deal!"

A wide smile spread across Sandra's face. "You have my private email, right?"

J. J. shook his head. "Uh, no."

"Really?" Sandra typed something out on her keyboard. "I was sure I'd given it to you."

A message popped up on the bottom of J. J.'s screen. Sexysandra15@yaheww.com. He swallowed hard. His eyes flicked back up to the screen just as the final button on Sandra's blouse popped free.

"Did you get that, sweetie?"

J. J. opened his mouth and closed it again, vaguely aware that he looked like a dying fish, but unable to form a single word. He could barely think a coherent word. In fact, he was fairly certain that, at that moment, he didn't even know his own name.

"J. J.?" Sandra sounded amused.

"Uh, yeah." Apparently he did know his name. "Got it."

He pulled up his email program, quickly shrinking the window and moving it to one side so he didn't miss a moment of the best night of his life. More than a little distracted, he had to backspace and retype Sandra's email address twice before he got it right, and then he struggled to find the files to attach, but he finally got the email sent off.

The moment it arrived, Sandra grinned. "Thanks J. J." She cocked her head to one side at some off-camera noise he couldn't hear, then called out. "Yeah, Mom. Coming." She turned back to J. J. "I gotta go. Thanks again." She leaned forward to plant a kiss on the camera; giving J. J. one last tantalizing view and he had the presence of mind to click his webcam's screen capture icon, freezing the image. He didn't mind too much that she was leaving; he had the most amazing screenshot of all time.

He was so mesmerized by what was in front of him that he didn't hear his bedroom door swing open.

"Hey, geek, Dad wants us downstairs in five."

J. J. squeaked and smashed his thumb into his monitor's power button so fast that he nearly knocked his monitor off his desk. He looked up to see his fifteen-year-old brother, Mr Perfect, Aaron, standing in the doorway, a mildly amused look in his brown eyes. As always, his golden waves had that tousled look that girls seemed to drool over.

The thought of drool caused J. J. to self-consciously wipe his sleeve across his mouth. "Yeah, sure, okay," he stammered. "I'll be right down."

Aaron rolled his eyes as he curled a forty-pound dumbbell he was carrying in his left hand. Aaron never seemed to be without some piece of exercise equipment, but he was their school's starting quarterback, so he was obviously doing something right. As he turned to go, Aaron said, "And stop surfing those websites, pervert. You're gonna go blind."

J. J. glanced at the screen to make sure it was black. He gave a sigh of relief. He doubted Aaron would have recognized Sandra, given her pose and puckered lips, but he still didn't want to take any chances. His "big, strong, handsome" brother had an easy enough time attracting girls; there was no reason to call attention to Sandra.

Not that he truly believed that his brother hadn't already noticed Sandra. And Karli, too, for that matter. Their families hung out at neighbourhood gatherings and tomorrow they were going to compete in a giant treasure hunt. In fact, all the teen boys in town would notice Sandra if she wound up on TV for winning the contest.

And if Digger found out he helped her win, well, J. J. didn't even want to think about what his military-minded friend might consider a just punishment for such a betrayal.

J. J. groaned. *What have I done?*

***

22

The outside of the Collins house looked like the others in the neighbourhood, with its carefully manicured lawn and neat garden. And like many of the homes, it was kept that way by Lopez Landscaping. Unlike the other properties, however, Carlos Lopez himself tended to the Collins property, and pretty much everyone knew that the reason was the Collins women. In her forties, Marsha Collins was still stunning. Her pale blonde hair was more bottle than natural and she had a few small lines around her eyes, but she hadn't yet resorted to plastic surgery and her figure was still desirable.

Inside, the décor spoke of high-end feminine taste without a trace of anything masculine. It had only been four years since her divorce had been finalized, but Marsha had made sure all evidence of Donald's presence was gone just days after he'd moved out.

Sandra stood in the doorway for a moment, looking into her mother's bedroom. Marsha sat at her vanity, scowling down at the Louis Vuitton bag that Sandra had bought her for Christmas the previous year. There were some advantages to having a father who used his chequebook to ease his guilt, even when it meant giving Sandra money to buy gifts for his ex-wife.

"Problem, Mom?"

Marsha didn't look up from where she was sorting through dozens of bottles and compacts. "Just trying to decide which of these to bring."

Sandra rolled her eyes. She liked her make-up, but she wasn't planning on taking an entire bag on the treasure hunt, only the barest essentials. Besides, most guys didn't spend much time looking at her face. She crossed to her mother's side and dropped a computer printout on the vanity.

"What's this?" Marsha asked.

"Just a complete inventory of every container for the Mackinac Island Treasure Hunt," Sandra said. "And a chart to where they're at."

Marsha looked at the paper, a smile spreading across her face. "How in the world did you..." Her voice trailed off as she watched Sandra button her blouse, a smug expression on the girl's youthful face. "That's my girl."

Sandra grinned. She'd known that her mother would not only understand but appreciate what she'd done. The Collins women knew how to manipulate men, that was for sure. Men always underestimated a pretty face and a nice body, no matter the age.

Chapter Two

J. J. made his way down the stairs, his mind still preoccupied by that last screenshot. He was halfway to the kitchen when he heard his parents' raised voices.

"You said you'd never touch the mutual fund! You didn't even ask me about it."

That didn't sound good. J. J. stopped. He could see his parents' reflections in the mirror across from the kitchen doorway. His mother, Gabriella, sat at the table, his father across from her. Aaron had inherited his mother's golden hair and brown eyes as well as her features. Just a hint too strong for her to be beautiful, they were just right for him. J. J., however, wasn't just his father's namesake. He'd seen pictures of his dad as a teenager and there was no mistaking their resemblance. Not exactly unattractive, but more on the plain side.

Jonathan Hanks Sr, shifted in his seat and J. J. saw that his father held a letter in his hand. J. J. couldn't tell what it was, but based on his parents' conversation, it couldn't be anything good.

"What are we going to do?" Gabriella asked her husband. "We can't move in with my parents, Jonathan. They don't have the room with my sister and her kids staying there to help Dad with Mom."

J. J. watched his mother stand and begin to pace, her steps taking her out of his sightline and back again. Why was she talking about moving in with Grandma and Grandpa Dyson?

"How long do we have before the bank kicks us out?"

J. J.'s stomach clenched at his mother's question. He couldn't have heard her correctly, could he?

"A few weeks, maybe a month," Jonathan answered. "I talked to my parents and they said we could stay with them until we got back on our feet... however long it takes."

Gabriella interrupted, "In Boca Raton? Jonathan, they have a two-bedroom condo in a retirement community."

J. J. really didn't like the way this conversation was going. It sounded far too much like everything in his life was about to change.

"I'm open to suggestions, Gabriella. We can't live in the car." Jonathan's voice had an edge to it.

J. J. felt ill.

His father continued, "And we can't keep this from the boys any longer."

J. J. had a sinking suspicion as to what the family meeting was going to be about.

Gabriella walked over to her husband and sat on his lap. Jonathan wrapped his arms around his wife's waist and rested his cheek against her shoulder as she spoke. "We're going to go on our trip and have a fun family vacation. No talk about any of this."

"Then we tell them when we come home." Jonathan finished the thought.

J. J. felt tears pricking at the back of his eyelids and he fought not to cry. He wasn't a baby. The sound of a chair scraping over their hardwood floor drew his attention back to the mirror. His parents were standing.

"I better check on the boys," Jonathan said. "I told them we were having a family meeting. We need to discuss our strategy."

J. J. slowly backed away. It wouldn't be a good idea for his parents to catch him eavesdropping. There was only one place he could go without being seen. He carefully opened the basement door and slid inside. He eased the door shut and listened as his father walked by. Still, he waited, wanting to give himself a bit more time just in case his mother decided to follow.

A noise from behind him made him jump. He spun around and peered down the stairs into the darkness of the basement. Only a thin sliver of light shone into the stairwell and it was far from enough to see by.

The sound came again, a shuffling that made his heart pound. After a quick internal debate, J. J. flipped on the light. He still couldn't see anything from the steps, but it made him feel a bit better. Cautiously, he made his way down the stairs. He hated the basement. Besides the fact that it was a breeding ground for the one thing J. J. feared – spiders – it looked like something out of a horror movie, one of the ones where the audience starts yelling at the idiot going down the stairs to investigate the strange noise because everyone knows he's going to die. A stack of dust-covered crates sat against one wall. An antique desk, also covered with a thick layer of dust, was hidden in the shadows against the far wall. Shelving units lined the wall above it, each one loaded down with a lifetime of sentimental family treasures such as the ugliest ceramic gnome ever made, and the hideous wreath Great Auntie Mabel had asked about every year until she died. The dim fluorescent bulb hanging from the centre of the ceiling cast its feeble light over all of it, somehow managing to be more menacing than if it had been utter darkness. He could almost hear the scritch-scratch of eight thin legs.

"Hello?" J. J. was impressed that his voice didn't crack. "Aaron? Is that you?"

As he took another step, J. J. had a new appreciation for the idiots in horror movies. He'd always wondered what would possess someone to keep going when they knew there was something creepy going on. Now, he understood that it was a sense of morbid curiosity. His eyes were automatically drawn to the closet directly across from the stairs. The door was partway open even though he knew that they kept it closed. A voice in the back of his head screamed that this was a very bad idea, but his feet kept moving. He slowly made his way past the mouldy chair his mother kept intending to reupholster but never got around to, then past his old crib to finally stand in front of the door. His hand seemed like it belonged to someone else as he stretched it out toward the handle of the door.

Just as his fingers brushed against the doorknob, it flew open and a hideous creature, face red with blood, jumped from the darkness, a piercing howl coming from its fang-filled mouth.

J. J. tried to scream as he spun around, managing only a thin, high whistle. His feet slid on the dusty floor and he nearly fell. He felt the creature make a grab for him as he stumbled toward the stairs. He was halfway there when he heard something else.

Laughter.

J. J. skidded to a stop, his heart still thumping wildly in his chest, blood roaring in his ears. He turned, eyes narrowing as he realized what had happened.

Still laughing, a perfectly human hand reached up and yanked off the rubber mask. Aaron had tears in his eyes as he doubled over.

"Aaron!" J. J. yelled. "You jerk! You scared the crap out of me!"

"I know." Aaron could barely speak he was still laughing so hard. "I could smell it as you ran for the stairs, you wuss."

With an enraged roar, J. J. launched himself at his brother, not caring that Aaron was older, bigger and could probably bench-press him without breaking much of a sweat. Fortunately for J. J., Aaron was still struggling to catch his breath and wasn't expecting to be tackled by his little brother.

J. J.'s momentum sent both boys careening into one of the shelving units, sending knick-knacks and keepsakes crashing to the floor. The world's ugliest gnome met its demise as it flew into a wall, but the wreath survived, bouncing into a shadowed corner. As a large statue of a wagon-wheeled cannon rolled off of the shelf and smashed to the floor, Aaron managed to get his arm around J. J.'s neck. The headlock effectively stopped the fight, but J. J. glowered up at his brother.

"Now you're going to get it." J. J. panted. "Dad's gonna be pissed that's broken."

Aaron threw J. J. aside in disgust and the younger boy scrambled to his feet. "Me? Who attacked who? I just came down to get a suitcase."

J. J. scowled, scuffing his toe on the floor next to a few of the shattered pieces. He knew Aaron was right, but he wasn't about to admit it. Something in the debris caught his eye and he crouched down. Keeping an eye out for spiders, he brushed away some of the debris.

"You're the moronic doofus that went totally psycho and came at me like a..." Aaron stopped when it became apparent that J. J. wasn't listening.

J. J. carefully extracted the scroll-like paper that had been sticking out of the cylinder of the cannon. He held it up.

Aaron said what they were both thinking. "What the heck is that?"

Chapter Three

The rising sun was barely visible through the thick spruce and pine trees, but the nineteen-year-old Express rider still urged his snorting steed forward. The spur dug into the horse's bleeding flank, pushing the creature harder than the rider liked, but the message that the boy carried was too important for him to lose time.

Less than a mile behind him, eighty canoes and bateaux full of British and Native American forces were drawing close to the shore of the island. Two miles in the opposite direction was Fort Mackinac where unsuspecting American soldiers were going about their morning routines. It was July 17, 1812, and things were about to get very interesting on Mackinac Island.

Approximately thirty years before, the British had built the garrison overlooking the harbour on the south-eastern end of the island and used it to control the Straits of Mackinac. For a military fort it was quite beautiful, its position on the one hundred, fifty-foot limestone making it picturesque, though not quite as strategically sound as perhaps it should have been. More than one soldier had wondered if the person who had built it had been more worried about looks than functionality, but for thirty years, it had held its position.

As the sun continued to rise, a small garrison of artillerymen performed their morning drills in the open yard. The breeze off of the water kept the men cool as they moved. Two older soldiers stood outside the two-tiered watch house, their weapons held in relaxed hands as they watched the exercises. There wasn't really much else for them to watch. Up at the tip of Michigan, they all understood the importance of the military presence on the island, but it wasn't a place known for its action.

The interior of the watch house was still lit by candlelight, the sunlight not quite having reached the windows with enough strength to allow its inhabitants to do their work. Soon, they would be able to extinguish the lanterns and candles, but for now, they burned.

On the first floor, Private Monroe wrestled with his backpack, an expression of extreme frustration on his youthful face. He'd been trying to get it packed for the past twenty minutes with limited success. He'd only been at the fort for a few weeks and his commanders were already wondering if the boy thought he'd made a mistake.

Forty-year-old Lieutenant Porter Hanks stepped out of the shadows and approached the private with a smile playing on his lips.

"Had breakfast yet, Private?" he asked.

The private shook his head. "No, sir."

Lieutenant Hanks kept his voice brisk. "You better have at it then before it's gone."

Private Monroe's fingers fumbled with the top of the bag as he attempted to close it over its bulging contents.

"Come on, soldier, get it together."

The lieutenant's bark made the young private jump. Frazzled, he yanked the tie closed on the bag, threw it over his shoulder and stumbled toward the door. His fingers scrabbled against the scarred wood before finding the latch and releasing himself out into the morning.

"You love to rattle him, don't you, sir?" twenty-five-year-old Corporal Miles Burke called down from where he'd been watching the interaction. The watch house's second storey had been built almost like a barn loft, with a wide space that allowed those on the top to look down at the first floor.

"Best part of my day, Corporal." Lieutenant Hanks was grinning as he stepped onto a wooden platform nearly invisible from the second storey. "The boy's got potential; he just gets in his own way." The lieutenant reached out and pulled a lever. With a creaking sound, a pulley on the second floor began to turn. As a boulder slowly lowered from above, the platform began to rise, lifting the lieutenant upward.

"You and your contraptions," Corporal Burke said.

"Once a blacksmith's son, always a blacksmith's son," the lieutenant said as he stepped off the platform onto the second floor.

"What's wrong with using the ladder, sir?" the corporal asked.

"Ladders are primitive, Corporal. This lift is the future. I've heard they have something like it in Moscow, although not quite so grand. I would like to see how it works." Lieutenant Hanks' tone was wistful.

The corporal fought to keep from smiling. "Still haven't figured out how to get down?"

Lieutenant Hanks didn't seem to be fazed by the younger man's amusement. "In due time, Corporal. In due time."

The pair stepped out onto a balcony that overlooked the outpost. On a clear day, they could see all the way across the island. This morning, however, the last of the fog was still hanging over the trees, still waiting to be burned away by the sun. Still, they could see the soldiers going through their paces.

"No sign of him?" Lieutenant Hanks asked.

"No, sir," Corporal Burke said. He hesitated, then added, "Sir, if the rumours are true... it's possible that Officer Dousman was captured before reaching St Joseph Island."

"Rumours spread worse than disease around here, Corporal." Lieutenant Hanks didn't look at his second in command as he spoke, afraid that his eyes would give away his own concern. A leader must be strong for the men under his command. "If the British forces were near, we would have already received communication from the Secretary of War."

A movement at the forest's edge caught the corporal's eye. He turned just as a horse and rider burst out of the underbrush.

"Sir, I think you may have spoken too soon." The corporal didn't wait for his superior officer to tell him to go. Burke raced down the ladder and through the yard toward the gates. As the soldiers at the gates pulled them open, the lieutenant started to make his way down the ladder, his own anxiety making it difficult to move slowly.

Corporal Burke waved his arms when the rider showed no signs of slowing as he raced toward the opening. "Whoa! Whoa!" He grabbed at the horse's reins.

The rider scowled down at the corporal as he yanked the reins out of the soldier's hands.

"Where do you think you're going?" The corporal tried to make his voice tough.

"I've got an urgent message for Lieutenant Hanks." The horse pranced as if its rider's impatience was contagious.

"Give it to me," Corporal Burke said. "I'll see that the lieutenant gets it."

The rider shook his head. "I have specific instructions to deliver this directly to Lieutenant Hanks himself."

The corporal's temper flared. He didn't allow the soldiers under his command, some older than he was, to question his authority. He wasn't about to let some boy barely old enough to shave to do it. "No one approaches the lieutenant in my regiment but me. Give me the dang letter."

After a moment, the rider reluctantly handed over the envelope, the expression on his face clearly saying that he didn't like being told what to do but that he had enough sense not to argue with an armed soldier.

"What do you have there, Corporal?"

Corporal Burke spun around to see Lieutenant Hanks just a few feet away, walking toward him. He suppressed a scowl. It never failed. He tried protecting Hanks and the lieutenant just did whatever he wanted. "Sir, who's attending the watch house?"

The lieutenant ignored the question and motioned to the envelope. "Well?"

Corporal Burke looked down at his hand. He'd almost forgotten the letter in his annoyance at his commanding officer. "Uh, an important message, sir."

Lieutenant Hanks took the envelope from the corporal and opened it. He was aware that Corporal Burke was watching him expectantly, but one glance at the handwriting and he knew it wasn't anything official. He shook his head in response to Burke's unasked question and then stepped away from the corporal, afraid that he would need the distance as he began to read.

My Dear Brother,

It is with a heavy heart that I write these words to you. This Sunday last, a terrible storm came through the town and at least a dozen people perished. Annie, I am sad to say, was grievously injured while protecting your son. She clung to life for two days before her strength finally failed. During those terrible days, I prayed that you would somehow arrive in time to comfort her, Porter, even though you had no way of knowing what had happened. Her final words were of you and your boy. We will care for him until your return. I am truly sorry to bear you this news. May the Lord comfort you in your grief.

Your Loving Sister, Martha.

The lieutenant put his hand against the trunk of a solid maple tree to steady himself. The strength ran out from his legs and he slumped against the tree, sliding to the ground as he clutched the letter against his chest. Grief warred with disbelief. This wasn't the way it was supposed to happen. He was the soldier, the one whose life was supposed to be at risk, not his Annie, so vibrant and full of life. He was the one who should be gone, his beloved the one grieving, though even that thought was painful. But that was how they had prepared themselves, that if one of them would be claimed before their time, it would be him. There had to be some mistake. She couldn't be gone. The world could not exist without Annie in it.

Even as he tried to deny it, he knew the words to be true. His sister would never have sent such news if it was not the truth. The tear stains smudging the ink shouted at him, the evidence of his sister's grief further confirming the veracity of the news. Annie and Martha had been close. He supposed he should be grateful that Martha had been there at the end, but all he could feel was the pain that he had not been present to protect her. Even if he had been unable to stop the tragedy from happening, he should have been the one holding her hand as the darkness took her. Even as he thought it, his hand went to his pocket where he kept the locket he'd traded a pair of warm woollen socks for, the locket that was supposed to be his gift to her when he returned.

"Annie," he whispered. "I'm so sorry."

Movement to his right caught his attention. Corporal Burke was approaching, all traces of previous emotions wiped away. His face was sombre, his eyes full of concern.

"Porter–"

The corporal never finished his statement. A familiar bang sounded from the forest, followed by the hiss of a musket ball as it streaked past the corporal's head. The Express rider barely had time to register any reaction to the sound before the force of the shot knocked him back in his saddle, a bright stain of red instantly appearing on his dirt-coated shirt. Corporal Burke drew his pistol and fired off a quick shot, taking the charging British soldier right between the eyes.

The corporal yelled as British and Indian forces poured from the forest. "Get out of here, Lieutenant! You can't be captured!"

Lieutenant Hanks didn't reply as he scrambled to his feet, drawing his own weapon. He stood his ground, firing into the oncoming troops. Beside him, he heard the corporal's gun going off again and another Brit dropped. A quick assessment of the situation told the lieutenant that he didn't have the time to reload and he dropped the pistol to the ground, drawing his sword the instant the gun left his fingers. The image of Annie's face, the last time he saw her, went through his mind.

He took a step forward and felt a sharp pain go through his side. He looked down, astonished as crimson bloomed across his shirt. He staggered and heard the corporal call out his name. As he dropped to his knees, he heard the unmistakable deep thud of cannon fire. He pressed his hand to his side and raised his head as the cannonball whistled toward the fort behind him. The men inside were barking orders, scrambling to try to do something even as the first shot fell short. It was obvious to all that the sixty Americans were vastly outgunned and outnumbered.

All of this seemed dim and faraway to the lieutenant and he looked down at his hand to see blood oozing from between his fingers. He pressed harder against the wound, the sharp flare of pain momentarily reviving his senses. He watched the corporal yank the dead Express rider from his saddle and grab the reins of the bucking horse.

"I am not leaving," the lieutenant tried to protest as Corporal Burke lifted him off the ground and shoved him up onto the horse.

"You can't be taken prisoner," the corporal repeated his previous sentiment as he tied the reins around the lieutenant's wrists. "You know as well as I do that they can't capture you. You're far too powerful to be taken by the enemy." Without waiting for any additional protests, Corporal Burke slapped the horse's hindquarters.

Lieutenant Hanks jerked in the saddle as the animal took off, cutting a path through a trio of Ottawa braves who dived out of the way just barely missing being trampled by the fleeing steed. The lieutenant was barely conscious of the shots being fired after him, even as they hit the tree trunks around him, spraying shards of wood and bark. The scratches on his face and hands hardly registered, little stings that faded behind the slowly dulling pain in his side. Finally, the distance grew great enough that the sounds of battle began to fade. Lieutenant Hanks struggled against the darkness that wanted to claim him and tried to concentrate on the fierce grunts of the horse as it dug into the underbrush, each push of its powerful legs driving them further from danger.

He wasn't sure exactly when he had lost his fight against unconsciousness, only that when he woke, he was on a small bluff, the sun was setting and the horse had stopped. He struggled to straighten, fighting a wave of nausea. The blood on his side was still tacky but none of it seemed fresh, so that was good. He felt around his back and frowned. No exit wound. That wasn't so good. The lieutenant reached into his pocket, breathing a sigh of relief as his fingers brushed against the locket and his father's pocket watch. He moved to his other pocket, bypassing his pocket knife to draw out a brass compass. He checked it and looked around, getting his bearings. He was closer to the north-eastern part of the island now, he was sure, deeper into the forest that the soldiers generally avoided.

A few feet away, hidden by a particularly dense line of pines, was a log cabin. In the rapidly declining light, he couldn't make out the details, but he saw enough to know that it was there. He yanked at the reins, cursing the corporal's quality knots. Finally, he managed to get his arms untangled and slid from the horse. His legs buckled and he grabbed onto the saddle to keep from tumbling to the ground. A stab of pain went through his side and he knew that he needed the bullet removed.

He stood there for a minute, gathering his strength. When he knew he could walk without falling, he let go of the reins and staggered toward the cabin. He thought about knocking but decided that he wasn't going to have the strength to stand and wait. He leaned against the door, using his weight to push it open.

The sight that greeted him sent a bigger shock through him than the bullet hole in his side had. Six ragged children, looking to be between the ages of eight and fifteen, stood just a few feet away, a massive chest between them. They appeared to be just as surprised to see him and the youngest gave a small cry.

Suddenly, the chest slipped from their fingers and crashed to the floor, the top flying open. Gold coins and jewels spilled out across the rough wooden planks. Seven sets of wide eyes stared at the treasure until the lieutenant's eyes rolled back in his head and he fell forward, face first onto the treasure.

Chapter Four

J. J. heard his brother's question but didn't answer it right away, too fascinated with what he'd just found. He walked over to a table and shoved aside a stack of musty old books, for once not preoccupied with looking for spiders. The space underneath them was devoid of dust and he set the scroll there. Carefully, he unrolled it, using just his fingertips to hold it flat, aware of how old the paper appeared. Only then did he speak.

"It's a map."

Aaron crossed to J. J.'s side and peered down at the yellowed piece of paper. "What's a map doing in a cannon statue?"

"How the heck am I supposed to know?" J. J. asked. He looked up. "We better show Dad."

Aaron slammed his palm down in the centre of the map, holding it in place. Apparently it was tougher than it appeared. "Are you crazy? You want Dad to know that you destroyed his statue? His grandfather gave him this stuff."

"It was a piece of crap statue."

"Yeah? Well, some people pay thousands of dollars for that kind of crap."

J. J. frowned, his stomach churning as his mind automatically went back to the conversation he'd inadvertently overheard. His dad could've sold the statue and maybe made enough money to keep them from having to move. The thought that he'd ruined his family's chances of staying in their house depressed him. He sighed. "You're right. We can't show Dad."

"I know I'm right."

As Aaron removed his hand, J. J. moved to roll up the map, stopping as he recognized something. He narrowed his eyes, looking more closely. "Aaron, look. Isn't this the U.P.?" He pointed. "And that's Mackinac Island? I mean, it looks a little different but–"

Aaron leaned in for a closer look, taking the opportunity to shove his little brother back up against the wall.

J. J. scowled but didn't complain, his attention grabbed by a handwritten note in the corner of the paper. "Eighteen twenty-seven. That explains why it looks different. The shorelines have probably changed since then."

Aaron's eyes were drawn to where J. J.'s finger rested on the corner of the map. "Is that a butterfly?"

"Looks like it." J. J. leaned closer and read aloud, "'Messengers of the Great Spirit.'"

Aaron pushed J. J. further away as he tried to get a closer look. "What does that mean?"

Surprising both boys, J. J. pushed back, moving Aaron's shadow from the map. J. J. read the words underneath the butterfly. "'To make a wish come true, whisper it to a butterfly. Upon these wings it will be taken to Heaven and granted.'"

Aaron snorted. "Really? Maybe we could send it on unicorn farts instead." He opened and shut one of the books, sending a puff of dust into the air.

J. J. glared at his brother. "It's a message. It's just cri... critic–" He coughed as he inhaled the book dust.

"That's cryptical, you butt-wipe."

"It's cryptic, raisin brain," J. J. said. He wiped the back of his hands across his watering eyes. Both boys leaned over the map again. "It's got a whole bunch more writing and charts. It's like a puzzle." His eyes widened. "Holy crap!"

"What?"

"It's a treasure map!"

Aaron straightened and rolled his eyes. "And you're an idiot. There's no such thing as a real treasure map."

Any retort J. J. might have offered was lost when their father called from upstairs.

"Boys, are you down there?"

The brothers exchanged glances, then J. J. dashed for the stairs. Aaron was half a step behind him.

"Dad!"

Aaron's hand slapped down over J. J.'s mouth, effectively silencing him. With his free hand, Aaron grabbed the map out of J. J.'s grasp.

"J. J.? Aaron?" Jonathan's voice sounded much closer. "What are you two doing in the basement?"

"Uh, just grabbing a suitcase, Dad. We'll be right up," Aaron said.

"Make it snappy," Jonathan said. "We need to go over our strategy for the weekend."

The floor creaked as he walked away.

"What are you thinking?" Aaron asked. "You show Dad that and he's going to want to know where it came from and I don't intend to spend the weeks after we get back being grounded because you couldn't keep your mouth shut."

J. J. pulled away from Aaron, furious. He hated being treated like a little kid and this was just another example of how Aaron used his bigger size to humiliate his little brother. More than that, he couldn't stop thinking about what a treasure could mean for the family. "We need money, Aaron! I heard Mom and Dad talking. They–"

Aaron interrupted, "You don't know it's a treasure map, but you definitely smashed Dad's antique cannon. Do you really want to have to explain that? And do you think for one minute that Dad's going to let you go on about some treasure map when he finds out?"

J. J. fell silent. Aaron was right and J. J. hated him for it. Being the little brother sucked.

"Look, hide those broken pieces in the closet and we'll see if we can get a replica of that cannon in Mackinac. If we can replace it, maybe Dad won't notice the difference." He held out his hand and J. J. took the map back with a scowl that said he wasn't happy. "And leave that stupid map here. We don't need you losing it. We have to stick it back in the new cannon in case Dad knew it was there."

Aaron grabbed a suitcase and headed up the stairs, unsurprisingly leaving J. J. to clean up the mess. He set the map down on the antique writing desk that sat against the wall in front of him and crouched down to begin cleaning up. If a spider crawled on him when he was doing this, he was going to kill his brother. He picked up the larger pieces and looked around, trying to think of somewhere he could hide the evidence of what he'd done. The desk in front of him had three drawers so he tried the bottom one first but it was locked. The second, however, opened and was empty. He dumped the statue pieces in there and bent to get more. It wasn't until he was halfway finished that his fingers brushed against something that was decidedly not ceramic.

Intrigued, J. J. shoved the drawer closed to give himself more light on the floor and found that, amid the debris, was a large old-fashioned key. He held it up, studying it in the dim light. He wasn't sure what kind of metal it was made out of, but one thing was for sure, it wasn't anything in this century and probably not even from the last. He glanced down and saw that he'd cleaned up the majority of the mess. The rest, he decided, he could just kick under the desk. He was in the process of standing when he saw it. The keyhole for the bottom drawer, the drawer that was locked, it appeared to be made of the same type of metal.

After a moment's consideration, J. J. inserted the key into the lock. It slid inside without any resistance. He hadn't realized that he'd been expecting it not to work until he turned the key and heard the lock click. He slid the drawer open and peered inside. He could just make out two shadows. Hoping there weren't any spiders, he stuck his hand into the drawer, ready to pull back the instant he felt anything crawling on him.

The first thing his fingers closed on was a soft, leather pouch. He drew it out, the shape and weight telling him that there were several small objects inside. Aware that his parents were waiting for him, he didn't bother to open it just yet, instead reaching inside the drawer for item number two. This was flat and rectangular so he had a guess as to what it would be before it came into the light. He wasn't wrong. The handmade leather-bound book had the look of a journal rather than the typical reading material. J. J. ran his fingers over the raised letters on the cover. Lt Porter Hanks.

"J. J.?"

His dad's voice made him jump. "I'm coming."

As he leaned over to close the drawer, something in the corner glimmered. J. J. reached down once more. His fingers closed on cool, smooth metal. He'd never seen anything like it outside of a history book and knew that the brass compass had to be an antique, maybe even worth some money. He shut the drawer and took the key from the lock. He stuffed the compass and key into his pocket, wrapped the pouch strings around his wrist and tucked the map into the journal. He hadn't wanted to fold it, but it seemed like the best thing at the moment. He started toward the stairs and then stopped. There was a better way to get all of this stuff upstairs without anyone getting suspicious as to why he was carrying a bunch of old odds and ends.

Less than five minutes later, the door to the basement creaked open and J. J. stepped into the hallway. He clutched the suitcase in his left hand more tightly as he turned to close the door.

A hand came down on his shoulder and J. J. screamed. He spun around as his mother screamed in response.

"Mom!"

Gabriella laughed, her hand on her chest. "Still spooky down there, huh?" She made as if to reach for the suitcase. "Need help packing?"

"Uh, no. I got it." J. J. pulled the suitcase back.

"Are you sure?" Gabriella asked.

"Yeah." J. J. took a step then paused. He leaned over and kissed his mother on the cheek, grinning at the look of surprise on her face.

"Just go put that in your room for now," Gabriella said. "Family meeting first. You can pack later."

J. J. nodded, hiding his disappointment that he would have to wait now to find out what was in the pouch and the journal. It was better, though, than sharing his findings with the family before he knew what they meant. The last thing he needed was to give Aaron any more ammo against him.

Once in his room, he set the suitcase next to the door and started to leave before thinking better of it. He knew his brother. Aaron would come take this suitcase just to screw with him. After a moment of consideration, J. J. slid the suitcase under his bed and draped his covers over the edge, effectively hiding the case from view. That done, he went back downstairs where his family was waiting in the family room, a laptop on the coffee-table in front of the couch.

Jonathan looked up when J. J. walked into the room. "Show us the map."

"Map?" J. J. glanced nervously at his brother.

Aaron smirked at him, his expression saying that he was enjoying watching J. J. squirm. "Yeah, you know... the one with all the container locations."

"Oh, the map. Yeah." J. J. dug into his pocket and pulled out a flash drive. He leaned over the laptop and inserted the drive. As the information popped up on the screen, J. J. sat down on the arm of the couch. From his perch, he watched a map of Mackinac Island appear. As the information finished loading, the high resolution picture showed distinctive red dots scattered across the nearly four mile island.

"Excellent," Jonathan said. "Now–"

"Jonathan, isn't this cheating?" Gabriella gave her husband a disapproving look.

Jonathan kept a straight face as he answered her. "No, honey. It's called strategy."

Aaron nodded earnestly. "Yeah, Mom. Strategy."

Gabriella turned her gaze to her sons and J. J. shrugged. He wasn't going to get in the middle of this. It wasn't like they'd listen to his opinion about it anyway. Besides, after hearing his parents' conversation, however, he was starting to think that he'd be willing to take any advantage he could get. A stab of guilt went through him as he remembered that he may have hurt his family's chances by giving the information to Sandra. If they lost because his hormones got the best of him, he'd never forgive himself. He resolved to do everything possible to make sure that they won.

"Gabby, I guarantee you that George is going to have military equipment and devices. Probably everything short of 'weapons of mass destruction.' Although, now that I think about it, he could have those too. Heaven only knows what he's been doing in that garage of his," Jonathan said. "And Hiroto will have every bit of his company's scientific, James Bond technology at his disposal. All he has to do is claim he's running beta tests."

Gabriella held her husband's eyes for a moment and then sighed. She nodded. "All right. So what's our plan?"

***

J. J. closed his bedroom door behind him and locked it. He'd told his parents that he was going to go pack, but the truth was, he'd already thrown most of what he was taking into a bag. All he had to do was dump the bag into the suitcase and it wouldn't be like he'd really lied. What he really wanted was the privacy to peruse the items he'd found in the basement.

He pulled the suitcase out from underneath his bed and opened it. He set the pouch, the journal, the key and the compass on his desk, then tossed everything from his bag into the suitcase. That done, he shoved the luggage aside and sat at his desk.

The compass was definitely brass, he decided as he studied it. Judging by the tarnish, scratches and dents, it had been old 200 years ago, but he had a suspicion it was connected to the map. After all, a compass and a map went together.

J. J. opened his desk drawer and rummaged through it before finding what he was looking for – a thin strip of leather he'd used for an art project a couple of years ago. He threaded it through the loop attached to the compass and then tied it off. It easily went over his head and the compass tucked nicely beneath his shirt. No need to raise questions if he didn't have to. In a way, it felt right having it around his neck, as if it belonged to him.

Next, he opened the pouch and dumped its contents onto the desktop. He sifted through the pile, examining each item. There was a round piece of metal that, at first, he thought was a ball bearing. Then, as he looked more closely, he saw the minute scratches and brownish-red stains. He'd spent enough time with Digger to realize that this was a bullet. Well, a musket ball. Now he was willing to bet that everything he'd found had all belonged to the same person who'd owned the map.

He set down the bullet and picked up a beaten-up pocket watch. It appeared to be made out of brass as well and he wondered if it and the compass had been a set. The glass was cracked and the watch had long since wound down, but it was still something to see. The intricate detail work was amazing. When he turned it over, J. J. saw an inscription on the back. *My love always, A.*

J. J. set it aside and reached for a pocketknife. Though in better shape and newer than the watch, it was obvious it was still at least 200 years old. It opened easily enough but the blade was dull and spotted with rust. If it was cleaned, it could be useful again.

The last item from the pouch was a gold locket. It was slightly tarnished, but the links in the chain were all good and the clasp still held. Unlike the watch, it had no inscription and, when J. J. opened it, there were no pictures inside.

J. J. put all of the items back into the pouch and added the key as well. The compass stayed around his neck. He picked up the journal and flicked through the pages. The handwriting was masculine, neat and orderly. J. J. wished his handwriting looked like that. His teachers were forever telling him that if they couldn't read his answers, they were wrong. His grades reflected that there was a lot they couldn't read.

He kicked off his shoes and sat down on his bed. He stretched out and opened the journal to the first page and began to read. Minutes turned into hours as J. J. made his way through the pages, certain passages sticking in his mind as he went.

...Sixty men have been dispatched with me to guard the fort, though I suspect my superiors find this number to be too great. Our weapons are low and the position of the fort itself worries me. My only ray of hope is that my second in command is a good man named Miles Burke. I believe we shall become fast friends...

...My heart aches as I look out toward the upper peninsula and know that my son is celebrating his birthday without his father. My darling Annie will make certain that John does not forget me, but I often fear that when I return, he will not know me...

...Rumors of war fly about, but still there is no official word. I worry that, should something happen, my small company would be unable to hold the fort. I can only pray that if a threat were to rise, support would be sent quickly...

...I was severely wounded during the attack on our fort and sent away by Corporal Burke, much against my will, but I had not the strength to stop him...

...When I woke, I found myself on a bluff. My horse had led me to a log cabin, hidden among the pines...

...To my surprise, the cabin was inhabited by a ragtag band of orphans. They hid me in a secret room in the attic and tended to my injuries, even removing the musket ball that had lodged in my side. They nursed me back to health and kept watch for British soldiers that never came...

...The children have told me that they survive by grave-robbing. Their largest bounty – a chest filled with gold and silver coins, jewels that had been buried by British troops in a shallow grave...

...My new-found family has begun to call me 'father' which I see as a mixed blessing since I fear I may never see my own son again. They share all they have with me, including a portion of their treasure. I will protect it for my son, though I have not chosen a place yet. By the grace of God, I pray that one day John will somehow retrieve his rightful inheritance and know that I never stopped loving him...

J. J. stopped suddenly and looked down at the map he'd taken from between the pages of the journal. His eyes widened. "John never found the map."

Chapter Five

The Shelby Court Estates had never been so busy, and certainly not so early in the morning. Before the sun had fully risen, four families were up and preparing. While the rest of the neighbourhood still slept, they gathered gear and loaded up vehicles. A Hummer was parked in the Franklin family's driveway, the rear hatch open. George carried a large camouflaged chest over and eased it into an open spot. At the Hanks' home, Jonathan finished latching luggage to the roof rack of their beat-up SUV. Hiroto pulled a Hi-tech Toyota Fine-X car from his garage, an impatient expression on his face. His wife, Sakura, hurried from the house, each hand carrying a large black case bearing the Tahama Corporation logo. A white Mercedes convertible pulled out of the Collins' garage and Marsha gave Sakura a forced smile. The two mothers couldn't have been more different, from their appearance to personality and parenting style. It was no secret in the Estates that the Collins and Kumai parents had a deep disapproval for each other.

J. J. stepped away from the window where he'd been watching the preparations. Neither of his parents noticed as he slipped down the stairs and out the front door, but that didn't surprise him. Even without the financial issues he knew were bothering them, they had a lot on their minds. He glanced around to make sure no one was watching him and then started toward the Franklin property. As he passed by the house, he could hear Karli and her mother talking.

"No cell phones allowed on this trip. It's against the rules and it's nonnegotiable," Beverly said.

"My life is ruined."

J. J. grinned as he imagined Karli flopping onto her bed, a tragic expression on her freckled face. His best friend's older sister could be a pain some of the time, but she was generally entertaining. Her mom didn't seem to be amused.

"Oh, don't be so melodramatic. It's only a cell phone. It's not the end of the world."

Karli's next statement was full of amusement. "Sandra's going to freak when she hears about this."

J. J. had to agree. The statement's veracity was proven only a few seconds later when a scream came from the Collins driveway.

"What kind of Neanderthal junket is this?"

J. J. turned slightly to see Marsha hug her daughter. The memory of his computer screen flashed through his mind, but he shook his head. As much as he loved that picture, this wasn't the time for daydreaming. He needed to talk to his friends. He'd texted them as soon as he'd gotten up, knowing they'd be awake already too. He'd told them everything from his parents' money issues and the possibility of moving to finding the map. Even though they knew their parents would be itching to leave right away, they'd agreed to meet in Digger's fort before they had to split into their familial teams.

The edge of the Franklins' backyard was overgrown with brush, and George had left it that way intentionally so that the fort he'd built when the boys were barely five would have a 'wilderness' feel to it. While the trio had more or less outgrown the pretend part of it, the fort still served as a private place for them to meet and talk about things they'd prefer their parents or older siblings not overhear. Behind a large shrub was an A-frame, redwood fort just tall enough for the boys to duck inside. At the rate they were growing, however, by the end of the summer, it might not be so easy. The outside walls were covered with camouflage, but the sign on the front door was anything but subtle. "Sleep well, America. My Army Dad has your back!" J. J. remembered helping Digger hang it about six years back.

Genius and Digger were already inside. The single window let in little light and J. J. blinked against the darkness until his eyes adjusted. Technically, he supposed he could have kept walking since he knew the place by heart. Even though the walls were shadowed, he knew they were covered with military paraphernalia, except one section of the eastern wall where an American flag hung. On the back wall was a "Military Brat" sign that J. J. had bought Digger for his seventh birthday. The main reason J. J. waited was Genius. It was impossible to tell where he would be or where he'd moved things to. The kid had a hard enough time sitting still, let alone leaving things where they were. Case in point, the beanbag chair that Genius was sitting in was about three feet from its usual place. Digger's was in the regular spot as was the empty one where J. J. plopped down.

"Florida?" Digger said, a glum expression on his face.

"That sucks," Genius said.

J. J. nodded in agreement as he pulled the map from his pocket. He'd thought about putting it in the leather pouch but had ultimately decided not to. He didn't want to risk the other stuff coming out until he'd talked about the map. It was more important than the rest. "I'm hoping that this map is the real deal. Then, maybe we can find the treasure and help my mom and dad. Maybe keep us from heading down to gator country. Have you seen the spiders in Florida?" He handed the map over to Genius. "What do you think? Is it real?"

Genius scrutinized the map as the other boys waited. "It appears to be a genuine artefact." He held up a hand before J. J. could get excited. "However, it would take some more testing in my lab before I could be absolutely sure."

Digger groaned. "We're leaving in, like, ten minutes, Genius. We don't have time for you to test the stupid thing!"

An idea popped into J. J.'s head. "Wait, what if you could see some things that were with the map, would that help you tell if it's real?"

Genius considered it and then nodded. "Multiple items could help prove the map's authenticity."

"Then check this out." J. J. emptied the contents of the pouch into his hands.

"Awesome!"

To J. J.'s surprise, Digger picked up the watch rather than the pocket knife.

Digger studied the watch with an unusual amount of focus. "This is so cool."

"Interesting," Genius said as he selected the key.

Before either of the boys could ask any questions about the object they were holding, a sound from outside made them all freeze. Just a few weeks ago, someone in the neighbourhood had spotted a skunk. The last thing any of them wanted was to spend hours in a car smelling like a skunk, not to mention the teasing they'd get from the older three or how pissed their parents would be.

"Shh," Digger said as he stood. He crept toward the door as quietly as possible. He grimaced as the door creaked when he opened it, but the sound didn't repeat itself. After a moment, he stuck his head out, listening for anything.

Suddenly, Digger was yanked off his feet and out through the narrow opening. The watch bounced on the compacted dirt floor as Digger screamed. J. J. and Genius scrambled to their feet and rushed outside, hearts pounding.

Panic turned to anger as J. J. saw Aaron clenching Digger in a headlock as the younger boy fought to get free.

"You're supposed to be a soldier?" Aaron mocked.

"C'mon, Aaron, leave him alone," J. J. said.

Aaron took a moment, appearing to consider the request, then rubbed Digger's head and released him. Digger glared, keeping his eyes on Aaron as he backed over to where his friends were standing.

"What's the matter?" Aaron asked. "Can't take a joke?"

A pair of hands came out of the brush and covered Aaron's eyes. He flinched and J. J. snickered.

"Guess who, sexy?" Sandra's voice was nearly a purr and J. J. took a moment to wonder how girls did that.

"Angelina Jolie?" Aaron grinned.

"Close." Sandra removed her hands as Aaron turned toward her. "I have fuller lips."

"Hey, Sandra." Aaron took a not-so-discrete step away from Sandra when he saw Karli standing just behind the blonde. "Hey, Karli." His grin softened.

"Hi," Karli said.

J. J. and his friends exchanged amused glances. It was nice to see Aaron uncomfortable for once. Digger scowled as Aaron and

Karli continued looking at each other and J. J. supposed he understood. If he had a sister, he wouldn't want Aaron looking at her that way either. Then again, if it was his sister, she'd be Aaron's sister too, and that just opened up a whole other set of issues.

Sandra must have sensed something between the other two as well because she took a step forward, breaking line of sight, and smiled up at Aaron. "Aaron, my mom said you can ride with us in the convertible if you want."

Karli rolled her eyes and crossed her arms. To Genius' amusement, Digger made a wrenching sound and bent over. Sandra shot the boys a dirty look, but Aaron just looked nervous. J. J. didn't laugh. He'd give anything to have Sandra offer him a ride. As Digger straightened, J. J. saw that his friend had picked up the watch. He turned toward Digger to ask for it back when Karli spoke up.

"What's that?"

Aaron used the distraction to walk away from Sandra and toward the boys, feigning interest. "Yeah, what do you have?"

"I found it," J. J. said, hating the defensive tone in his voice. "I actually found a lot of stuff." J. J. stretched out his hands.

"Where'd you find it?" Aaron asked suspiciously.

"When I was cleaning up the basement, I found a key." J. J. motioned toward the key Genius held up. "It went to that old desk and in the bottom drawer I found this bag of stuff and," he hesitated, "and a compass." He pulled the object out from under his shirt. He wasn't sure yet if he wanted to share the contents of the journal, especially with Aaron.

"What's this?" Karli plucked the bullet and held it up.

"That's a musket ball from 1812," Digger answered promptly. "Didn't you pay attention to any of Dad's weapons lessons?"

"Uh, no, not really." Karli stepped back, the bullet resting in her palm. A strange expression came over her face as she studied it, almost as if she recognized it. J. J. understood, he had the same feeling every time he looked at the compass.

"Is that a knife?" Aaron picked up the pocketknife, true interest now showing on his face.

"Ooh, look at that." Sandra snatched the locket. "How pretty!"

Impulsively, J. J. said, "You can keep it if you want." All eyes turned toward him and he felt his face heat up. "All of you can keep what you have, if you want it, of course."

Even as he said the words, he felt a rightness to them, as if this was the way it was supposed to happen. A sudden gust of wind blew through the group and they shivered as one. It wasn't until later that J. J. realized that nothing else around them had moved. Not the tree branches, not the grass, nothing.

Sandra broke the moment. "Well, I know my mom's going to be looking for me."

"We'd all better head back." Aaron switched into big brother mode. Otherwise known as bossy jerk mode.

Sandra smiled up at Aaron. "And, by the way, that offer to ride with my mom and I? Neither one of us would be sitting in the passenger's seat."

"Oh, uh," Aaron stammered.

As the others watched, Sandra put a finger on Aaron's lips and then raised herself on her tiptoes to press her lips against his cheek, leaving a red smudge. As she sauntered away, all four boys stared after her in shock.

After a moment, Karli sighed and followed the blonde.

It took Aaron a moment to realize that the other girl was leaving as well and he blurted out, "Bye, Karli."

She didn't bother looking back. "Bye."

J. J. glanced at his friends and they grinned. Together, they said, "Bye, Karli."

Aaron turned, eyes narrowed. He lunged and all three boys flinched. Aaron gave a derisive laugh. "Army, yeah right. The Few, the Proud... the Morons." He turned to walk away.

"That's the Marines, jerk," Digger mumbled.

Aaron spun back around and the boys made a run for it, cutting through the brush to come out on the other side of the Franklin house. It was a testament to how distracted their parents were that none of them said a word about the boys' dishevelled appearances or even bothered to ask where they'd been.

Without a word, the kids climbed into their respective family vehicles. J. J. glowered at his brother as the Collins' Mercedes passed and Sandra pursed her lips and waved at Aaron. The annoyance disappeared into amusement as the Franklins pulled out next and Digger mooned Aaron, earning a slap from Karli. Aaron muttered something about idiot kids and stuck his earbuds into his ears. As they pulled out onto the highway, J. J. retrieved his PSP from his bag and started in on an old favourite.

After an hour or so, J. J. set aside the PSP, bored with his game and unable to shake his curiosity about the things he'd found. He leaned forward and waited for a break in his parents' conversation.

"Hey, Dad, what's with all the Civil War stuff in the basement?"

Jonathan chuckled. "That stuff's from before the Civil War, J. J. Those are actual artefacts from the War of 1812. Which, if I remember correctly, first started here in Michigan. On Mackinac Island, as a matter of fact."

"The War of 1812?"

Jonathan shook his head. "What did you cover in history this past year? It was a war fought between the United States and the British Empire."

J. J. was vaguely aware that Aaron had removed his headphones and was also leaning forward, interested despite himself.

Jonathan continued. "Your great-great-great-grandfather, Porter Hanks, was a lieutenant in the U.S. Army and in charge of the garrison stationed at Fort Mackinac."

"So that's where I got my middle name 'Porter' from, right?" J. J. asked.

Jonathan nodded.

"Named after a great war hero. Cool." J. J. grinned. His pleasure was short-lived, however, as Jonathan shook his head.

"I wouldn't necessarily say 'war hero.' Historians say that when the British attacked Fort Mackinac, Lieutenant Hanks abandoned his post, leaving his men and the fort to be captured. His second-in-command surrendered after the first cannon shot."

Aaron couldn't resist. "Whoa. You weren't named after some war hero. You were named after a coward and deserter."

"Shut up, Aaron," J. J. snapped at his brother. He knew the truth, but if he shared, his family would want to know how he knew what happened and that would lead to the basement and the broken cannon statue. Not a conversation he wanted to have on a long car ride, especially with his dad's talent for lengthy lectures. Talk about a captive audience.

"Boys, that's enough," Gabriella said before Aaron could retort.

J. J. turned back to his father. "Do you think that's what really happened, Dad?"

Jonathan considered the question; J. J. had to give him that. "Well, your grandfather believed that Porter was seriously wounded and was forced to leave the fort by his men so he wouldn't be captured by the British. He was an officer, after all, but it wasn't common practice to send away officers to prevent capture." After a pause, he continued. "Later, it was found out that Porter and his troops had been betrayed by another officer – Dousman, I believe – but all of the blame still fell on Porter because he essentially vanished. No one ever heard from him again and nobody was ever found. He was declared a deserter. His son, John, kept the family name despite the grief he took for it. Everyone told him to sell the things that he inherited, but John refused."

J. J. felt a flare of anger that the truth had never been uncovered. His ancestor was no deserter, but the only proof of that was a journal supposedly written by Porter himself. It alone wouldn't be enough to prove his innocence, not without finding something else that proved the truth of the journal's contents. Which led J. J. back to the map. "Did you ever hear anything about a treasure map or a buried treasure?"

"Treasure map? Buried treasure?" Jonathan asked. "Hmm, now that you mention it..."

J. J. shot a look in his brother's direction before turning his attention back to his father. Jonathan peered over his shoulder and chuckled.

"No."

Aaron smirked. "See."

J. J. resisted the urge to flip his brother off and contented himself with sticking out his tongue before going back to his video game in disgust. There had to be more to the story. The journal was proof of it, wasn't it? It told the truth about what had really happened to Porter, so didn't it stand to reason that the story about the treasure was true too? That was, of course, if Porter had been telling the truth about what had happened and wasn't just some work of fiction, by Porter or someone claiming to be the lieutenant.

"Honey," Gabriella said. She used the map to gesture to an approaching exit sign. "Isn't that our exit?"

"Whoops. I think you're right." Jonathan started to veer toward the exit.

Out of nowhere, a yellow Land Rover roared past them and cut across to the exit. Jonathan slammed on the brakes, throwing everyone forward. The PSP tumbled from J. J.'s hands as he threw his arms up to keep his face from smashing into the back of his father's seat.

"What a freaking idiot!" Jonathan yelled.

Gabriella shook her head. "They'll give anyone a licence these days." She turned toward the backseat. "Boys, are you okay?"

"Fine, Mom," Aaron said.

"I'm good." J. J. pushed himself back into his seat. If this was any indication of how the rest of their vacation was going to go, it wasn't a good sign.

Chapter Six

The banana-yellow Land Rover took the exit at ten miles over the speed limit, but the three people riding inside didn't seem to notice that any more than they'd noticed the ancient SUV that they'd cut off to get to the exit.

Forty-three-year-old Melvin Dousman squinted at his map, trying to find exactly where he was heading next. Half of his attention was on the map, the other half on the conversation he was having with the person on the other end of the Bluetooth he currently had lodged in his ear. Unfortunately, that left nothing to be focused on actually driving.

"Mackinac Island," Melvin said. He paused to listen to a question. "Yeah, the wife has us on some scavenger hunt, or some crap like that."

Ki-Ki Dousman didn't appear to be concerned with her husband's assessment of her plans. In fact, she didn't seem to be listening to him at all, more concerned with fiddling with one of her large hoop earrings that had somehow tangled itself in her teased and tortured hair.

"What are you doing in the office on a Saturday, anyway?"

Ki-Ki snapped her gum as she finished fixing her earring and began rooting around in the fast food bag on her lap. Though she was forty, she didn't look old enough to have a teenage son, but she also didn't look naturally youthful. She knew that a lot of her friends referred to her as Barbie, and she believed it was due to her peroxide-blonde curls and surgically enhanced curves. No one said to her face that it was because the numerous surgeries she'd had made her look like she was made of plastic. Melvin was happy so Ki-Ki remained in blissful ignorance.

She pulled a hamburger from the bag. "Hunter, here's your triple burger deluxe."

The teenager in the back seat took his food with a scowl. "Yo, Moms, why do yous keep callin' me dat?" The words sounded odd coming from the pale, chubby thirteen-year-old with sandy brown cornrows. His clothes were pricey – designer jeans, a top of the line T-shirt and the newest, most expensive sneakers – but he wore them big and baggy like the gangsters he idolized.

"Oops, sorry, Hunter," Ki-Ki said. "I mean, Original-One."

"A'ight." Hunter's voice changed to something more natural. "It's got extra cheese, right?"

"Of course."

"Bet." Hunter lifted his chin and returned to watching the rap video that was currently playing on the overhead screen.

Suddenly, Melvin crumpled the map and threw it across the car, narrowly missing the nose he'd paid five thousand dollars for. His voice rose. "What? Mr Roberts? When did he call?"

Ki-Ki looked over at her husband, her face expressionless, though that was most likely due to the enormous amount of Botox she'd had injected into her face that morning. Her hazel eyes, however, conveyed the concern her face could not.

"Well, what did you tell him?" The tension in the car doubled as Melvin waited for an answer. "Don't worry, Frank. I'll figure out something." Melvin glanced at Ki-Ki and gave her a less than reassuring smile that vanished when Frank said something else that Melvin didn't like. "Stop calling it a 'Ponzi scheme' Frank! Those were sound investments!"

Ki-Ki shifted in her seat and darted a glance back over her shoulder to her son. Hunter wasn't paying attention to anything other than the bling on the screen and the burger in his hand.

"I know, I know. I'll take care of it. Yep, bye." Melvin hung up and looked over at his wife, his dark eyes worried.

***

Dousman and Dupree Investment Securities was located in a refurbished warehouse on the fringes of the Detroit business district. It had been there for only two years and still had an air of newness about it. Inside, it was clean and pristine. Looking decidedly out of place in the far office was the bloodied face of forty-five-year-old Frank Dupree. His right eye was swollen shut, his nose obviously broken and his top lip split. He glared up at the man holding the phone to his ear.

"Happy now?" Frank said.

The cell phone snapped shut and Charles Roberts took a step back from the chair to which Frank had been tied. In his early sixties, Roberts looked every inch the distinguished gentleman. His grey suit was well-cut, his shoes shone. Even his salt-and-pepper hair screamed of a haircut more expensive than some suits. In his other hand he held a skull-head cane.

"Now, do you see, Mr Dupree? That wasn't so difficult, was it?" His British accent was smooth and cultured, something that had taken years of practice. It wasn't easy getting rid of the sharp, low-class accent with which he'd been born. "I had expected better treatment from Mr Dousman at least. After all, his family does have such a good history with my people."

Frank spat a glob of blood at Mr Roberts, earning a weary sigh. Americans. Such barbarians.

"There is no need for such distasteful behaviour, Mr Dupree. We are gentlemen of business; let us move on with honour and dignity."

Frank let out a stream of expletives that left Mr Roberts shaking his head. Even English vulgarities had a class that was lost on Americans. "It truly is a shame that you would prefer to end our relationship this way, Mr Dupree. I had hoped for a different outcome." Mr Roberts nodded at the silent hulk of a man standing to his right, Frank's blood still fresh on the thug's meaty knuckles. "Bruno."

A slow, vicious smile spread across the man's face, his eyes alit with something other than his lack of intelligence. He reached into the waistband of his pants and produced a gun with a silencer.

"Thank you for your assistance, Mr Dupree. Your services are no longer required." Mr Roberts ignored Frank's pleas and curses as he turned and walked away, the click of his cane on the tile floor lost in the restrained man's shouting. Mr Roberts closed the office door behind him and continued toward the main door, not missing a step as he heard the muffled whump of a silenced gunshot. He pressed his thin lips together as he stepped out into the summer heat. At times, such things were necessary, much like the putting down of a dog or horse who had outlived its usefulness. In his opinion, had the British done so centuries ago, this land would not be overflowing with the 'huddled masses' that didn't know their place. Taking their money was one thing. Socializing with them was something else entirely. Mr Roberts straightened his jacket. He looked forward to the day when he was wealthy enough to be able to avoid rubbing elbows, so to speak, with those he considered beneath him. To be honest, that was most of the population, but he didn't see anything wrong with that.

***

Ki-Ki didn't like the expression on her husband's face. Something was wrong. She never asked many questions about business or finances. She told herself it was because she didn't understand those things and she'd rather invest herself in taking care of Hunter, but on some level she knew that it was because she preferred not to know the truth behind her husband's business dealings. She'd met Frank Dupree only twice in the four years he and Melvin had been working together and, both times, she got the impression that the two men were involved in something shady.

"What is it, Mel? Is everything all right?"

When Melvin didn't answer, Ki-Ki's concern grew. She started to speak again, but was interrupted by Hunter's decision to start belting out in an off-key 'human beatbox' style of rap. Whether it was his own or a bastardized version of what he was watching, she didn't know.

"*Yo yo yoooo! Listen up, y'all! Y'all better chill.. 'cuz the Original-One's about to get ill!! Say what.. you better not disrespect.. I'll bust'a cap in you.. and dat's a fact.. BANG! BANG!*"

Melvin jumped at the last bang, his hands jerking the steering wheel and causing the car to swerve. He quickly straightened out and threw a dirty look over his shoulder but Hunter didn't notice, too busy working his rhymes.

Chapter Seven

J. J. stared out the window at the massive suspension towers of the Mackinac Bridge. For once, Aaron wasn't harassing him for his interest. His older brother seemed as awestruck as he was. There was just something about seeing a structure that large and realizing all of the work that had gone into the building of it. For a brief moment, J. J. wondered if his friends were finding the bridge as fascinating as he did. He knew Genius would most likely be calculating the man hours that went into its creation as well as all of the maths used in its design. After all, that's what Genius did.

"Designed in the 1880s, the bridge wasn't opened until November 1, 1957. While it shares its name with the island, it doesn't actually connect the mainland to the island." Jonathan sounded like he'd memorized encyclopedia information. "At five miles long, it's earned the nicknames 'Big Mac', 'Mighty Mac' and 'The Magnificent Mac'–"

"We get the idea, Dad. It's big." Aaron sat back in his seat, his momentary interested gone.

J. J. returned to his game as well. They would be getting on the ferry soon and he still had one level to beat.

***

The air off the lake was welcomed after hours in stuffy cars and it whipped across the open-air deck of the Classic Ferry. All four families stood at the rails, relishing the beauty of the straits. All, of course, except Sandra who was fighting a losing battle with the wind regarding her hair. As much as he liked her, J. J. couldn't help but be amused by the futility of the action.

"My hair is ruined!" Sandra didn't appear to be complaining to any one person in particular.

J. J. was willing to bet that she did this often, just assuming that people would pay attention. Thing was, she wasn't wrong.

"I don't know why we couldn't just drive to the island."

Genius didn't look at her as he answered, apparently still concentrating on the geographical wonder around him. His words were matter-of-fact. "First of all, you can't *drive* to the Island, unless you have a floating car, of course." He paused for a moment, most likely pondering the possibility of such a vehicle, then added. "Plus, they don't allow motorized vehicles aside from emergency ones, of course."

J. J. didn't know how his friend did it. While Digger wasn't actually fond of Sandra, he didn't have a problem ogling her. Genius, on the other hand, for the most part, seemed oblivious to her charms. Perhaps, J. J. thought, Genius just used so much of his brain for all of the smart stuff he did that nothing was left to focus on girls, even one as hot as Sandra.

"How are we supposed to get around when we get there?" Sandra looked horrified at Genius' statement.

Karli was grinning as she looked up from the sketchbook she was drawing in. "See those things that are attached to the end of your legs? They're not just for wearing hooker heels."

Sandra was still so shocked that she let Karli's insult slide. "Oh, you've got to be kidding me."

As she turned, J. J. noticed that she was wearing the locket and he smiled. Aaron hadn't given her anything. "Nope," he said. "All travel is by foot, bicycle or horse-drawn carriage. That's it."

Sandra groaned. "No cars. No cell phones. This isn't a vacation... it's a freakin' nightmare. UGH!" She threw her hands up in the air and walked away from the railing.

J. J. watched her go. He was pretty sure Aaron and Digger were too.

***

J. J. actually kind of liked the horse-drawn carriages that took all of them to the Grand Hotel. He'd never been a fairy tale kind of kid, but he did like fantasy books and there was one particular scene that had come to mind when he'd seen the carriages. Granted, it hadn't been horses that had pulled those carriages, but it still made him grin.

The Grand Hotel lived up to its name, J. J. decided, as they arrived at the 660-foot porch. He'd never seen anything so massive. He lingered on the porch, wanting to soak in every detail.

"This place is unbelievable," Karli said as she carried her suitcase toward the stairs. "I'd love to draw it."

Sandra pushed past the older girl, still trying to untangle her hair. "Yeah, well, they better have air conditioning and room service." She glanced over her shoulder at the smitten-looking bellboy struggling to carry her bags. "Don't drop anything, sweetie."

J. J. followed Karli into the lobby... and stopped. If anything, the interior was more overwhelming than the exterior. It could have been the insane amount of pink and green in varying shades that adorned pretty much everything, but J. J. was pretty sure it would have been extreme no matter what the colour scheme had been. Pillars created a natural pathway and chandeliers hung from the ceilings. As J. J. walked toward the reservation desk where his family was waiting, he spotted a piano, a large fancy-looking cabinet, an array of paintings on the walls and dozens of potted plants scattered around the room. It was like nothing he'd ever seen before.

He reached his family just as a man in a suit practically bounced over to them. The man was grinning so widely that J. J. was sure it had to hurt. It was kind of frightening, actually.

"Welcome! I'm Edward, the manager here at the Grand Hotel."

J. J. glanced over at his brother to see Aaron trying to suppress a smirk and failing. Edward was what J. J. and his friends called 'shiny-happy' – the kind of person who was almost manically scary to the point of needing a punch to the nose to calm down.

"Are all of you here for the 'Geocache Treasure Adventure'?"

Edward said the name like it was vastly impressive, J. J. thought, like the opening of a new *Star Trek* movie or something. He had the sudden urge to express his sympathy to Edward for a lack of more excitement in his life.

"Yes, we are," Jonathan answered for the group and earned a dirty look from George.

"Excellent!" Edward beamed.

Digger came up on J. J.'s right, Genius trailing behind him. "A little too excited about this, isn't he?"

As the manager continued, the boys wandered over to the stack of island brochures.

"The teams are to meet in the Grand Pavilion for registration in about ninety minutes. That should give you time to get settled in your rooms and grab a bite to eat."

J. J. glanced over the papers, not really looking at them with any interest until something caught his eye. He grabbed the brochure and held it up.

"What?" Digger asked.

J. J. pointed to the title. *"The Original Butterfly House.* It's a clue to the treasure." Before J. J. could expound any further, his dad interrupted.

"C'mon, boys. We don't want to be late for registration."

J. J. and his friends exchanged meaningful looks. Digger nodded.

"Hey, Dad," Digger said. "Can we go scout the AO?"

"'AO'?" J. J. asked.

"'Area of Operation'," Genius translated the military-speak.

When George didn't immediately agree, Digger continued, "If we scout now, we can get going at zero dark thirty."

Without needing to be asked, Genius interpreted for J. J. "Way too early in the morning."

"Good thinking, soldier," George said, a proud smile on his face.

Jonathan still looked doubtful. "I don't know, J. J. We should probably all stick together."

George clapped Jonathan on his shoulder. "Nonsense. We're on an island, Johnnyboy. It's not like they could really get lost, right?"

Jonathan scowled, though more at the nickname and the condescending tone than the logic. He glanced at Hiroto who nodded. He sighed. "Yeah, I guess it'll be okay."

The boys didn't wait for their parents to change their minds. They dropped their bags on the floor and took off through the lobby.

George yelled after them. "Hey, soldier! I better not catch you and those 'boys' shamming around! Scope the AO and report... and don't be late for Chow Hall! Hooah!"

J. J. and Genius grinned, picturing the expressions on their fathers' faces as they shouted, "Hooah!" Then they were out the doors and up the street.

Chapter Eight

The sun was starting to descend as the boys walked through downtown Mackinac, towering trees offering some shade as they walked, but the breeze from the lake kept it from being too warm. As usual when they were on an 'adventure,' J. J. had fallen in step behind Digger. It wasn't something he really thought about, or even realized he was doing. The adventure may have been his, but Digger was the leader. Genius was, of course, the brains. J. J. wasn't sure what that made him.

A loud banging noise interrupted J. J.'s thoughts. He stopped and looked around.

"Holy crap!" Genius pointed. "Look at the size of that thing!"

J. J. looked. A giant woodpecker was hammering away at an oak tree. It was pretty cool, but they had better things to do than stare at a bird. Even as he thought it, the bird cocked its head so that one beady eye stared at him. J. J. shifted uncomfortably. It was like the bird had heard him call it stupid. "C'mon, Genius. There's no time to waste. According to my GPS, we still have half a mile to go."

"Seriously, I've never seen a woodpecker this big." Genius took a step closer to the tree.

Digger cut in, "Your mouth is moving, but all we hear is a lot of yadda, yadda, yadda. Now, let's move it!" He turned and ran up the hill, ignoring the amused looks from the other people out and about.

After a moment's hesitation, J. J. took off after his friend. Genius sighed and started off as well, the expression on his face clearly saying that he would have preferred to walk at a more reasonable pace.

J. J. and Digger rounded the bend neck-in-neck but J. J. spotted the small yellow building first. The sign hanging out front had the same logo and type of butterfly as the brochure tucked into his pants' pocket. The boys skidded to a stop and plopped down on the shaded bench to wait for Genius. A couple of minutes later, Genius appeared, his face red as he ran. When he reached his friends, Genius didn't bother with the bench and sat down on the cool concrete.

Genius glared at them as he sucked in air. "Not... cool."

Digger shrugged. "Told ya you should've opted for that training course I took in the spring."

"Bite me."

Digger grinned and stood. "There's that genius IQ at work."

J. J. rolled his eyes and got to his feet as well. He held out a hand and helped Genius up. Together, the trio walked around to the greenhouse and headed inside.

Whatever J. J. had been expecting, this wasn't it. The Butterfly House looked like something out of a dream. A very colourful, good-smelling dream. Flowers were everywhere and the air smelled like everything J. J. had imagined a girls' bedroom would smell like. No one else seemed to be around and the garden was filled only with the faint sounds of classical music and bubbling water from dozens of little waterfalls and ponds. Hundreds of butterflies of every shape and size seemed to dance to the music as they fluttered from flower to flower, tree to tree. J. J. had never seen anything like it.

"This place is for sissies." Digger folded his arms over his chest and tried to look tough. "And what's with the music?"

J. J. and Genius exchanged glances. Digger was a great guy, but sometimes he just didn't get it. But they both knew better than to argue with him.

"Yeah, sissies," J. J. said.

"Right. Give me some good old rock 'n' roll any day." Genius turned his face away from Digger as he spoke and J. J. knew it was to mask the sarcastic expression on his face.

"We need to hurry," J. J. said. He pulled the map from his pocket. "If we're late, my dad's gonna want to know why and I doubt he'll be happy to hear we were a mile away from the hotel."

"Yeah, mine wouldn't be happy about that either," Digger said.

J. J. unfolded the map and started to walk along one of the paths.

"So, J. J., what are we supposed to be looking for?" Digger asked as he began looking around.

"I don't really know. I guess something that..." His sentence trailed off as a large monarch butterfly floated down and landed directly on the map. J. J. froze. The butterfly was standing over a matching symbol on the map and he had the strangest feeling that the butterfly was looking at him. He didn't know much about the creatures, but he was pretty sure that wasn't possible. The butterfly flapped its wings and rose into the air, hovering for a moment before gliding forward. Without being able to explain himself, J. J. knew that they were supposed to follow it.

"Come on." He smiled at his friends and began to follow the butterfly. After a few steps, he turned toward the other two boys.

"Shh. Don't spook it. I think it's trying to tell me something."

He ignored the wide-eyed look that Genius and Digger gave each other. That wasn't important. What mattered was not losing track of his butterfly among all of the other ones. J. J. followed it along the brick walkway that wove through the tropical plants to end at the biggest of the waterfalls.

J. J. stopped abruptly, causing Digger and Genius to bump into him. He didn't look away, however, mesmerized as the monarch landed on the granite base of the structure. J. J.'s jaw dropped as he saw the inscription.

"What is it?" Genius was whispering. J. J. wasn't sure why, but it seemed appropriate.

"J. J.?" Digger put his hand on his friend's shoulder.

J. J. pointed and Digger read the words aloud. "'To make a wish come true, whisper it to a butterfly. Upon these wings it will be taken to heaven and granted.'"

"Is that the same –?" Digger started to ask.

A man's voice interrupted. "Magnificent, isn't it?"

All three boys jumped. An elderly man stood on the other side of Genius. None of them had heard him approach. His silver hair gleamed in the light.

"Uh, yeah," J. J. said. He glanced at the nametag on the employee vest. "So, um, Lloyd, can you tell us if the waterfall was made when this place was built?"

Lloyd looked at J. J., a curious expression on his wrinkled face. He glanced down, pale eyes widening as he saw the map and the compass that had come out from underneath J. J.'s shirt. He adjusted his glasses and cleared his throat. "Well... I'm sorry, what was your name again?"

J. J., seeing where Lloyd had been looking, folded up the map and tucked the compass back under his shirt. He tried to tell himself that it was just normal curiosity, but he couldn't help but think that Lloyd almost recognized the items. Impossible, he knew, but he couldn't quite shake the feeling. On impulse, he offered more than just his nickname. "I'm Jonathan. Jonathan Porter Hanks."

This time, J. J. was sure he saw Lloyd react, though the old man covered it well. J. J. motioned to the other two as he gave their names. "And this is Michael and Takumi."

The boys waved.

Lloyd nodded at each of them before addressing J. J. and his question. "Well, Jonathan, you'll be interested to know that this waterfall was constructed in the year 1827 in this very spot. The Butterfly House was built around it much later. Many see it as a fitting tribute to the Native American Lore of the time, much like the words etched into this middle stone."

The boys eyed the stone as if they hadn't just been staring at it.

J. J. hoped he didn't sound as eager as he felt. "What do you suppose it means?"

"The Indians believe that butterflies are messengers of all our unselfish wishes. If you believe, you make a wish and it will come true." Lloyd's voice gave no indication as to whether or not he believed what he was saying, but the shrewd expression in his eyes made J. J. think that the old man was gauging their reactions.

"But who are the butterflies' messengers for?" Genius asked.

"The Great Spirits," Lloyd said. "Guardian angels if you will. Those who watch over us and guide us every day."

A heavy silence fell for nearly half a minute before Digger broke it with an exasperated sound.

"Please. You guys don't really believe this load of –"

"Digger!" J. J. said.

Lloyd smiled at J. J., seemingly unperturbed at Digger's

protest. "Go on. Give it a try."

J. J. worked very hard at not looking at his friends as he took a step toward the fountain. The butterfly didn't fly away, not even when Digger snickered. His heart pounding in his ears, J. J. crouched down to be closer to the rock on which the butterfly was still resting, its wings slowly moving.

"If your quest is one, then you must all join in the wish," Lloyd said.

Digger laughed louder than before as J. J. turned toward his friends. Genius automatically took a step forward but Digger remained where he was.

"C'mon, Digger." J. J. was vaguely aware that he sounded like he was begging, but he couldn't stop himself. His head told him this was stupid, but something in his heart urged him to try. "Please. It's to help my Mom and Dad. I don't want to move away."

"Oh, all right." Digger sighed and allowed Genius to pull him forward.

Digger and Genius knelt on either side of J. J. and all three boys closed their eyes. J. J. made his wish, then waited a few moments, giving his friends time to finish theirs. He opened his eyes just a split second before they did and knew that the butterfly was looking at him. His friends stirred next to him and the creature took off. It fluttered around their heads as they stood, then flew down the path.

"Help us. Help my family," J. J. whispered as he watched it go.

J. J. turned toward Lloyd, another question on his lips, but the old man was gone. "Where'd he go?"

"Crazy old man," Digger said.

Genius spoke up, "We better be getting back to the hotel."

J. J. nodded in agreement. "We need to come back here tonight after everyone's gone. This is where the hunt begins, I know it. I can feel it." He looked at each of the boys. "Are you in?"

Genius and Digger both grinned and nodded, absolutely no hesitation. No matter how crazy they thought it was, an adventure was still an adventure.

"We better make sure we're prepared," Digger said as they left. "A mile walk when we don't care about being seen is a whole lot different than getting back up here in the dark without drawing attention to ourselves." He winked at his friends. "Lucky for you two, I know what I'm doing."

Chapter Nine

Aaron slumped down in his seat, trying to make himself look coolly aloof for the camera crews that were setting up all around the Grand Pavilion Room. He rolled his eyes. What a pretentious name. And, okay, the chandeliers were fancy, but what colour were the walls? They looked like pink and purple had some sort of mutated child. He was sure there was some fancy name for the colour, but he didn't know it and that was fine with him. For a moment, he wondered if Karli knew the name. She was an artist, after all.

As always, when he thought her name, he automatically looked around for her. To his surprise, he caught her looking back at him from where she was sitting between her mother and brother. She flushed, the colour deepening when he waved. He liked that she blushed when he paid attention to her. Sandra acted like everyone owed her attention. Aaron wasn't going to lie. Sandra was gorgeous. And that body... well, let's just say that she'd appeared in more than one of his daydreams, but never in a way that actually meant something.

A sharp elbow to his ribs caught his attention.

"Pay attention." Gabriella kept her voice low.

Aaron wanted to tell his mother that he really didn't care about what the event leader had to say, but he refrained and dutifully turned his eyes toward the stage. The event leader – Aaron was pretty sure his name was Edward – had been a cheerleader in a former life, Aaron decided. Either that or a motivational speaker, because he was having way too much fun for hosting something so lame.

"...so this event is part scavenger hunt, part geo-caching. A game of hiding and seeking treasures." Edward beamed a megawatt smile of teeth too white to be natural. "All right, that should pretty much wrap up everything. Are there any questions?"

George stood up and Aaron saw Karli cringe. He didn't blame her. He wouldn't want his dad drawing attention to himself.

"Just to be clear, we're not restricted to just using our GPS devices, right?"

The megawatt smile faltered slightly. "Absolutely no cell phones. If any team member is caught using a cell phone, that entire team will be disqualified." Edward paused to regain his prior enthusiasm. "Other than that, as long as the apparatus meets the requirements listed in the guidelines, you should be fine."

George nodded and sat back down. He leaned over to Jonathan and spoke in a whisper loud enough to carry down the row, further embarrassing his daughter. "What the heck's an apparatus?"

Jonathan pressed his lips together in what Aaron knew was an attempt to keep from laughing. A look of amusement flitted across Hiroto's face as Jonathan quickly answered George's question. "A device, George."

"Right." George nodded and turned his attention back to the event leader.

Edward continued when no one else stood. "Okay, now remember, this was not designed as a race, but an exercise to strengthen families and help them work together." After a moment's pause, he added, with a laugh, "Who am I kidding? It is a race! The winners will receive this awesome trophy." A young man wearing the Grand Hotel uniform walked onto the stage, a model-fake smile plastered on his face. "And, of course, they'll be spotlighted on ESPN 5."

The crowd roared at that and Aaron caught a glimpse of Sandra tossing her hair and winking at one of the male camera operators. Based on the direction the camera was pointed, Aaron thought it was safe to say that she'd had the man's attention for a while. As he looked away, he saw Karli sneering at Sandra's antics and couldn't help but grin. He liked a girl with attitude... just not that catty, manipulative attitude that most girls had. Something about Karli told him that she could be tough if she wanted to be. And he liked that thought.

The event leader had paused again, this time to build tension before announcing the final prize. "Our winners will also receive a cheque for ten thousand dollars!"

The crowd erupted again as a pretty brunette in a stunning red dress came onto the stage carrying a giant cheque. It was a toss-up as to whether or not the men in the audience were cheering for the model or the check.

"So, tomorrow, at nine a.m. sharp, we're all going to start the hunt and have some fun!" Edward pumped his fist in the air. "Yeah!"

Some sort of canned music that Aaron assumed was supposed to be rock blared over the PA system and people began getting out of their seats. He stood as well, trying to catch Karli's eye. He wanted to find out what she was planning on doing for the rest of the night. It was still fairly early and he was hoping that he could convince her to take a walk with him.

"Aaron!" Jonathan's voice was sharp. "Did you hear a word I just said?"

Aaron shook his head. "Sorry, Dad. What did you say?"

"I said we're all heading up to the room and turning in."

Was his dad serious? "It's not even nine o'clock."

"Which means we'll have a head start."

Aaron didn't bother to remind his dad that the hunt was going to start at the same time for everyone. There really wasn't a point, not when he was like this. Instead, he resigned himself to glancing over his shoulder at Karli and then following his parents out of the room.

Almost three hours later, Aaron was stretched out in his bed, staring at the ceiling. His parents had done exactly what they'd said and went to bed almost immediately after returning to the room. They'd turned off the television and turned off the lights, leaving the room in near darkness and relative silence. Aaron had forgotten his charger for his iPod so there wasn't even any music to distract him from his boredom.

The bed next to him creaked as J. J. shifted again. Aaron suddenly realized that he'd been hearing J. J. moving around for the last hour, almost as if he was anxious about something. A suspicion rose as Aaron remembered that the map his brother had shown him had been for Mackinac Island. He was willing to bet that J. J. was going to do something that had to do with that map. Something stupid.

The only way J. J. would act, Aaron realized, was if he thought everyone else was asleep. Aaron closed his eyes and called on his one semester of theatre freshman year. The snore he let out almost startled him, but he managed to keep still.

The moment he heard the floor creak, Aaron opened his eyes.

Even though he kept his eyes opened, he continued to make snoring sounds as he watched his little brother creep over to the door. The hall light illuminated J. J. enough for Aaron to see that his brother was fully dressed and carrying a backpack.

Aaron counted to ten, guessing how long it would take J. J. to get to the end of the hallway, then crawled out of bed. He pulled on the first things that his hands found and hoped that he hadn't accidentally grabbed his dad's clothes. If he wanted to follow J. J., he couldn't waste time. As it was, by the time he peeked his head out of the room, J. J. was at the end of the hall. Aaron glanced down. His own jeans and T-shirt. That was good, just in case anyone saw him.

He waited until J. J. rounded the corner and then hurried down the hall, thankful that he'd chosen his tennis shoes instead of his sandals. These were much quieter. Aaron stopped as he reached the corner, the soft voices of his brother's friends alerting him to their presence. He leaned against the wall and listened, catching snippets of their conversation.

"...did you really need to go full camo?" That was Genius and Aaron didn't need to see the trio to know that Digger was the one being addressed.

"...everyone have their equipment?" That was Digger.

"...don't leave me behind this time..." Genius' voice was fading, as if the boys had started walking.

Aaron waited another couple seconds and then peeked around the corner in time to see the stairwell door closing behind Genius. Aaron stepped into the hallway, his eyes drawn to a piece of paper lying on the ground. He bent to pick it up and recognized the brochure from the lobby. He slipped it into his pocket.

"What are you three stooges up to?"

***

84

The boys slipped out of the stairwell and flattened themselves against the wall as J. J. peeked around. The pair at the desk immediately drew his attention. One was massive, with a face right out of a horror movie. The other looked more like Batman's butler with a skull-tipped cane. Neither one of them looked pleased with the clerk at the desk. J. J. didn't blame them. He could hear the conversation she was having on the phone.

"... Can you believe it? She loses twelve pounds in one week and they still send her packing. I went through an entire box of tissues after that episode."

The man with the skull cane cleared his throat and J. J. thought that if those two men were looking at him like that, he'd put down the freaking phone in a hurry. The clerk, however, didn't seem to be as easily intimidated.

"Uh, huh... hold on a sec, Mama..." She gave the men a plastic smile. "Can I help you?"

J. J. scanned the rest of the lobby as the clerk conversed with the two men. Or, at least, the conversation was with one of them anyway; the other didn't appear to be talking. After ascertaining that the lobby was otherwise empty, J. J. motioned for his friends to follow him. They made it halfway to the doors when Genius stopped.

"Fudge!" He took a step toward a large table loaded with pastries and other desserts. "Mackinac Island is known for its fudge. It has seventeen fudge shops, each one with its own..."

J. J. spun around to hush his friend, but just then, they all heard the sound of the elevator doors dinging open. Two people, obviously a father and son, stepped out into the lobby. J. J. froze. The boy, who for some strange reason was dressed like some wanna-be rapper, looked directly at J. J.

"Go!" J. J. made a dash for the doors and heard his friends following. A quick glance over his shoulder told him that the boy wasn't watching them anymore. Rather, he seemed to be making a beeline for the dessert table. A rush of relief went through J. J. as all three boys ran out into the warm summer night. They'd gotten away without being noticed.

Chapter Ten

Charles Roberts despised Americans in what he considered menial jobs. Most believed that their jobs were beneath them, as if they deserved better than the pleasure of serving those of more noble birth and bearing. It was obvious from the way the woman at the desk prattled on that she considered herself his equal and it took all of his considerable self-control not to educate her in the proper place of her kind. Just then, a movement from the hotel entrance caught his eye. He turned slightly to see three adolescent boys disappearing through the doors. It was as he was turning back that he spotted the person he'd come to find. Melvin Dousman was currently filling a plate with desserts that he did not need. Roberts tapped Bruno on the arm and gestured. As expected, Bruno said nothing, but his smile spoke volumes. He did enjoy his work.

As Roberts and Bruno walked toward the unsuspecting man, Roberts could hear the conversation Melvin was having with the stout boy at his side.

"C'mon, Hunter. Easy on the sugar, will ya?" Melvin said as he popped a Pecan Ball into his mouth and reached over to fill a Styrofoam cup with coffee.

The boy, who Roberts felt safe to assume was Melvin's son, ignored his father and ran off with an overly full plate. The only thing Roberts hated more than the American workforce was

American children. Lazy, unappreciative, and with no respect for their betters.

"Would you care for cream with your coffee?" Roberts asked.

Melvin was answering even as he turned. "No, thanks. I like my coffee bla–" The plate and cup trembled in his hands as he saw who had spoken. A few drops of coffee splashed up over the rim, scalding Melvin's hand, but he didn't react.

"Fancy meeting you here, Mr Dousman."

***

All of the lights were on in the Dousman suite, but no one inside was particularly concerned about that as they weren't sleeping. Roberts walked through the room at a leisurely pace, enjoying the way Melvin and his wife, the oddly named Ki-Ki, watched him. He didn't consider himself a violent man, though his current position in this world required him to resort to violence more often than he'd have liked. One of the benefits, he'd found, did tend to be a unique opportunity to see people in a way that others did not. For example, he sincerely doubted that any of the Dousmans' friends had ever seen the couple looking so terrified. Not that Roberts could blame them. They were, after all, both tied to chairs and Bruno was currently leaning over Ki-Ki to fasten a gag into place.

"I trusted you, Mr Dousman." Roberts kept his voice quiet. Over the years, he'd found that the contrast between a soft voice and a harsh touch was more productive than shouting. "As did my partners. Even my associate, Bruno, trusted you with his meagre life savings."

Bruno mumbled what Roberts had learned during their time together was nothing that should be uttered in the presence of a lady. Fortunately, Bruno's inability to speak properly due to an unfortunate encounter with an angry Russian, prevented any of the words from being understandable.

"As you can see, he's beyond words." Roberts ignored the glare Bruno sent his way. It was all for show. As much as he could for someone of Bruno's standing, Roberts respected his associate and knew that the feeling was mutual.

"Listen to me." Melvin's voice wasn't just tinged with panic; it was saturated. "I believed the investment was sound. The stock market is going through a difficult time right now. I lost money too!"

Roberts nodded his head ever so slightly and Bruno sank his fist into Melvin's soft abdomen. There was a rush of air as Melvin's lungs emptied and Ki-Ki screamed, the sound muffled by the gag. Roberts waited until Melvin started taking deep, gulping breaths before he began talking. No need to waste time repeating himself when the first few minutes would be consumed by pain and fear.

"Two million dollars should roughly convert into euros equalling what you stole, plus interest, of course."

"I told you, it's gone." Melvin was gasping. "Every penny. Honest."

"How unfortunate." Roberts sighed. He motioned Bruno toward Ki-Ki. "I am sorry to hear that Mr Dousman. Truly sorry."

Bruno slid his gun from his belt and stepped directly in front of Ki-Ki before screwing on his silencer. Ki-Ki's eyes kept widening until the effect was nearly comical.

"Perhaps you have an insurance policy on your wife that could assist you with paying your debts."

"Wait, wait!" Melvin's desperation was clear. "I can get it."

Roberts was pleased to see that Melvin was a man more

concerned with the welfare of his wife than himself. Roberts could respect that. There was nothing he loathed more than having Bruno inflict pain upon someone's partner or child, only to have them break only after the harm was turned their way. He always had difficulty leaving those people alive. A true gentleman would always sacrifice for a lady or child.

"You can get it?" Roberts gave Melvin a small smile. "Mr Dousman, two million dollars is a lot of money. Where could you possibly–"

The sound of the door being unlocked cut through what Roberts had intended to say. As the doorknob jiggled, Roberts motioned to Bruno who flipped off the main light, leaving only the glow of the bathroom light. A moment later, the chubby boy from the lobby appeared. Hunter, Roberts remembered.

He was already talking before the door shut behind him. "Pops. Moms. I found these kids who have a treasure map, for reals. They's outside talkin' 'bout it and how they's goin' to some butterfly place. I'm thinkin' there be gold, silver and jewels here on the island. I'm gonna follow 'em and get me some gold for my grill... just came for some supplies first."

Hunter opened the refrigerator and pulled out a soda and a slice of pizza. Roberts took a moment to wonder why Americans were so surprised about their obesity problem, particularly among their children. As the boy turned, Roberts held up a hand to Bruno, waiting for the opportune moment to turn the lights back on. It came a moment later when Hunter's eyes widened as he saw his parents. As the lights came back on, the food dropped from Hunter's hands. The can of soda burst open and sprayed the sticky liquid everywhere, but Hunter didn't move. Roberts had a moment to feel bad for the maid service.

"Did you hear that, Bruno?" Roberts was intrigued by the boy's story but didn't want to reveal how much. If the child spoke the truth, Roberts could at last have the life he deserved. "A buried treasure."

"It's true!" Melvin blurted out the words and Roberts turned toward the man. "There is a treasure! That's why we're here. It's enough to cover all of our losses."

Roberts' eyes narrowed as he studied Melvin. Nothing about this man spoke of the intelligence needed to create such a fantastical lie. And the children of whom Hunter spoke had to have something real if they were talking about having to leave the hotel grounds for the butterfly place over a mile away. If they were merely playing at treasure hunting, surely they would stick to the area close by. Why walk so far at night when they could have just as many nooks and crannies available here?

"Fair enough," he finally said. "You'll remain here in this room, while we take in the sights of the island... with your son for company, of course."

The protests of the Dousmans confirmed his decision to take the boy. They clearly loved their son and would do nothing to bring him harm. Leverage was a beautiful thing.

"Bruno," Roberts said. "Collect their phones."

Roberts walked over to Hunter's side as Bruno dug through Ki-Ki's purse to take out her pink bejewelled phone. The one from the nightstand was the usual businessperson's smartphone. After Bruno handed both devices over to Roberts, he grabbed the landline and ripped it from the wall.

"They will make you pay for that, I'm afraid," Roberts said. "Now, if you leave this room or attempt to contact anyone, you will never see your boy again." He drew a small electronic device from his pocket. "I will receive a notification if your door opens, so, if I were you, I would refrain from ordering room service."

Chapter Eleven

J. J. glanced over his shoulder again. When they'd stopped just outside of the front doors to take a look at the map, he could have sworn he'd seen someone following them. Digger and Genius had thought he was paranoid, but J. J. wasn't about to let someone else in on the secret. Now, the three boys were huddled at the far corner of the hotel's massive porch and J. J. was fairly confident that they were safe. He slid his backpack from his shoulder and unzipped it. The hotel grounds were well lit, but they were at enough of a distance that he retrieved his torch as well as the map.

"You really think that map is going to lead us to a buried treasure?" Digger asked, his tone sceptical.

J. J. unfolded the map and laid it flat on the porch. "In my great-great-great-grandfather's journal, he spoke of a chest filled with gold and silver coins and jewels that he and some kids stole from the British Army. He never left this island, so the treasure must be buried here somewhere."

"Wait, if your triple-great-grandfather never left the island, how did you end up with the map and his journal?" Genius asked.

J. J. shrugged. He'd asked himself the same question. "I don't know. Maybe one of the kids did it. He said that they were like family. Somehow, they got this stuff into the hands of his only son, my great-great-grandfather, John Hanks, and it eventually got passed down to my grandfather and then my dad. They must not have known where the treasure was and no one ever found the map or journal until now. The journal kind of ends abruptly."

"So this map leads to a stone in a waterfall that's now in the middle of a butterfly garden and that's how we're going to get rich?" Genius put it all together.

J. J. gave his friend a dirty look.

"Just asking."

"Okay, enough talking," Digger said. "Let's get over to the Butterfly House and check out that waterfall. If you're right, that's our first clue."

The other two agreed and J. J. deposited the map back into his bag. As they stood, J. J. looked around one more time to make sure that no one else was around. He still had the strangest feeling that they were being watched. He didn't see anyone and set off without another word. The boys set the easy jogging pace they'd agreed upon earlier that day. Genius looked relieved while J. J. and Digger fought the urge to go faster. Something was waiting for them ahead, J. J. was sure of it.

***

Karli wasn't sure why she'd agreed to go on a walk with Sandra. Maybe it was because they were the only two girls their age. Maybe it was because, despite Sandra's often abrasive personality, Karli actually kind of admired the blonde for the way she went after what she wanted. Whatever the reason, it had landed her walking around the Grand Hotel fountain late at night.

"Isn't this place just beautiful?" Karli tried for small talk.

"Yeah, I guess, if you're into primitive culture. And, what the heck, it's July and it's freaking freezing!" Sandra complained.

Karli tried not to smile. "It's at least sixty-five and it's the middle of the night."

"Exactly!"

Lightning flashed in the distance and was followed by the low rumble of thunder.

"Great," Sandra said. "A storm is just what I need for my hair."

Karli shivered and folded her arms across her stomach. "I don't like storms. Never have."

Sandra grinned at her. "Bet you wish Aaron was here to make you feel safe, huh?"

Karli felt the heat rush to her face as she played dumb. "What do you mean?"

"I see the way you two are." Sandra's voice changed to an almost wistful note. "I wish he looked at me like that."

"Like what?" Karli could hardly believe what she was hearing. Every guy stared at Sandra, including Aaron.

"Are you really that naïve?" Sandra asked. "When guys look at me, they just see big boobs, and most of the time I'm okay with that. But, every once in a while, I'd like to have a guy look at me and see me. The way Aaron does with you. He's totally into you."

A wild hope rose in Karli's chest. "You think so?"

"Duh." Sandra's expression grew serious for a moment. "Look, I like to flirt, but there's nothing between me and Aaron."

A lighthouse foghorn echoed across the lake and both girls jumped. Karli looked over at Sandra and was pleased to see that the blonde looked just as sheepish as she felt herself. They both laughed and sat down on the edge of the fountain. Sandra dug into her pocket and pulled out a pack of cigarettes.

"Want one?"

"Sandra, where'd you get those?" Karli knew she sounded disapproving, but she was honestly surprised. She hadn't thought Sandra would do anything to risk her precious health.

Sandra shrugged and held them out. "Snuck 'em out of my mom's purse. I was bored."

"Uh, I don't know–"

Karli screamed as a shadow lunged toward them.

Sandra threw her hands in the air, fumbling with her torch. Before either girl could get the beams pointed in the right direction, Aaron stepped out of the shadows.

"Geez. You both scream like girls."

"Aaron, you jerk!" Sandra turned around, looking for her cigarettes. "You scared us half to death."

Karli would've laughed at the expression on Sandra's face when she saw the pack floating in the middle of the fountain, but her heart was still racing from the scare.

"Sorry."

Aaron gave Karli a sheepish grin as he apologized and her heart skipped a beat for a completely different reason. Suddenly, panic seized her. "What are you doing out here, Aaron? You didn't hear us talking, right?"

Sandra giggled and Karli shot the girl a fierce look. Or, at least it was supposed to be fierce. She wasn't entirely sure if she'd gotten any colour back in her face. Not that she'd had much to lose in the first place.

"What? No." Aaron shook his head.

Karli could breathe again.

"I was following the Three Mouseketeers. They're up to something." His eyes lit up. "Hey, you two wanna have some fun? I think I can get one of those carriage guys to give us a ride."

***

95

Genius started complaining when the rain began halfway to the Butterfly House, but Digger actually liked the way the mist gave everything a surreal look. It made the entire mission seem more stealthy, more secretive. He could almost imagine that he was on a classified assignment, one that he wasn't guaranteed to live through. Besides, it was more of a sprinkle than actual rain, though judging by the lightning in the distance, more was coming.

He led the way, of course, with J. J. right behind him and Genius last. They crept around the little yellow house to the greenhouse in the back. He wasn't sure what he was thinking when he reached for the door, maybe that it wouldn't be locked because the only thing inside was butterflies, but then J. J. tapped him on the shoulder and pointed to the digital door lock. Both of them turned toward Genius who was already digging through his backpack. After a moment, he pulled a strange-looking electronic device from his bag, a wide grin on his face.

"This could take a while," J. J. said. "Why don't Digger and I go take a look around for another way in while you take care of that lock?"

Genius nodded. "Okay."

Even though he was the leader, Digger was glad that J. J. had said it. Genius tended to take things better from J. J. The pair left Genius hooking the device to the lock and circled around the back of the greenhouse. By the time they rounded the last corner, Digger was contemplating other ways to get inside.

"Let's just bust out a few of these windows and crawl through."

J. J. gave him an exasperated look. "If we damage the greenhouse, the butterflies will escape."

Digger snorted. "They're butterflies, J. J., not killer bees." For a brief moment, his imagination took over and he saw thousands of butterflies attacking his sister. The mental movie was still playing as he and J. J. returned to where they'd begun. A beep brought him back to reality and the click that followed was loud in the night air.

Genius grinned, looking rather pleased with himself. "Simple."

Digger rolled his eyes. "Yeah, simple. Right."

As he took a step forward, a sound came out of the darkness and Digger froze. The hairs on his arms and the back of his neck stood up and a shiver went through him. A series of images flashed through his mind as a sense of danger filled him.

A bright light.

Figures emerging from the darkness.

The flash of a weapon.

"Get down," J. J. hissed, yanking on Digger's arm.

The three boys crouched down, trying to make themselves as small as possible.

"What is it?" Genius asked.

"Shush!" Digger pushed aside the lingering foreboding and let his training take over. Granted, with the exception of a couple of 'survival classes,' most of that training had been listening to his father, watching war movies and playing video games, but he still knew more than the other two. "Someone's there."

"J. J., let's go back to the hotel. I don't want to go to jail." Genius sounded like he was close to panicking.

"Hush," J. J. said.

"It's all good for you. Give you a scar or something and you'll look badass. Pretty boys like me and Digger don't do well in jail."

Digger glared at his friend. "Shut up."

His ears strained against the darkness, listening for any

indication that they weren't alone. He heard nothing and, after a moment, stood. "Whatever it was, it's gone now."

Genius gave a sigh of relief that Digger thought was a bit too melodramatic. It wasn't like they were in any actual danger.

"All right," J. J. said. "Let's get inside."

As soon as the words left his mouth, a deep voice came from the shadows. "Put your hands on your heads and get down on the ground."

Bright lights shone in their eyes and all three boys winced. Digger's heart gave a thump as his mind flashed back to the images he'd seen. Weapons would be next. His stomach twisted.

"Uh, sir," J. J. said. "I can explain–"

"Now!" The voice left no room for argument.

All three boys dropped to the ground and Digger heard Genius whimper. The lights moved closer and Digger set his jaw, determined not to cry. He'd take his punishment like a man. He was still young enough that he could have his record sealed so it wouldn't affect his military career. It wasn't like they'd killed anyone. A little B&E could be dismissed as childhood pranks.

"I knew it," Genius said. "I'm gonna end up a jailhouse boy toy. Digger, don't let J. J. trade you for smokes."

A new sound cut through the darkness. A familiar sound.

J. J. lifted his head. "What the..."

Digger looked up to see his sister with Sandra and Aaron. The girls had their hands over their mouths. It had been Karli's giggle that Digger had heard. Aaron burst out laughing.

"Aaron, you jerk!" J. J. scrambled to his feet.

Digger was just a split second behind, the memory of what he'd felt still fresh in his mind. Genius took a minute longer.

"What are you doing here?" J. J. asked.

Aaron shook his head, still laughing. "What am I doing here? J. J., what the heck are *you* doing here?"

Sandra snickered. "Looks like B&E to me." To pretty much everyone's surprise, she winked at Genius. "That's about five to ten in the slammer for a pretty thing like you."

Genius' jaw dropped.

"Michael!" Karli's voice was sharp and Digger turned away from his dumbfounded friend to his glaring sister. "Dad's gonna be pissed."

"He doesn't need to know what we're doing, Karli," Digger said, trying to hide the nervousness in his voice. The last thing he needed was his father to know he'd been running around at night. Military school would very quickly become a real possibility and, as much as he liked the whole military thing, Digger did not want to go to military school.

"What *are* you doing?" Aaron asked.

"Look, can we get out of the rain, please?" Sandra asked.

Digger sighed. "Tell 'em, J. J."

J. J. looked at Genius who nodded as well and pulled the map from his backpack.

"Holy crap, J. J. Not that again." Aaron ran his hand through his damp hair.

"Come on," Digger said as the mist began to turn into rain. "Let's talk inside."

Since it didn't look like anyone else was going to lead the way, Digger did. He tried to walk through the illegally opened doorway as if he didn't care. Surprising himself, he managed it even though the entire time, his heart was in his throat, as if he expected to hear an alarm any moment. Then again, it was just a room of butterflies so the lack of an alarm system wasn't exactly surprising.

The group paused just inside the door as J. J. unfolded the map.

"Now we're all accessories to a crime," Sandra said. "I'll tell you this right now, I will sell you out in a minute for a plea bargain. I refuse to go to jail for you guys. I would not do well in jail."

Despite her complaint, Sandra joined the rest as they followed J. J. down the path the boys had taken earlier that day.

"I told you to leave that dumb map at home, J. J.," Aaron said as he walked behind his brother.

Digger glanced over his shoulder to check on his sister. He may have been the younger one, but his father had drilled into his head that it was his responsibility to look after Karli. That's what men did. A large black butterfly with bright green stripes landed on Karli's shoulder for a moment before taking off again.

"They're so beautiful."

Yeah, she was fine. Digger turned his attention back to J. J.

"Here." J. J. handed him the map as he dug the journal from his backpack.

Aaron's eyes widened as his brother flipped through pages of handwritten notes and drawings. "What in the world is that?"

"Porter Hanks' journal," J. J. spoke without taking his eyes off of the journal. "I found it in our basement, locked in the old writing desk with the rest of the stuff I showed you guys back home. The journal is filled with clues that will lead us to the treasure."

"Treasure?" Sandra was suddenly very interested in what they were doing.

"Yeah," Digger said. "Gold, silver and diamonds."

"There's diamonds?" Karli asked doubtfully.

"We'll need them to hire the best defence attorneys," Genius said mournfully.

"All right!" Aaron's voice was sharp. "This is going too far. J.

J., what did Dad say in the car? There is no treasure."

J. J. held his ground. "Grandpa Porter Hanks hid the map in that cannon statue for his son, but John never got it. No one did until we broke it. The journal has some information about his life on the island, but it's mostly clues and drawings that we can use with the map to help us find his treasure."

"You are such a child, J. J.," Aaron said.

"C'mon, Aaron." Karli touched Aaron's arm and Digger almost gagged at the sickening look that passed between the two. "Give him a break."

"What can it hurt?" Sandra's eyes gleamed and Digger knew that she was thinking of the treasure. "We're already here, right?"

Aaron looked from Sandra to J. J. and then down at Karli who was staring up at him with those big grey eyes of hers. Aaron smiled and Karli blushed.

Digger was now sure that he was going to throw up. That was his sister for crying out loud! To further his annoyance, J. J. was grinning like an idiot, as if he was now certain he was going to get his own way. These guys seriously needed to man up!

"Okay, J. J.," Aaron said. "You've got five minutes."

"Hooah!" Digger shouted, as much to break the mood as anything else. Aaron really needed to stop looking at Karli that way. It was gross.

Chapter Twelve

Mr Roberts marched through the nearly deserted streets with a confidence that would have made people get out of his way, if there had been anyone else out and about. As it was, the few people who were still around gave him a wide berth and averted their eyes, as well they should in his opinion. Bloody Americans always had thought too highly of themselves. The only ones worse were the French. He'd never understood how his countrymen could tolerate being around these people for extended periods of time. They were the low class, the criminals and outcasts that other countries didn't want. He, on the other hand, was descended directly from royalty. Granted, through a bastard, but royal blood nonetheless.

He sighed. "What kind of cursed place is this? No means of transportation anywhere."

Behind Roberts, Hunter squirmed in Bruno's grip. "Let me go you creepy tongue-tied Frankenstein!"

At least the child had enough sense not to scream. Roberts would have hated to have needed to instruct Bruno to snap Hunter's neck. The boy did still have a part to play before his final demise. Based on the child's terrible vernacular and inexplicable fashion sense, Roberts was sure he would be doing the world a favour. Heaven forbid the boy grow up and breed.

Roberts stopped and turned. "He's just a child, Bruno." Bruno was scowling down at Hunter with an even more unintelligent expression on his face than usual. Roberts respected the man's brute strength and ability to cause pain, but intellect was not part of the package. "Are you unable to handle even a single child? Perhaps I should dissolve our partnership and find someone more capable?"

Bruno made a sound very much like a growl and shook Hunter who let out an undignified squeak. Roberts closed his eyes, repulsed by the boy's weakness. While he appreciated the progress of civilization, there were times he could see the logic of drowning certain children at birth. When Roberts opened his eyes, his gaze fell on a horse-drawn taxi waiting for the final fare of the night. At last, something was going right. "Ah, come along, Bruno, and bring our little friend. Our carriage awaits."

"I ain't going nowhere with yous and I ain't tellin' you nothin' about no treasure neither."

"What a delightful child," Roberts said.

Hunter twisted in Bruno's hand and delivered a sharp kick to Bruno's shin. The big man groaned.

"That is about enough of that." Roberts yanked the skull head off of his cane to reveal the seven inch blade that had been concealed within the cane. Hunter's eyes widened as Roberts took a step toward him. When Mr Roberts grabbed Hunter's braids, the boy let out a frightened yelp that turned into a whimper as cool steel came to rest on the tender skin of his throat.

"P-please."

"Let us come to an agreement, shall we?" Roberts leaned close enough to smell the boy's sweat and the stench of whatever food was smeared on his clothes. "You will come along with us, peacefully, mind you. There will be no more resistance, whether physical or verbal. No more assaults. You will tell us what we want to know when we ask. In return, I will not peel the flesh from your bones, remove your tongue and eyes, and then throw you into the lake, still alive." The acrid smell of urine filled his nostrils and he knew that he'd gotten his point across. Still, he waited for an answer. "Do we have an understanding?"

"Yes, yes, yes." Hunter was crying now, tears streaming down his pudgy face.

Roberts released the boy and stepped back, disgusted. He walked ahead of Bruno and Hunter, slipping the blade back into its sheath as he went. The cab driver looked at Hunter and raised his eyebrow in question.

"The boy decided to sneak out. His mother coddles him." Mr Roberts folded an extra bill in with the fare. It would be well worth the fifty dollars if the cabbie forgot all about the crying boy. "Now, my good man, will you take us to the Butterfly House? And be quick about it."

Chapter Thirteen

J. J. looked up at the waterfall, mesmerized by the constant sound of the water bubbling up through the rock and spilling down over nearly eight feet of stone. Unlike the other structures in the greenhouse, this one didn't look as if it were man-made. In fact, J. J. couldn't tell what kept the rocks together, only that they appeared to have been fitted in such a way that they didn't need anything else to maintain their shape. This was it, the start of the adventure; he was sure of it. Now he just had to figure out what to do next. The fact that everyone was staring at him wasn't helping him think. He could smell Sandra's perfume and it was really distracting. She smelled so good. Like flowers and soap. A slap on the back of his head brought him back to the problem at hand. He didn't have to look to know it had been Aaron. He knew better than to complain, especially if he wanted to see this through. J. J. flipped open the journal to the page that bore the symbol of the monarch butterfly.

"Okay, we're right here. This symbol on the map matches the symbol on the top of this page in the journal. It's not a coincidence. They're pieces to the puzzle. I'm sure of it."

"You think the treasure's under here?" Digger asked.

J. J. shrugged. "I don't know. Maybe."

"C'mon, J. J. How are we going to break through this stupid fountain?" Aaron sounded like he was ready to call the whole thing quits.

Sandra leaned over J. J.'s shoulder, her chest brushing his arm. He nearly jumped out of his skin. "What's this writing under the picture?"

"It's a riddle." J. J.'s voice cracked and he blushed, desperately hoping that no one could see how red his face had gotten. "There's a bunch of them in here." This time, his voice held steady.

"This is a joke," Aaron said. "Look, it's late. We have to leave, now."

The others ignored him.

"What does this riddle say, J. J.?" Karli asked.

"There's two parts. The first part says," J. J. read, "'The journey begins with four coloured rocks. One is correct, the others are not. Turn once to the left and thrice to the right, push down so hard to seal it tight. Err once, brave the bore. Err twice, err no more."

"Oh-kay," Karli said slowly. "I really don't like the sound of that."

"Me either," Sandra agreed.

"Hold on, you guys. Let's see what else it says." Digger turned to J. J. "What's the second part?"

"Umm... 'Look to the end of forever, and the beginning of eternity and you'll find a passageway halfway through the middle.'"

As J. J. finished, all eyes turned from him to the waterfall. After a moment of straining in the dark, Karli shone her tourch at the top of the water. She did a slow, careful pan from left to right, moving down a little at a time. When she reached the section at eye level, the dull stones shimmered for a moment as her light passed over them. Aaron touched her shoulder, but she was already moving back. There, in the middle of the stones, were four that didn't match the rest. These were larger... and they were red, green, blue and gold. They weren't bright, like they had been painted, but almost as if the colour had been worked into the rock itself.

"Take a look at that. She found it," J. J. said.

"So, which one is the right one?" Sandra asked the question they were all thinking.

Digger reached out to grab one of the rocks. "It's gotta be the gold one."

"Don't touch it!" Aaron shoved between J. J. and Digger, knocking Digger aside. The others took a step back. "Don't touch any of them! I mean, if we're gonna do this, we need to decide together... take a vote."

J. J. gave his older brother an admiring look. For the first time since this adventure had begun, J. J. was glad that Aaron was with them. Even if J. J. had protested, Digger would've just went ahead and did what he wanted like always. Usually he liked his friend's go-for-it attitude, but with something like this, it could mean the difference between finding a treasure or something bad happening.

"The gold one makes sense," Sandra said immediately. "Gold for treasure."

Karli was shaking her head in disagreement. "Why not the green one? Emeralds are green."

The girls looked at J. J.

"I'm not sure." He started to give an answer when a soft whispering sound distracted him. He turned his head and saw a huge monarch butterfly, easily bigger than his hand, hovering in the air. It remained there, just a few inches away, so close that he could have reached out and touched it.

Red.

J. J. blinked. Had he just heard a butterfly say 'red'? No way. That was impossible. It was crazy. And yet...

Red.

J. J. shook his head and the butterfly flew away. For a moment, he could have sworn he heard the butterfly sigh. Maybe he did need to head back to the hotel and get some sleep. Talking butterflies? What was next, dancing iguanas and singing tuna?

"J. J.?" Aaron's impatience was tinged with a small amount of brotherly concern.

Pushing aside the thoughts of talking animals, J. J. turned back to the group. "I agree with Sandra. Gold for treasure."

"Shocker." Digger ignored the dirty look J. J. sent his way. "You should've just let me turn it then. I was going for the gold anyway."

"Shut it, Digger." Aaron turned to Genius. "That's three votes for gold and one for green. What about you, Genius?"

Genius shifted his weight from one foot to the other, looking decidedly nervous. "I... I changed my mind. I think we should hightail it outta here before something bad happens."

Aaron shook his head. "Useless." He turned back to the others. "Okay. We'll go with the gold one."

No one moved as they all looked at each other while trying not to make eye contact. Finally, J. J. asked, "Who's going to turn it?"

After a moment, Aaron spoke up, "I'll do it. I'm the oldest."

J. J. took a step back to give his brother easier access to the waterfall. Aaron put his knee on the edge of the base around the fountain and leaned forward. His hand parted the flowing water and, after a slight hesitation, he touched the gold rock. Everyone tensed, but nothing happened. Aaron, bolstered by the lack of disaster, looked over his shoulder.

"Someone hold on to me."

Before anyone else could step forward, Sandra wrapped her arms around Aaron's waist, pressing her cheek against his back.

"Um, maybe just hold on to my belt loops?" Aaron's face was red and J. J. resisted the urge to laugh.

"Oh, right." Sandra giggled and let go of Aaron. She hooked her fingers into the belt loops of his jeans. "I gotcha."

Aaron looked doubtful at Sandra's ability to prevent him from taking a header into the fountain, but he didn't say anything. J. J. thought that was wise. Sandra could be a bit scary sometimes.

"J. J., what's the book say again?" Aaron asked.

"Turn it once to the left and then three times to the right," J. J. answered promptly.

Aaron plunged his other hand through the water and grasped the rock. He took a deep breath and tried to turn the rock. Nothing happened. Aaron made a face and tried harder, the cords on his neck standing out as he strained. Suddenly, the skin on his arms rippled as if his muscles were doing something new and, with a loud creak, it gave way. Surprise flashed across his face and was gone again as he completed the counterclockwise motion. He paused, holding his breath, then exhaled slowly as nothing happened. He glanced behind him and grinned at the girls, a smug expression on his face.

"Once to the left," J. J. said, rolling his eyes. "Now, three times to the right."

Digger picked up the count as Aaron began to turn the rock slowly in the opposite direction. "One."

A grinding sound came from behind the waterfall.

"Two," Digger said.

"Do you hear that? It's working!" J. J. could barely contain his excitement.

"Yeah! We're all gonna be rich!" Digger pumped his fist in the air.

"Three," Sandra said.

"It's not too late to turn back, you guys." Genius stayed off to the side, the expression in his face saying that he didn't think any of this was a good idea.

"Shut up, all of you," Aaron said. His breath was coming in pants. "What do I do now?"

J. J. glanced down at the journal and then back up at his brother. "Push down real hard and seal it tight."

"Be careful, Aaron." Karli sounded worried.

Aaron gave her a charming smile as he placed both of his hands on the rock and pushed down. Sandra scowled and, for one brief moment, J. J. was sure that she was going to let go of Aaron. Then the moment passed and the rock Aaron was pushing gave way, disappearing into the fountain with a heavy clang.

"What was that?" Sandra asked.

"Uh-oh." Genius began backing away.

"Get back!" Aaron tried to straighten as Sandra let go of his belt loops and jumped to the side. Before Aaron could do anything, a jet of water shot from the hole the gold rock had disappeared into. It hit Aaron square in the chest and knocked him backward. He tumbled off the edge of the fountain and onto the brick walkway. The water continued spurting for a few seconds more, then stopped as abruptly as it started. For a moment, there was only the sound of running water in the distance and their own harsh breathing. Then Karli and Sandra both hurried to help Aaron.

"Oh my gosh!" Karli reached him first. "Are you okay?"

Aaron scrambled to his feet, his tennis shoes sliding on the wet brick and threatening to take him down again. He glared at the boys as he regained his balance.

Digger couldn't quite hide his grin as well as the other two. "Oops?"

"We're leaving. Now!" Aaron's voice took on the authoritative tone that their father used when he was fed up with their behaviour.

"No, Aaron, please?" J. J. knew that it was risky pushing it, but now that he'd seen that something had happened, he was more certain than ever that the treasure was real. "It's gotta be the green rock."

"Actually, it's the red one," Genius said.

Before he could stop himself, J. J. said, "The butterfly was right?"

"What?" All eyes turned to J. J. and Genius.

"Um, nothing." J. J. hurried to cover his impetuous statement. He directed his question to Genius to deflect the attention. "How do you know it's the red rock?"

"I was thinking about the clue and it came to me just before Aaron got blasted by that water."

Aaron took two steps and yanked Genius up by his collar until the younger boy's feet were barely touching the ground. "You knew the answer?"

"Aaron, stop. Wait." Sandra grabbed Aaron's arm and spoke to Genius. "How do you know it's the red rock?"

Genius' eyes darted from Sandra to Aaron and back again. "Well, 'look to the end of forever.' At the end of the word forever is the letter R. And the beginning of eternity is the letter E. And you'll 'find a passageway halfway through the middle.' The letter halfway through the word 'middle' is D." The explanation poured out of him.

"Uh huh." Aaron still seemed sceptical, but he lowered Genius to the ground and released his grip on the young man's collar.

Genius straightened his shirt. "It's really kinda easy if you think about it."

"Easy?" Aaron scowled. "Whatever. We're leaving."

"C'mon, Aaron." J. J. knew which button to push, especially with the girls here. "I'll do it if you're too scared."

"I'm not scared!" Aaron reacted exactly as J. J. had wanted. "I'll do it." He turned to Genius. "You better be right."

Genius' face paled and he swallowed hard. For his friend's sake, J. J. hoped Genius was right. If Aaron got another blast of water, things were not going to end well for Genius. Or for him, for that matter.

Aaron grabbed the red rock, hesitated, then turned it counterclockwise once. Another groaning sound came from the fountain. Aaron flinched, but kept going, turning the rock clockwise three times. Either it wasn't as tight in as the gold one or Aaron had gotten in the rhythm because it turned much easier than the previous one.

"Here it goes." Aaron closed his eyes and shoved the red rock into place.

The entire waterfall shook and Aaron jumped back, nearly stumbling as his feet slid on the brick. None of the others paid any attention to his near wipe-out as they watched the fountain begin to move. Down a seam that had previously been invisible to the naked eye, the stones split apart, revealing a passageway that sloped down into the earth.

"Whoa," Genius said.

"Holy crap!" Digger's eyes were huge.

"Now do you guys believe me?" J. J. clutched his ancestor's

journal to his chest. If the passageway was real, the treasure would be too.

Genius stepped forward first, an expression of wonderment on his face. He tilted his head, looking up one side and then the other. "This is beautiful. Pure genius!"

"Guys, we gotta call someone," Aaron said. "Mom, Dad...the police."

The idea appalled J. J. "What? No! We need to go down there and follow the map to the treasure."

Sandra shook her head and crossed her arms under her ample bosom. "I'm not going in there. It's cold and wet." She wrinkled her nose. "And what in the heck is that smell?"

J. J. ignored Sandra's comments, which said something about his dedication to finding this treasure. Not much could've distracted him from the blonde, but this was more important than trying to look good in front of Sandra. He had to keep everyone from leaving. They needed to keep looking. They needed to find that treasure. "In case you're forgetting, Aaron, we broke in. I don't think the police are going to overlook that little piece of information."

"First of all, *we* didn't break in. *You* did," Aaron said. "But it doesn't matter, J. J. We can't just ignore this."

"Aaron's right," Karli said. "This is a big deal."

Before J. J. could argue, Digger spoke up, "But we said we'd help J. J.'s mom and dad. They need this."

Aaron turned to his brother. "What's he talking about J. J.?"

J. J. hesitated. He hadn't wanted to tell Aaron what he'd overheard, but it seemed like he didn't have a choice now. It might be the only thing to get through. "Mom and Dad lost everything, Aaron, including the house. As soon as this trip's over, we're moving to Florida to live with Nana and Grandpa."

Aaron shook his head and glared at his brother. "You're lying. Mom and Dad wouldn't have told you and not me. You're just saying that so we'll follow you on this stupid adventure."

"It's true, Aaron. I overheard them talking before we left. They didn't tell us because they didn't want to ruin our trip." He knew the moment Aaron believed because his brother's face fell.

"This is crazy." Aaron raked his hands through his hair. "I can't believe this is happening."

J. J. stared. He'd never seen Aaron so upset. His big brother had always been a tough guy, the one who'd bash him over the head and tell him to walk it off. Last year, during a football game, J. J. had seen Aaron take a hit from a defensive player who was more than twice his size, get up and finish the game. Later, they'd found out that Aaron had cracked two ribs. Now, knowing that they'd lost their house and would be leaving their friends, Aaron appeared to be at a loss as to what to do.

Karli reached out and took his hand. "I'm sorry, Aaron."

For once, Digger didn't have a smart comment and even Sandra looked genuinely sympathetic. Genius awkwardly patted J. J. on the shoulder.

"Look, Bruno," a clipped British accent came from the top of the path. "We've wandered into an after-school special."

114

Chapter Fourteen

If J. J. had thought he'd been scared before when Aaron had shown up and tricked him, it was nothing compared to the stomach-dropping terror he felt when he turned to see the two men from the hotel lobby standing behind them. Also there, for some reason, was the chubby boy who J. J. had last seen stuffing his face. The two men, J. J. had found creepy before. Now, they were freaking terrifying. A quick glance around at his friends told him that their feelings were very similar to his.

Karli clung to Aaron's hand and he pulled her close. At the same time, he stepped in front of Sandra, as if to shield her as well. J. J. had to respect his brother's willingness to protect both of the girls. Digger was staring at the men, his eyes wide. It was a pretty safe bet, J. J. thought, that his friend was trying to figure out what military strategy would best work in the current situation. Genius was backing up, climbing up over the fountain wall when he ran out of room on the path. J. J. caught a glimpse of Genius looking intently at something before the boy from the hotel spoke and drew J. J.'s attention.

"See. I told yous." He pointed to Digger. "And that kid's holding the treasure map. Now, let me go. I told yous what you wanted to know. I gots to go and –"

"Hush, Hunter."

"I done told yous that it's Original-One." The boy struck a pose that J. J. assumed was supposed to be gangster though it simply looked ridiculous. "Yo, yo, yo."

"And I have told you that you mustn't be demanding." The British man pulled the boy to him and held the skull head of his cane against Hunter's face. The boy whimpered as the British man looked at Digger. "Be a good lad and hand over the map or, I'm afraid, this dear boy will meet a rather unfortunate end."

"Who the heck are you guys?" Digger asked. His sister let out a nervous squeak.

"Oh, so sorry, quite rude of me. Do let me make introductions," the British man said. "My name is Mr Roberts and my silent companion is Bruno. Lovely to meet you all. Now, do as I ask or I shall be quite cross with you and, believe me, that is not something you wish to experience."

"Give him the map, Michael," Karli said.

"No way!" J. J. couldn't believe that they were considering giving up the treasure to a couple of thugs.

Roberts did something that made Hunter whimper. "P-please. Help me."

"Just give it to them!" Aaron snapped. "It's not worth anyone dying over."

"The young man is right. No one needs to die tonight." Mr Roberts smiled at the kids and J. J. was reminded of the way a cat would look at its prey before it pounced. "Now, give me the map!"

Digger looked to his friends, clearly torn. When J. J. shook his head, Digger turned to his sister. Her face was white, her lips pressed tightly together. She nodded.

"Give it to him!" Sandra's voice was shrill.

"Here, take it." Digger held out the map.

"Digger, no!" J. J.'s heart dropped as he watched his last shred of hope offered to these two men in exchange for a kid none of them knew. A kid who, for all they knew, could be in league with the men. Or men who wouldn't keep their word not to hurt any of them.

"Thank you." Hunter was almost in tears.

"Get it," Mr Roberts said to Bruno.

The large man lumbered forward and J. J. felt tears pricking at the backs of his eyelids. He told himself that he wouldn't cry, not even if everything he'd dreamed about since finding the map was taken away. Suddenly, a movement in the shadows above caught J. J.'s attention. The monarch butterfly that J. J. thought had spoken to him was hovering in the air. J. J.'s eyes locked onto it as it descended to land... directly on Bruno's nose.

The man stopped with a grunt of surprise. He shook his head, but the butterfly didn't move. Another butterfly, this one electric blue with black trim, flew out of the darkness and perched on Bruno's forehead. Before anyone could react, hundreds of butterflies swarmed around Bruno. Big ones. Small ones. Ones with bold, bright colours, others nearly camouflaged by the dark. Yellow with black spots. Black with yellow spots. Oranges and blues. Striped and solid. Every single one of them flew in circles around Bruno's head.

Bruno panicked – not that J. J. could blame him. He liked butterflies and the idea of them surrounding him freaked him out. Making sounds that J. J. assumed were supposed to be words, Bruno swatted his large hands in the air, the gestures too slow to make any contact. His hands moved closer and closer to his face until, with one wild swing, the gun in his right hand smashed into his face and the butterfly floated away unharmed. J. J. winced as

Bruno staggered backward. As the big man's feet came down on the wet floor that had nearly taken down Aaron, Bruno's shoes slid. Even as they all watched, his legs flew out from underneath him and he slammed into the ground with a bone-crunching thud, taking Mr Roberts and Hunter down with him.

"Get up, you clumsy oaf!" Mr Roberts shouted at his assistant.

Startling all of them, Genius yelled, "Guys! Run through! Hurry!"

None of them stopped to question or to even think if they should be following the instructions. Digger made it through first, followed by his sister and Aaron, still holding hands. J. J. was halfway over the fountain wall when he realized that Sandra hadn't moved. Ankle-deep in water, he turned toward her.

"Sandra!"

His voice jarred her out of whatever had been holding her in place and she turned to run. As J. J. watched in horror, Mr Roberts shot out his hand and grabbed Sandra's ankle. She let out an ear-piercing shriek and a loud crack echoed in the greenhouse, sending a ripple of electricity through the air. The hairs on J. J.'s arms stood up as Mr Roberts yelped and released Sandra's leg. Automatically, J. J. held out his hand to help Sandra over the wall and the two stumbled past Genius into the tunnel. J. J. saw Genius pull on something and heard a loud creaking sound as the fountain began to close behind them.

"Get up! Get up!" Mr Roberts was yelling at Bruno. "The entrance is closing!"

J. J. paused and turned, needing to see if the men were going to follow. Mr Roberts was shaking his hand as he tried to get up and Bruno was still struggling to get his feet beneath him. J. J. felt a surge of hope. There was no way either man was going to get to the opening in time. It was down to less than a foot now. Suddenly, he saw Mr Roberts throw something toward the fountain and the skull head of the British man's cane lodged between the stone walls. J. J. didn't know if it would hold or if the men would be able to pry the walls open again, but moving on seemed like a good idea. He hurried to catch up with his friends.

The tunnel sloped downwards and J. J. put a hand on the wall to steady himself, snatching it back at the feel of something damp and slimy. He'd read enough adventure books to know that it was probably moss, but he didn't really feel like testing that theory. He wiped his hand on his trouser leg, trying very hard not to think about how many different types of spiders could be lurking in the darkness. Ahead of him, he heard Karli, her voice tinged with hysteria.

"He had a gun. He was going to kill us. Why?"

"Seriously. This can't be happening." Sandra was shaking.

Digger half-turned and saw J. J. "They knew about the map. How?"

J. J. shook his head. "I don't know. Maybe that kid overheard us or something?" He gulped in deep breaths of the musty air in an attempt to calm his racing heart.

"I knew we should have gone back to the hotel," Genius said. "But *no*... we needed to see what would happen if we followed the map."

"Would you all just shut up for a second?" Aaron stopped suddenly, his free hand held out in front of him. Karli was still hanging on to the other one. "Everyone stop. I can't see a thing. Who has a flash...?"

Four beams cut through the darkness and shone directly on Aaron's face. "Hey, not in the face!" He shielded his eyes as he stepped back and stumbled over something on the floor. He yanked his hand from Karli's as he threw out his arms to stop himself from falling.

"Are you okay?" Karli asked.

"Yeah," Aaron said. J. J. could tell his brother was trying to be cool about it, but that he was still as rattled as the rest of them. "I tripped over something. J. J. – and only J. J. – shine your light at my feet."

J. J. let his torch follow Aaron's hand pointing down to the floor... and nearly screamed. Sandra did scream, as did Genius, their voices indistinguishable from one another. Digger gasped, or whatever the guy version of gasping was. Karli made a sound like a strangled sob and buried her face in Aaron's chest. Aaron didn't say anything, but his face was pale and, to be honest, a bit green. J. J. wasn't sure what he looked like, but he knew it was better than the remains on the ground.

There were two of them and, as J. J. panned the light across them, he saw that they were both wearing the same type of tattered clothes, most likely a uniform. Both bodies had decomposed down to the bone, leaving grinning skulls with empty eye sockets staring up at the kids. One still had a tomahawk buried in the top of its head. J. J. had never seen anything like it. And, as he took a deep breath, he'd never smelled anything like it either. It was a sickly, sweet smell that only made his stomach rebel when he realized that it was the bodies that made it. He gagged as Digger took a step forward, his expression intrigued rather than disgusted.

"These are old British military uniforms." He reached toward the Native American hatchet.

"Don't touch it!" Karli yelled at her brother.

Digger froze automatically and J. J. tensed. He knew his friend well enough to know that the only time Digger listened to his older sister was when he knew that something was wrong. Younger brothers and sisters, J. J. knew, had a kind of sixth sense when it came to their older siblings giving them commands. There was a certain tone that all younger siblings knew not to disobey. It wasn't about behaving or anything like that. When an older brother or sister sounded like that, it was important.

As Genius' shaking beam of light moved over the second body, J. J. saw why Karli had told Digger to stop. Half-rotted ropes had been tied around the skeleton's wrists and ankles, suspending it several feet above the ground.

"What the heck is this place?" Aaron said what all of them were thinking.

The torches were roaming now, revealing that the passageway they'd been taking had opened up into a much larger area. J. J. estimated the ceiling was around fifteen feet high and cavern at least thirty feet wide. What looked like two dozen grey boxes lined the floor. J. J. shone his light toward a silhouette on the far wall. As soon as he saw the intricately carved statue, he understood where they were.

"This is an Indian burial ground."

***

Roberts eyed the place where his cane had wedged between the two slabs of stone before they'd closed. It had been a lucky shot, he knew, and he'd been surprised he'd had the presence of mind to try it, what with his hand almost numb from whatever that blonde girl had done. He was still trying to work that one out. The only thing he could think of was that she'd had something electrical that she'd dropped into some water that he hadn't realized he'd been touching. It was the only logical explanation. He got to his feet and walked toward the fountain.

"We'll pry it open." He turned toward Bruno. "Find something we can use for leverage."

Bruno grumbled something and finally managed to get to his feet. Roberts shook his head. The man may have been strong, but agile he was not. As Bruno headed toward a wooden bench, Roberts glanced over at Hunter to make sure his hostage was still there. The boy was sitting on the path, his hands making random motions as he began to make that horrific sound that some Americans considered music.

"A'ight, I'm gonna break it down to y'all. It goes a lil' somethin' like this: *Yo, I was jumped, kidnapped, hands tied behind my back. One of the Nappers is Bruno the Mute, the other's just plain whack!*"

Roberts resisted the urge to remind the child that his hands were free, and motioned to Bruno to hurry up. The more time they wasted here, the further away the kids with the map were.

Muscles straining, Bruno ripped the bench from its supports. He made a sound that Roberts interpreted as asking what he should do next.

"Get that door open."

Hunter laughed. "You can understand that?"

Bruno turned and glared at the boy. Roberts sincerely hoped that the child used common sense.

"What?" Hunter looked up at Bruno. "Cat got your tongue?"

Apparently not.

Bruno let out what could only be described as an inarticulate roar and slammed the bench over his knee, snapping it in two. Hunter's mouth fell open and all of the colour drained from his face. Roberts shook his head. Idiot.

Chapter Fifteen

While a jealous-looking Sandra watched, Aaron lifted Karli onto his shoulders. As his hands wrapped around her legs to hold her steady, her face turned red, but she wasn't distracted from her task. The fear of not seeing what was around her appeared to be bigger than anything else. Carefully balancing, Karli lit a match and placed it into what Genius had identified as a 'sconce'. He'd then quickly explained what the word meant and asked for matches.

Much to the relief of everyone, fire instantly flared up from the sconce, casting a warm, orange glow on Karli's face. Immediately, Aaron moved on to the next one, eager for more light.

"It's a good thing you had those matches, eh, Sandra?" Digger grinned.

"Yeah, whatever," Sandra said, glaring at the pair currently lighting a second sconce. Apparently, she didn't like it when anyone except her was receiving attention.

As the torchlight revealed their surroundings, even Sandra forgot to be annoyed. The walls weren't dirt here as they had been in the passageway leading to the tomb. Someone had taken great care to line the walls with stones very similar to the ones that had made up the fountain. And, like the fountain, J. J. couldn't see anything binding the rocks together.

Cobwebs hung from the ceiling and some of the rocks were

green with moss, but the tomb appeared to be in relatively good shape. The box-like things that J. J. had seen in shadow he now realized were coffins made of stone. At the head of each one was another intricately carved statue. It looked like the statues were made of the same stone as the coffins.

J. J. took a step toward the coffins, ignoring the sound of protest his brother made. Genius followed and the two examined the strange symbols carved into the lids.

"Whoa," J. J. said. He reached out as if to trace one of the symbols and stopped short of actually touching the stone, mindful of what had happened at the fountain when Aaron had touched the wrong thing. "What do you make of the symbols on these coffins?"

"Sarcophaguses." Genius didn't even look up to make the correction.

"Sarcopha... what?" Digger asked.

Genius explained, sounding, as usual, like an encyclopedia. "These are sarcophaguses, cut from limestone which helps the flesh to decompose. Since embalming wasn't a common practice among the Native Americans of this time period, it was actually quite smart for them to utilize this particular resource."

"What?" Karli, who had just quit looking like she wanted to run, now looked nauseous.

"Oh, that's just gross." Sandra made a face of disgust.

Genius continued without acknowledging the girls' revulsion and J. J. had to grin. When Genius got going about something he found interesting, he'd share everything he knew, completely oblivious to how people were taking it. "This type of burial was typically used for royalty and war heroes."

Aaron pointed to the two skeletons. "What happened to these two, then?"

Digger crouched down for a better look at the tomahawk and Karli made a gagging noise. He reached out and, after a moment's hesitation, rested one finger on the handle. "This is an authentic Native American iron-head tomahawk. Cool."

"You're a freak," Sandra said, holding up her hands.

"I'm not sure what happened to the soldiers." Genius answered Aaron's question. "The British Empire and the Indians joined forces to fight against the United States, but these two soldiers appear to have been killed by the Indians."

"Maybe they were killed because they trespassed on an ancient Indian burial ground." Karli shivered. "All the more reason for us to get out of here."

An image suddenly popped into J. J.'s head. "The map! Digger, the map!"

"It's right here." Digger pulled the map from his duffel bag.

J. J. crossed to his friend's side as Digger unfolded the map. J. J.'s gaze was automatically drawn to the Butterfly House and then he saw it. A line.

"Look at this!" Digger pointed at the spot where J. J. was looking, seeing the same thing. "This is the tunnel underneath the Butterfly House." His finger traced along the line. "And it leads here, where the sarc... sarcoph... the flesh-eating coffins are."

"Okay, you cannot call them that, 'cause I'm gonna puke." Sandra's face did look a bit green.

Digger ignored her. "There's another symbol here on the map, J. J. It's a... skull with crossbones."

"We're dead," Genius said. "I should've just taken my chances in jail. Maybe I could still trade Digger for smokes."

"The two dead soldiers are on the map too," Digger said as he flipped up his middle finger in Genius' direction.

J. J. pulled out the journal and began flipping through the pages. There had to be answers in it.

"How do you know they're the same two?" Aaron asked.

"'Cause one of them has a meat cleaver in his head," Digger said matter-of-factly.

"Ugh," Karli groaned. "Now I'm gonna puke."

"Give me that, GI Jane." Aaron snatched the map from Digger's grasp.

J. J. stopped turning the journal's pages. His heart began to pound and it had nothing to do with the two men chasing them. He was right. The journal and the map together had the answers. "Check it out, guys. This page in the journal has the same symbol: a skull with crossbones." He waited until everyone was looking at him. "Porter Hanks left another clue." J. J. began to read. "'Warriors in line buried with pride, dragoon traitors rot at their side.'"

"Well, now we know what happened to Phineas and Ferb," Aaron said. When Karli looked up at him, eyebrow raised, he flushed. "The kid watches them."

J. J. glared at Aaron for a moment and then resumed reading. "'Find the exit with no door, through a chamber of bones that blanket the floor. Commence with the mark of a Ruler, then by eight. Too many gaffes, a tomb be thy fate.'"

"'Chamber of bones'?" Karli's voice was weak.

"'Tomb be thy fate'?" Sandra said.

Genius repeated his previous sentiment. "We're dead."

"No, you guys." J. J. shook his head. They were doing so well. They couldn't give up now, not with so much at stake. "We just need to figure out these riddles. C'mon, we did it before. We can do it again. Right?"

"We're doomed." Genius leaned back against the wall. "I could've had a nice, comfy cell with an eastern view of the sky. Gotten buff lifting in the yard."

J. J. looked at Aaron. No matter what the others said, J. J. knew that whatever Aaron decided would be what they would do. The girls would go with him because, well, he was Aaron. Digger would go along with it because he wouldn't want Aaron to come out looking tougher than him. And J. J. knew that Genius, even complaining, would never leave his friends, even it wasn't for the two men between Genius and his comfy prison cell.

Aaron looked down at the map in his hand and then at J. J. Their eyes met and J. J. saw that Aaron understood what giving up would mean for their family. That knowledge was warring with Aaron's responsible side, the part of him that said it would be crazy to keep going, especially with the whole group. J. J. held his breath, waiting for the decision that could mean the end of the adventure and the end of any hope they had of saving their home.

"I hate to admit it," Aaron said, "but J. J.'s right."

J. J. suppressed the urge to let out a whoop of triumph and settled for grinning at Aaron. They were going to keep looking for the treasure! He knew they could find it, as long as no one gave up.

Sandra looked at Aaron in disbelief. "You can't be serious."

"Look, we can't go back. Those goons are waiting for us. We can only go forward." Aaron shrugged. "The way I see it, we might as well see this thing through... to wherever it takes us."

Digger stuck out his hand. "So we're all in?"

J. J. put his hand on top of Digger's and Aaron followed, forming part of a circle. Once Aaron's hand was in, Karli and Sandra both sighed and placed their hands in the circle. Karli scowled as Sandra got hers in first, but didn't say anything.

"In it to win it?" J. J. asked.

"To win it," Aaron agreed.

"To win it," Karli and Sandra both echoed the declaration.

All eyes turned to Genius who was still standing outside the circle, his reluctance written on his face. His gaze slowly travelled around the circle before coming to rest on J. J.'s face. With a resigned sigh, he placed his hand on top of Karli's.

"Hooah," he said quietly.

Aaron rolled his eyes, but the smile on his face said he wasn't truly annoyed. "On three?" The others nodded. "One, two, three–"

"Hooah!"

The sound echoed through the tunnel, followed by the nervous laughter of a group who had no idea what they'd just got themselves into.

Chapter Sixteen

Roberts reclined on the remaining bench while Hunter sat at his feet. Bruno's little stunt with the bench had scared the child badly enough that Hunter had tried to run, wasting precious time and energy. Now, the boy was tied with ropes that had been used to hang the signs along the walkway. Roberts was at an impasse regarding what to do with his hostage. He wasn't yet sure if it would be wise to eliminate him at this juncture. There was always the possibility that he could be useful in the future and Roberts was loath to lose any advantage. He just needed a way to ensure that Hunter became easier to control. An idea was beginning to form in his mind when a loud rumble emanated from the boy.

"Yo, I'm hungry." Hunter was still trying to sound tough.

"Turn around." Roberts yanked off the top of his cane, exposing his blade again. Perhaps it was a bit overly dramatic, but the boy was getting on his nerves.

"W-wait a minute." Hunter eyed the knife with a terrified expression on his chubby face. "Be easy. You don't have to do this. I could actually afford to lose a couple of pounds." He tried to scoot away.

Roberts grabbed Hunter's shoulder. "I said, turn!" He pushed the boy around.

"No, please don't." Hunter was blubbering now, the tears

streaming down his face doing nothing to strengthen his case. "I'll join Weight Watchers. Really."

Roberts pushed Hunter's head down so the boy was bending forward. As more nonsense spewed from the child's mouth, it was all Roberts could do not to just put an end to it all with one quick slice through the base of Hunter's neck.

"I'm comin', Biggie! This one's for you...' *I love it when you call me Big Pop-pa... Throw your hands in the air, if yous a true player...'*"

Roberts cut through the ropes around Hunter's wrists with one clean slice. "Now, shut your bloody mouth and listen." His accent was slipping back into the rough one of his childhood. He slid his knife back into his cane as Hunter turned toward him, sniffling but otherwise silent. "You may be able to prove yourself useful after all." He tried to give the boy a fatherly smile, but wasn't quite sure if he succeeded. He'd never related well to children. "I'll tell you what, you help us and we'll cut you in on some of that treasure."

"H-how much?" Hunter wiped his arm across his face.

Roberts tried not to grimace. "Enough for a lad like you to purchase something you truly desire."

"A grill and some bling?" Hunter straightened.

He had no desire to know what 'grill' or 'bling' were, so Roberts merely smiled. "Of course." He reached into his pocket and pulled out his wallet. After leafing through his American currency, he retrieved several bills. He held them out to Hunter. "Now, why don't you run along to those vending machines and purchase some supplies for the three of us. And, while you're there, take a look around and see if you are able to find any torches for us."

"Torches? Yous whacked man. Nobody uses no torches." Hunter snorted.

Roberts bit the inside of his cheek to keep himself from backhanding the boy. It was one thing not to understand another culture's colloquialisms. It was quite something else to be rude about it. "Torches are what the British call flashlights."

"Why didn't you just say so? I'll see if I can find any." Hunter snatched the bills and rushed off to the vending area faster than Roberts would have thought possible.

A loud grunt from Bruno drew Roberts' attention. As he turned toward his employee, the gap between the two sections of rock gave just an inch.

"Put your back into it! That's a good man!" Roberts stood.

Bruno's face began to turn red as he strained every muscle putting force on the wood he was using for leverage. The cords of muscles in his neck stood out and a long, drawn-out groan came from his mouth. A loud clang came from inside the passage and, without warning, the two halves popped apart. Bruno fell into the entrance, barely breaking his fall with his hands. For a moment, it seemed as if his arms would hold him, then they gave way and he collapsed into the basin of the fountain.

"Well done," Roberts said. The man may have been a brute, but he was a strong brute. "Come along, Hunter. We have a treasure to steal."

A moment later, Hunter came hurrying back, his arms filled with cakes, chips and sweets. Hanging from one finger was an old-fashioned lantern. "Booya! Didn't need the vending machines. This stuff was behind the counter."

"Excellent," Roberts said. He took the lantern from Hunter and shook it. Perfect. It was full. He reached into his pocket and retrieved an old-fashioned lighter. As soon as the lantern was burning, he stepped over Bruno and into the passageway.

"Wait for me, yo." Hunter struggled to pull up his trousers without dropping anything.

A stream of unintelligible expletives told Roberts that Hunter had walked over Bruno with less grace than himself. Still, there was no point in waiting. Bruno was resilient. He would catch up.

Chapter Seventeen

It came to no surprise to anyone when Genius pulled a laptop out of his backpack. He set it on top of one of the sarcophagus lids and turned it on. As it was booting up, Aaron and the girls began to look around the tomb for an alternate exit while J. J. and Digger moved to stand on either side of their friend. Once the computer was ready, Genius tapped on a few keys.

"No Internet signal, though that's hardly a surprise. We are underground." He opened up a file. "Not to worry, I have the entire Mackinac Island wiki on my hard drive."

J. J. and Digger exchanged amused glances over their friend's head. Leave it to Genius to be overly prepared. He could've taught the Boy Scouts a thing or two.

"Searching 'Missing British Soldiers,'" Genius said as he typed in the words. He was silent for a few minutes as he skimmed the information that came up. "Okay. It says here that a British military post called the Fourteenth Dragoons used the natives to track down AWOL soldiers. Even put a price on their heads." He looked up. "Kinda like bounty hunters."

"Maybe that's what happened to these two guys." Digger gestured at the skeletons.

Aaron and the girls came up behind the three boys, the frustration on their faces saying all that needed to be said about the search for another way out.

"What about the 'chamber of bones' mentioned in that riddle?" Aaron asked.

"On it," Genius said. His fingers flew across the keys.

J. J. was glad Genius was typing and not him. He wasn't quite at the hunt-and-peck rate, but he still wasn't very fast. His prowess on the computer mostly came from playing video games, a slightly different skill set.

"There's a 'Skull Cave' here on the island that was used to store human remains during the early 1800s." Genius frowned.

"'Skull Cave'?" Karli said. "Does anyone else have a problem with that?"

J. J. had to admit, the name did make him a little nervous, but he wasn't about to give up just because something had a creepy name. "I think that's it, the 'chamber of bones.' That's our way out of here."

"No way in the world am I getting anywhere near anything that has the word 'skull' in its name."

J. J. looked over at Sandra. "Do you have a better idea? Some way to get past Psycho One and Two and their little wannabe mascot?"

"Wait," Genius said. His shoulders sagged. "Sorry, Skull Cave is further north-west, like the middle of the forest. There's no way anything from here connects to it."

"So what now?" Aaron asked.

"'Chamber of bones'," Karli repeated. "Guys, do you think, maybe it's just as simple as it sounds?"

"What do you mean?" Genius asked.

"I mean, maybe it's just referring to a coffin." Karli gestured to the stones behind them.

"You think the way out of here is in a sarcophagus?" Genius asked. "That's an interesting theory."

"So let's look at the coffins," Aaron said.

"That's just gross." Sandra made a face.

"Well, as J. J. pointed out, we don't really have much of a choice," Karli said. "Might as well give it a shot. I just hope it works."

"It's gonna work, guys. We're going to escape the guys behind us, find the treasure and Aaron and I won't have to move." J. J. tried to put all of his conviction into his words. "I can feel it."

"Take it easy, J. J.," Aaron said with an amused smile. "We don't know where this bone chamber thing is and we still gotta figure out 'the mark of a ruler.'"

"That sounds simple enough. Just look for some sort of measurement," Sandra said. Everyone turned to look at her, surprised. "What? I can't have a good idea?"

Genius stuffed his computer back into his bag as the others fanned out around the room. As Sandra and Karli went to opposite sides of the room, Aaron hesitated, then went straight down the middle. J. J. glanced at Digger who grinned and the two started to walk toward one of the further coffins.

Digger paused by the tomahawked soldier and J. J. heard him whisper, "I gotta have it." He crouched down and J. J. knew that it was hopeless to get his friend away. When Digger saw a weapon, he had hyper-focus.

J. J. walked away, leaving Digger to admire the old hatchet. He stopped at the sarcophagus next to the one Karli was circling and looked down at the lid. At least an inch of dust coated the top of the stone. He bent down and blew, sending a cloud of dust swirling off of the coffin and right at Karli.

***

This was not how Karli had imagined she'd be spending her night. She'd been having fun, even with Sandra flirting like crazy with Aaron after saying that she wasn't interested. Even after they'd followed the boys into the Butterfly House, it was still a good night. They weren't going to steal anything or vandalize the place, so they could've gotten out without anyone knowing. It was just a little not-so-legal excitement, something they could talk about when they went back to school. Then they'd started messing in that stupid fountain and everything had gone downhill from there.

Now, she and the others were in a crypt, complete with skeletons, and two nasty men were behind them. As she studied the coffins, she kept looking down to make sure she wasn't stepping on anything gross. She was so intent on switching her gaze from coffin to floor that she didn't notice where her arms went and, suddenly, she felt a sharp pain along her forearm.

"Dang it," she muttered as she looked down. It didn't seem deep, but it was bleeding. She turned, intending to ask her brother or Genius if either of them had any bandages in their packs. She wiped her arm off on the side of her trousers to get a better idea of how big the wound was and...

She blinked. The blood was smeared, but the source was gone, as was the pain. Her arm was smooth and unmarked. What in the world had just happened? She could've sworn she'd just cut her arm, but now it was like nothing had happened. Had she just imagined it? Before she could think about it too much, J. J. blew dust off of a coffin lid and right into her face.

***

"AAAAHHHH AAAAHHHH CHOOOOO!" Karli let out a violent sneeze.

"*Gesundheit*," J. J. said. Oops. Karli glared at him and he offered her an apologetic grin. He really hadn't meant to do it.

The moment her gaze turned from him and fell on the sarcophagus, her face changed and J. J. knew that she'd found something. "Uh, Genius? Could the 'mark of a ruler' mean, like, some important guy?"

Genius looked up from the stone he was studying. "Yeah, I suppose. Why, what'd you find?"

Everyone abandoned what they were doing to see what Karli had uncovered. Everyone, that was, except Digger who had grabbed onto the handle of the tomahawk and was now trying to pull it free. J. J. didn't think that was a good idea, but monitoring Digger's behaviour wasn't really his top concern at the moment.

Genius ran his fingers over the carvings and letters. "This sarcophagus belongs to Chief Pontiac. Ruler didn't mean measurement, it meant like a king or chief." He turned to Karli. "You found it!"

"Way to go, Karli!" J. J. felt the sudden urge to hug his friend's sister.

Aaron beat him to it and J. J. was glad that he did. He didn't like Karli, not that way. He'd just been excited by her discovery. Aaron, on the other hand, seemed to appreciate having an excuse to hug Karli.

"Oh, please." Sandra, on the other hand, didn't seem to share the sentiment. "She sneezed."

J. J. decided that the best thing to do was to get everyone's attention back on the matter at hand. The last thing they needed was the girls to start fighting and Aaron to get caught in the middle. No matter how gorgeous he thought Sandra was, he didn't want to end up buried next to her in an ancient Native American tomb. "Now we just have to count out eight coffins from this one, right?"

"That makes sense," Aaron agreed, then frowned. "But in which direction?"

Genius eyed the coffins on either side of the one they were standing around. "There's only seven that way." He pointed to his left.

"So it's gotta be to the right, then," J. J. said.

Together, they counted out loud until they reached the eighth sarcophagus and then they began to circle it, searching for some clue as to what to do next. It was just as dirty as the others, J. J. noted, and didn't appear to be anything special. He had a bad feeling where this was going to go next and knew that no one, least of all the girls, would be happy with it.

"Now what?" Karli asked.

Genius answered her question with the response J. J. had been dreading. "We open it up."

"Let me get this straight," Sandra said. "We're about to take the cover off of a flesh-eating coffin?"

"Yeah, pretty much," J. J. said.

"Okay. Just wanted to make sure." When everyone stared at her, Sandra shrugged. "Like J. J. said, it's either this or face the two guys back there. As gross as it is, I'll take the decomposing corpse over two whack-jobs with weapons."

"So, how do we do this?" Karli asked, the expression on her face clearly stating that she really didn't want the answer.

Once again, Aaron took charge and J. J. let him. The others were going to be more likely to follow one of Aaron's suggestions than one of his own.

138

"Line up on this side." Aaron motioned to the side he was standing at and the others did as he asked. "Now, on three, we're going to push together."

"Wait," Genius said. "Most sarcophaguses don't have sliding lids. They were designed to keep people out. We actually need to lift up and then push." He moved from one end to the lid to the other. "Just to let you all know, based on my calculations, this is going to weigh over two thousand pounds. There's no way we're going to be able to get it off on our own."

"Genius, you're really smart and all, but shut up," Aaron said. "If this is some secret entrance, maybe Porter made it lighter so people could get in."

"That is a possibility," Genius admitted.

"Great. Now that we're all agreed, maybe we could try to get the lid off of the coffin so we can get away from the two psychos behind us before we get shot and need a coffin?" Sandra spoke up.

"On three." Aaron set his feet. "One... two... three."

With a chorus of groans, the kids began to push. After several seconds of nothing, they stopped, frustrated. Genius opened his mouth to say something as Aaron slammed his hands against the lid, and, with a suddenness that threw them all forward, the lid gave and began to slide off of the coffin.

"Push!" Aaron's voice was strained as he leaned further across the coffin. Karli and Sandra were now on their tiptoes.

With one final shove, the lid reached its tipping point and fell over the side of the sarcophagus. The resulting bang hurt their ears and reverberated off of the walls. The girls clapped their hands over their ears and J. J. resisted the urge to do the same. If Genius could tough it out, so could he.

"Hooah!" Aaron let out a yell.

All eyes turned to him.

"What? Seemed appropriate." He grinned. "C'mon."

While the girls watched, the three boys leaned over the edge and peered inside, each one preparing themselves for whatever they might see. J. J. was so convinced that he was going to have to fight throwing up that it took him a moment to process what his eyes were seeing.

"It's empty."

"Thank goodness." Sandra stepped up to the coffin. Karli followed and both girls peered inside.

"There's a wood floor," Genius said.

"Yeah. And?" Aaron gave Genius a puzzled look.

"And," Genius said, "it should be limestone."

Aaron looked down at the bottom of the sarcophagus and, after a moment, jumped inside.

"What are you doing?" Karli asked. "That floor looks like it's half rotted through."

Aaron didn't respond. He leaned back against the edge of the coffin and braced himself with his hands. While the others watched, he lifted his foot and slammed it down. The rotted wood gave way easily, the pieces tumbling through the hole. Taking care not to get his feet too close to the edge, Aaron bent down to inspect the opening. He cocked his head to one side, a puzzled expression on his face.

"Well?" J. J. asked, impatient.

"Wind," Aaron said.

"It's a passage!" J. J. gave an excited jump.

Aaron stuck his face closer to the hole. "It's completely black. I think it's deep."

"Let me take a look," Genius said. He picked up a rock from

the ground as Aaron lifted himself back out of the sarcophagus. He held the stone out over the hole. "'S' is equal to the depth. 'T' is the time it takes for the rock to reach the bottom. Taking into consideration 'G' for the acceleration of gravity –"

Sandra cut in, "Just drop the freaking rock already!"

Looking a bit sheepish, Genius did as he was told and dropped the stone down into the hole. Immediately, he started counting. "One one thousand... two one thousand... three one thousand –"

J. J. didn't like the sound of this. If the passage was straight down, they'd never make it.

"Six one thousand... seven one thousand... eight one thousand."

A faint splash rose up from the darkness.

"Water," J. J. said.

A strange ripping sound came from behind them.

"Awesome," Digger said. "Hey guys, look!"

J. J. heard Karli choke even as he was still turning. The moment he saw his friend, he understood the reaction and sympathized. Digger had apparently decided that he couldn't extract the tomahawk easily and had just yanked on the weapon, taking with it the skull and part of the spinal column. As Digger took a step forward, J. J. caught a glimpse of something hanging from the bottom of the spine and, for a moment, thought that the body was still attached. His eyes followed it down to the floor and he realized then that it was a rope. He opened his mouth to warn everyone, and that was when everything went crazy.

There was a dull crack from inside the wall, then a sizzle that sounded a lot like a firecracker being lit. Almost in slow motion, all eyes turned toward the wall. A series of small holes had appeared in the stone and J. J.'s stomach dropped. There was a bang and, suddenly, an arrow exploded from one of the holes, hissing through the air past Digger's head.

Digger yelled out, dropping the skull, but it was too late. Another explosion sounded and a second arrow fired. J. J. watched, horrified, as it flew through the air, heading right for Genius. The young man threw up his hands and, suddenly, the arrow veered away. Before J. J. could try to figure out what had happened, another bang echoed and he knew what was coming next.

"Get down!"

Everyone dropped immediately and a series of arrows flew over their heads, clattering off of the stone wall on the other side of the tomb. As J. J. turned his head toward the closer wall, he saw his brother do the same. He and Aaron saw the same thing at the same time. Another row of holes lined the bottom of the wall. J. J. heard the now-familiar hissing sound and scrambled to his feet even as Aaron called out.

"Get up!"

The others obeyed, jumping out of the way as another series of arrows shot out.

"J. J.!" Genius pointed.

J. J.'s heart almost stopped as he saw a third row of holes appear – in the middle of the wall. They were too high to jump and too low to duck, especially if another round came from the bottom row. There was only one option.

Genius must've realized it at the same time because he gave the next direction. "Get in the sarcophagus!"

The kids jumped over the side of the coffin and the floor creaked beneath their feet. J. J. swallowed hard as he remembered how easily Aaron had broken through the floor and the distant splash of the rock below.

"You could've just said coffin, you know," Sandra said to

Genius.

"Where's Digger?" Karli asked frantically.

J. J. poked his head up over the edge of the coffin, sure that, at any moment, the middle row was going to start firing. Digger was still standing next to his dropped prize, frozen in place.

"Digger! Come on!" J. J. yelled.

A bang behind him broke through and Digger took off. As the arrows were released from their tubes, he dived over the edge of the coffin. Karli grabbed his arm to keep him from tumbling into the hole Aaron had made. Digger didn't protest as his sister hugged him close, the sound of the arrows clattering off the sarcophagus making it all too clear what would have happened if he'd stayed.

There was a moment when all of them breathed a sigh of relief and J. J. thought that the worst was over. Then, a creak, a crack, and the floor buckled beneath them. They all screamed as they plummeted into the darkness below.

The falling took on a surreal quality. J. J. saw Aaron reach for Karli. Watched Sandra trying to keep her hair from flying about. Genius clutched at the bag with his laptop. Digger was rifling through his bag, and then tugging on a string. There was a whooshing sound and something unfolded in the darkness beneath them.

J. J. identified the object even as they raced toward it. Their screams were swallowed up in the rubber as, one by one, they landed on the raft. As the raft thudded into the water, something hit the edge and then there was a loud splash. Then all that was left was the sound of their harsh breathing.

Aaron broke the silence. "Is everyone okay? J. J.?"

"Yeah, I'm fine." J. J. winced as he tried to get onto his knees. He had a feeling they were all going to be bruised. "Digger? Genius?"

"Good," Genius said.

"Karli?" Digger's voice was breathless, as if the wind had been knocked out of him.

"I'm okay." Karli sounded more scared than hurt. "Sandra?"

The silence was deafening.

"Sandra?" Aaron spun around and J. J. could feel the atmosphere in the raft shift as they realized they were missing a member of their group.

The water next to the raft suddenly parted as Sandra's head broke through the surface. Her hands scrabbled against the slick sides of the raft as she coughed and spluttered.

"Sandra!" Karli leaned over the side and grabbed the other girl's flailing arms. "You're okay."

"Okay?" Sandra was seething. "We just got shot at by arrows! Arrows! Then we jumped into a coffin and fell through the floor! I landed in a lake! Look at me! My hair and make-up are ruined! I am anything but okay!"

A bubble popped up next to Sandra and she glared at it, as if it was the source of all of her problems. A second bubble popped and, this time, they could all see what had caused the eruption. Half a dozen skulls bobbed up from the water, grinning up at the kids.

"Get me outta here!" Sandra screamed, thrashing about as more skulls appeared.

Aaron hurried to help Karli pull Sandra into the raft, but J. J. couldn't move. This was not how things were supposed to go.

Chapter Eighteen

The tunnel was damp, musty and dark – and it reminded Roberts of the cellar back in England that his father had used whenever the children had misbehaved. There were still nights Roberts woke in a cold sweat, the darkness closing in around him, the memory of hours spent without being able to see his own hand in front of his face. Now, as he hurried along, it was only the dull illumination of the lamp and the steel of his own resolve that kept the memories and panic at bay. He breathed a sigh of relief as they reached the wide cavern that Roberts immediately recognized as a necropolis. The sconces burning high on the walls provided enough light that Roberts no longer felt his past pressing on him, and he could think once more.

He stopped just a few feet in and heard his two companions do the same. He quickly scanned his surroundings. The place was full of recently disturbed dust and the floor was littered with arrows. A glance at the closest wall revealed lines of small holes that appeared to be the correct size to have stored the weapons.

Behind him, he heard Bruno sniff. "Gunpowder."

"Quite right, Bruno." Roberts too smelled the unforgettable stench of gunpowder.

"A'ight, I gots ta ask," Hunter said. "What's wit the big man's speech problem?"

Roberts closed his eyes and pinched the bridge of his nose between his thumb and forefinger. Perhaps if he answered the child honestly, he'd stop asking inane questions. "Some years ago, Bruno had been employed by members of the Russian mob and they took exception to his pointless and maddening questions." He didn't feel the need to add that the questions had been about the mob boss's very attractive nineteen-year-old daughter. "I must warn you that, should you insist on continuing to ask questions which are not relevant to the matter at hand, I will be inclined to follow their example." He turned back toward Hunter. "How well do you think you will be able to create that infernal nonsense without a tongue?"

Hunter gulped.

"Now," Roberts said, "let us attend to the business of our little group of friends."

Hunter, perhaps trying to make amends, offered his opinion. "Looks like the Scooby Doo gang went all buck wild up in here."

Roberts paused for a moment to mourn the brutalization of what had once been the English language and then he spoke. "It would appear that our friends had a little misadventure."

"Ain't that what I said?" Hunter asked, honestly confused.

Roberts reached into his jacket as he looked around the tomb. He didn't normally indulge when on a mission, but this obnoxious American child would drive even the most sober man to drink. He pulled a silver flask out of his inside pocket and took a sip. The amber liquid burned a trail down his throat and he made a small sound of enjoyment. The one good thing about this accursed country was the abundance of alcohol from which to choose. This one was particularly fine.

"Search the area." He gave his instructions. "They may be hiding. Or better yet, they may be dead." He smiled at the thought.

Nothing would give him as much pleasure as taking that map from the hands of a corpse.

"Dead?" Hunter echoed.

Well, almost anything. Watching Bruno end the life of that little nuisance was going to be quite enjoyable. He might even do the deed himself if the child continued to push.

Bruno laughed at the shocked expression on Hunter's face and gave the boy a little shove. Hunter tripped and tumbled to the floor, what remained of his junk food spilling onto the floor.

"Aw, man, why ya gotta disrespect like dat? Now I gotta get up in your grill." Hunter was still talking when he raised his head... and came face to face with a skull. The spine was still attached and a tomahawk had been buried deep into the bone.

The boy let out what Roberts could only describe as a near banshee-like shriek of terror. This time, Roberts joined with Bruno in laughing at Hunter as he scrambled backward on his hands and knees, desperation and terror written on his pale face.

Chapter Nineteen

"You guys, go to the back of the raft," Aaron said as he and Karli began to pull Sandra out of the water. "We need your weight back there to balance us."

The boys did as they were told without a word of complaint.

"We got you," Karli said.

"Hurry! It feels like the Cryptkeeper's tugging at my feet." Sandra gave a half-sob of relief as she toppled into the raft, half landing on Aaron.

In J. J.'s opinion, Sandra lingered on his brother a bit too long, but he was glad that she was safe. The enormity of what they'd undertaken was making itself all too real to him. He was sure that it would be worth it in the end, but he wasn't sure the others would see it that way. He pulled the map from his pack as Sandra rolled off of Aaron and sat up.

"Guys, we need to get to the next clue," J. J. said.

"No." Aaron shook his head. "We need to get back to the hotel. Geez, J. J. Are you blind? We're in a raft, surrounded by dead bodies and this is the safest we've been since you convinced us to go along with this crazy adventure!"

"B-but we made it through another stage." J. J.'s heart sank. Had they really just gone through all of that only to give up now? What had happened to 'in it until the end'?

"Barely," Genius said. His head was down when J. J. looked over at him, but the defeated tone in his voice said it all.

"Come on, J. J., what kind of father would put his son through that?" Karli spoke up. "Something about this just isn't right."

J. J. hurried to defend his ancestor. "Porter Hanks would never do that to his son. He must not have known about the Indians' booby traps. They probably didn't trust him since he'd been an American soldier." He turned to Aaron, pleading silently for his brother to understand.

Aaron's voice softened, but his words were still not what J. J. wanted to hear. "Who knows what else Porter Hanks didn't plan for? The treasure could've been moved or already found. The hiding place could've been destroyed. A lot can change in 200 years, J. J. I don't think it's going to be as easy as answering a couple of riddles about where to go next."

"I'm cold," Karli said.

"And tired," Genius added.

"And wet." Sandra was trying to wring out her hair when all eyes turned her way.

Four sets of eyes widened and four jaws dropped. All thoughts of treasure and money and saving his family's house disappeared from J. J's mind. The only thing he could think of was how Sandra's wet T-shirt clung to her very nice curves. Her breasts were bigger than he'd realized during their little webcam session, and there was just something different about there not being a computer between them.

"What?" Sandra suddenly realized that everyone was staring.

Karli gave a discreet cough and crossed her arms over her much smaller chest. Her eyes darted from Sandra and down to herself.

149

Sandra looked down and shook her head. "Idiots."

Karli inserted herself between Sandra and the guys, shooting Aaron a dirty look. He had the decency to blush and look away. J. J. knew he should be embarrassed too, but he was still having difficulty processing anything other than the image burned into his retinas.

"Uh, hello?" Karli waved at the boys. "One of you want to be a gentleman and give Sandra your shirt?"

The guys exchanged glances. Out of the four of them, only Aaron was big enough that his shirt wouldn't be almost as tight as the one Sandra was already wearing, though it would at least be dry. All of them but Genius were only wearing T-shirts and J. J. knew that Digger was thinking the same thing that he was. While far from scrawny, neither boy had the type of physique that they wanted to show off, especially in front of Sandra. Aaron did, but he seemed to be debating what would upset Karli more, giving Sandra his shirt or not. They each processed all of this in just a few seconds so when Genius pulled off the button-up shirt he was wearing over his T-shirt, less than a minute had passed since Karli had asked her question.

"Thanks." Sandra took the shirt and turned her back to the boys. Since it was barely going to fit as it was, she quickly pulled off her wet shirt and put on the pale grey shirt.

J. J. averted his eyes. Something about her turning away from them had reminded him that Sandra deserved privacy. From the shuffling of his friends and brother, he had the feeling that they'd done the same.

"All right, I'm done," Sandra said.

When the guys looked back up, Sandra was covered. The buttons strained a bit across her chest and the material was darkening from her wet bra, but it was far from the same thing as before.

The thought of Sandra and water triggered J. J.'s memory of what had happened in the Butterfly House when Roberts had grabbed Sandra's leg. Another image flashed into his mind, this one of the arrow flying at Genius before inexplicably diverting.

J. J. cleared his throat. "Hey, guys, I was just wondering, have any of you noticed anything weird happening to you recently?"

"Seriously?" Aaron gave J. J. an incredulous look. "This entire thing is weird."

"No, that's not what I mean." J. J. held a brief internal debate over whether or not he should say what happened. A desire for answers trumped his fear of appearing crazy. Besides, if they weren't going to go after the treasure, at least he could satisfy his curiosity. "When we were up there and the arrows were coming at us, I could've sworn I saw one heading right for Genius." He glanced at his friend. "He threw up his hands and it turned and went another way."

"Are you sure you didn't hit your head?" Karli sounded as if she were only half joking. Her left hand went to a spot on her right arm, her fingers nervously rubbing at her skin.

J. J. continued, "And before that, when we were first running from those two guys. Sandra was behind all of us. That Roberts guy grabbed her leg and I heard a cracking sound, like lightning. He yelled and let go of her."

Sandra shifted, clearly uncomfortable with the conversation.

"And then, when we were trying to figure out what stone to turn." J. J. hesitated, then took a deep breath. If he was going to suggest that Genius and Sandra had strange things happening to them, he had to admit his own too. "That big monarch butterfly told me to choose the red stone."

Aaron stared. "It told you?"

J. J. shrugged. "I don't know what's going on with us, Aaron, but it's not normal." J. J. suddenly remembered seeing Aaron's muscles ripple when he was trying to turn the stones. "Like, how did you manage to push over two thousand pounds of limestone? And you got those stones turned after hundreds of years of not being used."

"I saw something," Digger said in a soft voice.

"What did you see?" J. J. asked, eager to hear someone else's story. It meant he wasn't nuts.

"I saw a bright light. Figures coming out of the darkness and a weapon of some kind."

"What are you talking about?" J. J. didn't understand.

"I didn't see someone else do something. I *saw* something." Digger's eyes were wide. "It happened back in the greenhouse, just before Aaron and the girls showed up. It was like I saw something that was going to happen."

Karli shivered. "Stop fooling around, Michael. It isn't funny."

Digger shook his head. "No, it's not."

There was an edge to Digger's voice that J. J. didn't recognize at first. Then he saw the sheen on Digger's eyes and realized that his friend was close to tears. That alone scared J. J. more than anything else that had happened that night. There were two people in this world who he counted on to be rock solid and, tonight, both Aaron and Digger had shown that they weren't as tough as J. J. had always thought.

"Look, I don't know what you guys think you saw or did, but we don't have the time to discuss it or analyse it or whatever." Aaron's tone was firm, his voice taking on an authoritative note.

152

"We have bigger things to discuss. We need to decide what to do next. Do we let the river take us away from the town or do we try to paddle against the current to see if we can find a way out that's closer to the town?"

***

Roberts handed the lantern to Hunter and reached down to yank free one of the skeleton's femurs. He ignored the choking sound the boy made and set to work wrapping the end of the bone in the tattered military cloth. It took Bruno a moment to realize what Roberts was doing, but once he did, he followed suit.

The material caught instantly, blazing up into a light brighter than the dim glow of the lantern. Roberts turned toward the rest of the tomb and let the torch reveal the rest of what lay inside. At the same time, he and Bruno saw the sarcophagus without a lid and walked over to it.

"What do you think, my inarticulate friend?" Roberts asked.

Bruno lowered his torch into the coffin, revealing the gaping hole where the bottom had been. He pointed unnecessarily as he nodded.

"I agree," Roberts said. "It's the only way they could have gotten out. Now, we just need to –"

A crunching noise cut off the brilliant suggestion Roberts had been about to make. He and Bruno raised their heads to see Hunter peering down into the hole... and noisily munching from an open bag of those things Americans insisted upon calling potato chips. Crumbs tumbled from the boy's mouth into the hole and disappeared.

"That's deep, yo."

"Is there anything or any time that you don't eat?" Roberts asked.

Hunter shrugged. "I like variety as long as it tastes good like candy and cake and chips and stuff. And I eat when I'm nervous or scared or bored or tired," he eyed Bruno, "or being held against my will."

Roberts was again strongly reminded about why he'd never wanted one of these little urchins. He picked up Hunter's lantern without a word and smashed it against the stone coffin. Hunter jumped, losing his grip on his bag of chips. He watched as they disappeared into the hole.

"Hey, man. Those was my last chips, yo."

"Pay attention," Roberts snapped as he poured the kerosene from the lantern through the hole. When the lantern was empty, Roberts tossed it aside. He held his torch over the hole. "You may just learn something."

Seconds later, there was a flash of light far below and then the unmistakable cries of the frightened. Roberts smiled. "Ahhhh. There is nothing so sweet as the terror in a young one's voice." He turned from the sarcophagus and began to walk back toward the tunnel. "Come along, then. Don't dawdle."

"B-but, they're down there. Where we goin'?" Hunter picked up one of the snack cakes he'd fallen on when Bruno had shoved him and seemed to be sizing up whether or not the squashed pastry was worth eating.

Roberts made a face as Hunter tore open the package and squeezed the now unrecognizable substance into his mouth. "We are going to find where the river comes out and meet our dear friends there."

Chapter Twenty

"How can you even think about wanting to keep going?" Karli asked J. J. "We've almost died tonight! More than once!"

"I don't think we really have a choice." J. J. tried to present the argument from a different angle. "We're stuck in this raft, on an underground river. We don't know where we are or where we're going. The only map we have is the treasure map, and it goes along with the current."

"He does have a point," Digger said.

J. J. turned to thank his friend and stopped, his mouth open, as something caught his eye. "Look!" He pointed as something fell from above. "Is that... fire?"

Everyone turned just as the flame hit the water. Instead of extinguishing, it burst into flames, sending a wave of heat washing over the kids. J. J. instantly understood what it meant.

"They found us."

"What?" Sandra asked.

"Those two guys." J. J. looked at Aaron. "They must've dropped something flammable down here first."

"All right, move! Move!" Aaron leaned over and began to paddle.

J. J. wasn't sure that was a good idea considering whatever the fire was using to burn was apparently spreading across the surface of the water, but the flames were getting closer so they didn't have much of a choice. As he stuck his hand in the water, he saw Digger calmly reaching into his duffel bag. Before he could yell at his friend to stop fooling around, Digger pulled out two yellow sticks. He held them out and pressed a button on each. With a twang, the sticks extended into paddles.

"Aaron," Digger said as he held out a paddle.

"What the –?" Aaron reached out automatically to take it, his expression one of surprise.

"Army strong!" Digger grinned. "Be all you can be –"

"Yeah, yeah," Aaron said. "Shut up and paddle."

The boys dug the paddles into the water and propelled the raft away from the fire, pushing skulls out of the way as they went.

"How do you know if we're going the right direction?" Sandra asked.

"How do we even know what the right direction is?" Karli came up with a better question.

"Well, we're going with the flow of the current," Digger said. "It's slow, but it's moving. I think that's probably our best bet. Away from danger and letting the river do most of the work."

J. J. bolted upright. He could tell them which way they were going. He pulled the compass out from underneath his shirt. After a moment, he had a reading. "We're heading north-east."

"How do you –" Aaron started to ask, then saw the compass and stopped. "Never mind."

Silence fell over the group, the only sound was the gentle lapping of the paddles in the water. The fire faded behind them and darkness fell again. J. J. felt that eerie sense of the loss of time. Without being able to see anything, there was no way to know how much time had passed, how long they'd been afloat. Logically, he knew it couldn't have been more than an hour or so, but it felt so much longer, as if the only thing that had ever existed was the river and the raft and the people around him, and the rest of his life was only a dream.

Karli broke the silence. "What time do you think it is?" she asked. "It's got to be getting close to morning."

Genius looked at his watch, pressing one of the little buttons to make the screen light up. "It's four thirty."

"I should so be getting my beauty sleep right now." Sandra sighed.

J. J. peered ahead. "Is it just me, or is it getting lighter up there?"

"Woohoo!" Digger cheered as he and Aaron dug deeper into the water.

"I can't wait to take a shower," Sandra said.

"Me too," Karli agreed.

"J. J., let Genius take a look at the map." Aaron didn't look at his brother as he spoke.

J. J. could hardly believe his ears. "Are we still on the hunt?"

All eyes turned to Aaron.

"Just give him the map, doofus, before I change my mind."

J. J. pulled out the map and handed it over to his friend.

"Aaron, what are you doing?" Karli's whisper was loud enough for the others to hear and she blushed when they looked at her.

"The kid's right," Aaron said. "This is the only way out, but we don't know where we are. The only map we have is that stupid treasure map. We might as well use it, and if we find a treasure in the process, all the better."

"We're here," Genius pointed to a spot on the map, squinting to see in the ever-growing moonlight. "There's another symbol here next to the entrance. I can't quite make it out. J. J.?"

J. J. narrowed his eyes. "It's a circle."

"Yeah, I can see that." Genius rolled his eyes as he lifted the map closer to his face. "I think it's a sun."

"I think there's something about a sun in the journal," J. J. said as he flipped through the book's pages.

"Ah, the sun." Sandra sighed. "I could use a tan." Her gaze ran down over her arms, then paused at her hands. She grimaced. "Ew. And a manicure."

"Here it is!" J. J. felt his previous excitement returning as the dangers behind him grew further and further away. He began to read. "'An Indian ruler's shameful deed, anger the gods, the sun will bleed. Strike the rock on the Eastern shore, hollow the earth to an open door.'"

"That's a little melodramatic, don't you think?" Aaron glanced over his shoulder at J. J. "You must've gotten Porter's wuss genes."

J. J. glared at his brother for a moment and then returned to the journal. "'The key, an Ostracon, broken in three, difficult to find, yet easy to see. Find the first piece above the lake, hidden in stone at heaven's daybreak.'"

"'Heaven's daybreak?'" Digger asked.

The entrance to the cave was growing closer and the current had picked up enough that the boys no longer needed to paddle. Digger and Aaron set down the oars and leaned back against the side of the raft.

"I think 'heaven's daybreak' means dawn," Genius said.

J. J. nodded. "That sounds about right."

"So, what time is it?" Aaron asked. "Because it looks like it's getting pretty close."

Digger reached into his pocket and drew out the battered pocket watch J. J. had found. J. J. raised his eyebrows in question.

"What?" Digger said as he checked the time. "I wound it and it works. It's nearly five o'clock."

"According to my calculations," Genius spoke up as he looked from the entrance to the raft and then down at the river, "we should make it in time."

"I really should get a pedi too." Sandra's statement drew the attention of the others, but she seemed oblivious to them as she examined her toes. "It's been nearly three weeks. I never go that long without a trip to the spa."

"Sandra, shut up." Karli surprised everyone, including herself. "This is important!"

Sandra gave Karli a superior look. "Well, so are my French tips." Her eyes dropped to Karli's hands. "Not that you'd understand."

Karli opened her mouth to provide a sharp comeback, but, at that moment, the raft passed through the entrance of the cave and into the open air. The eastern sky was lit up purple and pink, but the sun had yet to be seen. Everyone took a deep breath of the fresh air. J. J. had never considered himself claustrophobic, but he couldn't deny the relief that rushed through him now that he was out of that tunnel.

"Digger, paddle to shore." Aaron got back onto his knees and picked up the oar.

The boys dipped the paddles into the water and began to row. The raft, however, continued forward without the slightest movement toward the eastern bank.

"Why aren't we going to shore?" Karli asked.

Digger peered over the side. "Looks like there's a strong

undertow."

"Let me do it, Digger," Aaron said, his voice strained. "Take your paddle out and I'll bring it around."

Digger did as he was told and lifted his paddle from the water. Aaron dug deep, fighting the current. For a brief moment, it looked like he would win and then the raft spun, nearly yanking the oar from Aaron's hands.

"What's happening?" Karli fell sideways.

"I can't hold it!" Aaron tumbled backward, barely managing to keep hold of the paddle.

"What's that?" Sandra's voice shook as she pointed downriver.

Less than ten yards ahead, the river dropped away and disappeared into a white mist. Digger pushed himself up onto his knees and peered ahead. The minute his friend's face went white, J. J. knew that they were in trouble.

"Uh-oh." Digger grabbed his paddle. "Aaron, look!"

J. J. didn't think the instruction was necessary. They were all looking, unable to tear their eyes away from the rapids that had suddenly emerged from the mist. The raft whipped around, throwing them all off balance and crashing into one another. Aaron and Digger thrust their paddles back into the water, fighting to keep the raft away from the biggest of the rocks. The forest sped by in a blur as the kids were thrown back and forth. They grabbed at one another, desperate to keep themselves from flying overboard.

J. J. found himself holding onto Digger's ankle and watched with horror as the river yanked the paddle right out of his friend's hand. Digger stared ahead of the raft, apparently at the paddle.

"Guys?"

It was nearly impossible to hear Digger over the rapids.

"Guys!" Digger yelled this time and everyone looked at him.

He pointed.

Fighting the violent tossing and turning of the raft, everyone pushed themselves up enough to see what Digger had so freaked out about. J. J. immediately understood and started to freak out himself.

"No." Sandra started shaking her head as if she could negate the truth simply by denying it. "This can't be happening."

"We're gonna die for sure this time!" Genius clutched his backpack to his chest.

"J. J., if this kills us, I swear I'm gonna kick your butt!" Aaron yelled.

J. J. thought about pointing out the absurdity of that statement, but he didn't bother. At the moment, he was more concerned about the waterfall he was currently hurtling toward.

"Get down!" Aaron said suddenly. "Get down and grab onto the raft with one hand, the person next to you with the other."

Everyone did as they were told and J. J. had a second to think about how, just a couple of days ago, he would've given anything to have Sandra's arm linked through his, her body pressed against his back. Now, all he could think was that he'd prefer to have his mom hugging and embarrassing him someplace nice and safe.

"Brace yourself!" J. J. squeezed his eyes closed as the river dropped from underneath them and the raft took them all, screaming, over the falls.

Chapter Twenty-One

Melvin's snores had grown more unbearable with each passing hour. Around two o'clock, Ki-Ki had decided that she would try to get free. Melvin wouldn't be able to do it. He couldn't do much of anything, really, so it was down to her. At first, she tried pulling her right hand free, then her left, but the ropes were too tight. She flexed her wrists, trying to loosen them, but that didn't work either. She kept trying until her wrists were rubbed raw and then she stopped. She would need to figure out another way to get free, something that didn't involve removing unnecessary flesh in a painful manner.

It wasn't until nearly three that she remembered about the nail file in her back pocket. After nearly a half-hour and quite a bit of manoeuvring, she managed to retrieve the thin piece of metal. For a moment, she was tempted to poke Melvin with it and see if that woke him up since her squirming apparently hadn't, but she refrained. There was something much more important that she needed to be thinking about. Those monsters had her baby.

It was Hunter's face she kept in her mind as she worked the file into the knot. After poking herself several times, she succeeded in the insertion and began to work on loosening the knot enough for her hands to get free. The clock on the nightstand read five o'clock by the time she pulled her left hand out of the loop. She made short work of the right and then removed the gag from her mouth.

"Melvin!" Her voice was hoarse, her mouth dry. She grabbed a bottle of water from the table next to her and took a swig. "Melvin!" Stronger this time. She got the last of the ropes off and jumped up from the chair.

When her fingers started to work at the knots holding his hands together, Melvin stirred. "Hunter?"

Ki-Ki began to cry as she untied her husband. "My baby. They took my darling angel. My poor innocent baby."

***

A glob of sunflower seed mess landed on Bruno's left shoe.

"Oops." Hunter grinned, his teeth speckled with pieces of the seeds he'd been munching for the last twenty minutes. Roberts had asked about them since Hunter didn't seem like one who cared at all about eating healthy. The boy had shrugged and said that they'd been free, so there was no point in passing up free food.

Bruno glared at Hunter.

The boy shrugged. "My bad."

The sound that came from Bruno's mouth was half obscenity, half growl. Either one could have been responsible for Hunter immediately rushing to Roberts' side.

During the exchange, Roberts had been standing on the bank as close to the tunnel entrance as he could get. He'd watched the pair for a few minutes while he gathered his thoughts. Now, as Hunter approached, he spoke to one of them. "There's no sign that they exited the water."

"So now what?" Hunter smugly enquired as he shoved another handful of seeds into his mouth.

Roberts turned away from Hunter and gazed downstream, a thoughtful expression on his face. "They're around here somewhere. I can smell it."

"You can smell that?" Hunter asked. "Wow. That's pretty good. I ripped that one back there a ways. Shouldn't have had that beef jerky. It always gives me the silent 'n' deadly ones. Ya feel me?"

Roberts made a noise of disgust. He'd never understood the American male's fascination with body functions. They were far too crass for his own amusement.

"What?" Hunter had apparently heard the sound Roberts had made. "You got rainbows and skittles shootin' outta your rear like some sorta unicorn?"

The boy took another hand of sunflower seeds and Roberts momentarily imagined himself shoving the seeds down Hunter's throat. They really needed to find those kids and that treasure before he lost his temper and killed Hunter just for the sheer pleasure of doing it.

Chapter Twenty-Two

Rubber rasped against rock as the raft bumped up against the shore, the calm pool of water rocking it gently back and forth. The sky overhead was slowly dawning and the smallest hint of orange could be seen on the eastern rim. Six bodies lay on the floor of the raft, each one soaked and unmoving.

A Canadian tiger swallowtail hovered over the raft, its yellow and black wings gently moving as it circled the kids below. It fluttered down near the face of each one, as if examining the features to find one particular person. It circled J. J. a second time before moving lower to gently land on his nose.

***

It was nice in the silent dark, J. J. thought. Nothing hurt. Nothing was scary. Everything was just nice and quiet. No worries. No fears. If he woke up, he'd be cold and wet, probably even hurt. He didn't want to wake up. He was completely content to stay right where he was.

Wake up.

J. J. twitched. Someone was calling him. It was his mother, he told himself, telling him to wake up and come down for breakfast, that she'd made pancakes with fresh strawberries just the way he liked them. After breakfast, he'd hang out with Genius and Digger, maybe sneak a peek at Sandra sunbathing.

Wake up!

The voice was more insistent this time and it no longer sounded like his mother. In fact, it didn't sound like anyone he knew. The memory of the two men back at the Butterfly House flashed through his mind and adrenaline flooded his veins.

The butterfly flew away as J. J. stirred. He sat up, blinking blearily around at his friends. As he turned, he saw that the raft had grounded itself... and then he saw the large hollowed rocks that formed an arch.

"'An open door,'" he whispered. He raised his voice. "'An open door made from stone.'" He scrambled to his knees, excitement chasing away the fright of what had happened just minutes ago. "Guys! We made it! Wake up!"

"J. J., what are you yelling about?" Aaron's voice was thick.

"We made it!" J. J. repeated.

"Mommy?" Genius said as he stretched. The moment his eyes opened, he bolted upright, cheeks turning red. "J. J.? We're alive?"

"Karli, are you okay?" Aaron gently shook the girl's shoulder until her eyes opened.

"Yeah." She nodded and immediately crawled over to Digger who was coming to. She grabbed him in an embrace and, without any hesitation or embarrassment, he returned the hug. There was nothing like a little near-death experience to negate normal sibling annoyances, J. J. thought. He and Aaron might not be hugging, but he'd seen the relief in his brother's eyes when they'd seen that he was okay.

"J. J.?" Sandra murmured as she opened her eyes.

J. J. turned toward her, shocked and pleased that his name was the first thing she said.

"Sandra?"

She opened her eyes and pushed herself into a sitting position. "I'm going to kill you." She lunged at him and he fell backward, nearly falling out of the raft. "You're dead, you little –"

Genius reacted on pure instinct and threw his arms around Sandra, pulling her back. She struggled in his grip, reaching for J. J.

"Sandra!" Karli snapped her fingers in front of Sandra's face. "You keep doing that and you're going to give the boys a show they won't forget." She looked down meaningfully.

Sandra did the same and saw the buttons on Genius' shirt were straining. One wrong move and they'd pop. Immediately, she stopped... and realized that Genius' hands were very close to that same part of her. He must have realized the same thing because his hands fell away as if he'd been burned.

"Sorry," he said, his face flaming.

"Don't mention it." Sandra's cheeks were pink.

J. J. decided the best way to relieve the situation was to move on. It also seemed like the best way to live a little longer. He scrambled over the side of the raft, his feet splashing into a couple of inches of water. "Look!" He pointed. "An open door made of stone! Just like the journal said. That's where the first piece of the Ostracon is hidden."

The others followed him onto the shore, Aaron and Digger pausing to pull the raft further up on the rocks before joining the rest of the group. Their only remaining paddle sat forlornly on the wet bottom of the raft. Genius peeked into his backpack and then gave a sigh of relief. J. J. knew that meant his friend's laptop was okay. That was good; they might need what Genius had on there.

"Water resistant?" Digger asked as he slung his duffel bag over his shoulder.

"Yes, thank goodness. Yours?"

"You know it! Army strong!" Digger pumped his fist into the air.

"Shut up," Aaron said.

"Hooah!" Digger yelled as he ran toward the archway.

J. J. immediately followed, though he refrained from yelling. He had a feeling Aaron would throw something at him if he did. A moment later, he heard Genius behind him. This was one of the reasons why he was pushing so hard to find this treasure. If he didn't and his family had to move, he'd lose the two best friends he'd ever had. No matter who else he met, he knew he'd never find anyone like Digger and Genius. The other three followed at a slower pace, but J. J. could still hear their conversation as they walked.

"Just so you guys know," Sandra said. "If there's no treasure and all this crap has been for nothing, I'm gonna kill those overexcited pubescent nerds without thinking twice about it."

"I'll help," Karli said.

"No court in the land would convict us." Aaron stooped and picked up a rock.

J. J. ran a little faster.

Digger was already in the centre of the archway when J. J. arrived and the pair watched Genius run the last few feet. He glared at them as he caught his breath.

"This is cool," J. J. said, looking up over his head at the arch.

Karli was a few steps ahead of the other two and some of the annoyance faded from her face as she saw the magnificent structure. Her jaw dropped as she spotted a clear, gleaming rock at least an inch wide embedded in the limestone. She ran her fingertips lightly over it, as if afraid that touching it would make it disappear.

"You guys," Karli said softly, "it's the largest diamond ever!"

Sandra appeared behind Karli. "Holy crap!"

Aaron stepped past the girls to stand next to his brother. As he scanned the arch, his eyes widened. "Whoa. There's a bunch of them in here. We're freaking rich!" He punched his brother's shoulder. "J. J., I take back all of the mean stuff I ever said or did to you."

Digger was telling J. J. all of the cool new military equipment he was going to buy with his share when Genius walked up to the wall, his eyes narrowed as he studied one of the crystals. Without a word, he leaned forward and licked it.

"Did he just –?" Karli asked.

"Yeah," Sandra said, "he did."

"Guys, these aren't diamonds," Genius said. "Sorry, but they're halite."

Everyone stared at him blankly and J. J.'s stomach dropped. Whatever it was, halite didn't sound like it was going to be able to keep his family from losing their house.

"It's rock salt," Genius clarified.

"Rock salt?" Sandra echoed. She ran a hand through her hair.

Aaron delivered a stinging slap to the back of J. J.'s head. "Butt-wipe. You got us running around this island and almost getting killed for some stupid wild goose chase."

As everyone around him began complaining about how everything they'd been through had been for nothing but some lousy rock salt, J. J. closed his eyes. The back of his head hurt a bit and his body ached from the ride on the raft, but that wasn't important. He needed to concentrate. He was missing something, he knew it.

Sure enough, that something just popped into his head. "Wait a minute!" He raised his voice. "Wait a minute!" The others turned to him, all five looking decidedly annoyed, but they were at least paying attention. "Remember, we're supposed to be looking for a piece of the Ostracon, not diamonds in rocks."

"Uh, J. J.?" Digger raised his hand.

"Yeah?"

"What in the world is an Ostracon?"

J. J. blinked. He hadn't even thought to ask that. "I don't know." He turned to the same person he always did when he had a question to which he didn't know the answer. "Genius?"

Genius pulled out his laptop and punched a few keys. J. J. wondered if Genius actually needed to look up the information or if he just wanted to be sure that the computer hadn't been damaged during the most recent leg of their adventure. Whatever the reason, after a minute, Genius had the answer to their question.

"The Ostracon dates back to ancient Egypt and Greece. Usually pottery, it contained words or pictures relating to an issue of the day. Because it was used to cast votes in Athens, including decisions regarding exiling people, it is the origin of the word ostracism –"

"Genius, give us something useful," Aaron said. "I doubt Porter wants us looking for some old school voting ballot."

"True," Genius said. He paused and skimmed further down in the article he was reading. "Ah, here we are. Native Americans used Ostracons for leaving messages. They were usually just pieces of stone with words and pictures scratched onto them."

"All right," J. J. said. "Good to know. Thanks, Genius. Okay, everyone –" The rest of the sentence died in his mouth. Aaron and the girls were walking back toward the raft. "Aaron. Please wait." If he lost his brother, no one else would even consider helping. Maybe not even Genius or Digger.

Aaron stopped and turned to face J. J. "You want us to search this whole area, made out of stone, for a broken piece of stone. That's the dumbest thing I've ever heard."

"J. J., that's like finding a needle in a haystack," Karli said.

Sandra didn't even bother speaking; she just shook her head.

J. J.'s head fell and he felt tears welling up in his eyes. They were giving up.

Psst.

J. J. jerked his head up. That was the voice that had woken him, he was sure of it. There, near the top of the arch, was a yellow and black butterfly. He could see the unique way its wings formed something like a tail at the end of either one. And he was pretty sure that it was staring at him. It fluttered down toward him and circled his head. J. J. remembered the belief about asking a butterfly for help. He took a deep breath. What could it hurt?

"Please," he whispered. "I believe. Help me make them believe."

Sunrise.

As he watched, it fluttered off toward the eastern horizon as the first sliver of sun showed itself. The others watched it go as well, though no one else gave any indication that they'd heard it speak.

"Look at that sunrise." Karli sighed. "Like a piece of heaven peeking through the sky. I'd love to paint it."

Sunrise. Heaven. Everything clicked into place.

"'Heaven's daybreak!'" J. J. nearly shouted the words. "Remember? The riddle said that 'it could be seen at daybreak.'"

Even as the words left his lips, a beam of sunlight broke across the water and straight into the arch. It hit one of the crystal rocks and darts of prism light shot out to touch five more of the rocks, each one sparkling and sending rainbows dancing across the limestone. Each rock sent one ray of light toward the floor and, as the kids watched in amazement, the combined light bounced off another crystal and shot straight up to the ceiling of the arch.

"Unbelievable," Sandra breathed the word, her eyes wide.

As suddenly as it came, it was gone.

"It's here!" J. J. bounced on his toes. The butterfly had been right again! As weird as it was, he wasn't going to question it, not if it led him where he wanted to go. "The piece we're looking for is right up there!" He pointed to where the last beam of light had landed.

"So how do we get up there and find it, Sherlock?" Aaron asked.

"I may be able to help with that." Genius handed his laptop to Digger and dug in his backpack. A moment later, he pulled out a plain black case. With all eyes on him, he opened the case and removed a pair of sophisticated-looking sunglasses.

"I don't think it's really bright enough to need those," Sandra said.

"These are infrared glasses with a five-element lens and ultra-digital zoom, and they transmit directly to the laptop." The group gathered around the laptop as Genius stepped under the arch. "Let me know if you see anything."

After a moment of adjustment, the picture of the arch ceiling appeared on the monitor, crystal clear.

"This is some wicked James Bond crap," Aaron said admiringly.

"Q Branch crap," Genius corrected. "Without Q, James Bond would have been killed on his second assignment."

"Who knew geeks could be so sexy." Sandra gave a throaty chuckle.

J. J. was sure that his friend would ignore it. Genius wasn't exactly known for his prowess with the opposite sex, or, honestly, really even acknowledging them. He was just as likely to be dumbstruck and embarrassed as anything else. In fact, J. J. wondered sometimes if Genius even realized how gorgeous Sandra was. Then, Genius turned and J. J. knew that his friend did indeed understand the beauty of the neighbourhood hottie. The image on the screen suddenly zoomed in on Sandra's chest.

"Oh please!" Karli threw her hands in the air. "Enough with the boobs already! She's got them! Big freaking deal!" She shot Aaron a dirty look. "And no more James Bond crap either. He was a snide womanizer that deserved being slapped more than kissed. If he ever hit on me, I'd give him a piece of my mind."

Aaron blinked, his jaw dropping open. A dark red flush was slowly creeping up Genius' neck and J. J. was pretty sure that they all felt about an inch tall.

Sandra grinned and winked at Genius. "Time to get back to work, Geek Boy."

Genius nodded dumbly and turned back to the arch. Aaron, however, couldn't seem to take his eyes off of Karli who, try as she might, kept stealing glances at him. J. J. couldn't stop grinning. It was nice to see a girl catch his oh-so-cool brother off guard. He was starting to like this whole Aaron and Karli thing for reasons other than wanting Aaron to ignore Sandra.

"See anything yet?" Genius' question drew everyone's attention back to the computer screen.

"Nothing," J. J. said. "Move a little to the left."

"Hey!" Digger pointed at the screen. "I saw something! Go back."

Genius panned back and a jagged-edged stone appeared on the monitor.

"There. What's that?" Digger asked.

J. J. bent his head closer to the screen. He tilted his head slightly and the shape of a bird became recognizable. "That's it."

"So, how do we get it?" Karli asked.

Digger grinned. "My turn to go all James... um, I mean, MacGyver?"

Karli gave him an approving nod. He reached into his duffel bag and produced a hammer and chisel. He looked around and then turned to Aaron, an apologetic look on his face. "I need a ladder."

"No." Aaron shook his head. "No way in this life."

Karli reached out and put her hand on his arm. "You are the tallest, and how else are we going to get to it?" He still looked doubtful. "If you don't find this treasure, your family's going to move away and we'll never see each other again."

Aaron looked torn. His eyes moved from Karli to her brother and back again. Finally, he groaned. "All right, I'll do it." He turned to Digger. "No pulling on the hair."

"Gotcha," Digger said.

Digger got onto Aaron's shoulders with relative ease, but as the younger boy tried to shift to find the best angle, his foot caught Aaron in the jaw.

"Ouch! Easy, Rambo."

"Sorry." Digger looked like he was trying not to laugh. "At least it wasn't your hair."

Aaron looked murderous, but didn't retaliate. The other three stayed at the laptop, watching along with Genius as Digger began to chisel around the edges of the stone.

"It looks like a puzzle piece." Karli traced her finger along the lines showing on the screen.

"Careful," J. J. called to his friend.

"What's that drawing on it?" Sandra asked.

"I'm not really sure," J. J. said. "It's a bird, I'm sure of that, but I don't know what kind. A bald eagle maybe?"

"It looks like a woodpecker," Sandra said, squinting her eyes.

"Naw, it's a falcon." J. J. tilted his head at a different angle.

"No." Karli shook her head. "I think Sandra's right. It's a woodpecker."

Digger paused in his chiselling to peer at the rock. "A woodpecker? This is a clue to a historic treasure. You guys need to be thinking fierce 'birds of prey', not Woody Woodpecker. It's gotta be a hawk or a –"

"Woodpecker," Genius interrupted. "It's definitely a woodpecker. They're indigenous to the island. Remember I saw that huge one banging away when we first went to the Butterfly House?"

"I hate to interrupt this lovely nature discussion," Aaron said. "But can Digger just get on with it? He's not exactly light."

"Oh, right, sorry." Digger sounded anything but sorry as he resumed chiselling.

The next several minutes were filled with the sounds of chisel against stone and hammer against chisel, each hit echoing off the archway walls. J. J. kept glancing around, sure that someone was going to hear them, maybe the two thugs from the Butterfly House, maybe just the Island authorities. Either way, he was sure that neither scenario would end with them getting to the treasure.

"Got it!" Digger announced. He dropped the stone into his backpack, along with the hammer and chisel, and proceeded to climb down Aaron like a jungle gym.

"Easy!"

"Sorry." Digger didn't sound very apologetic. He pulled the stone from his bag as everyone gathered around.

"There's writing along the side." Aaron pointed.

Genius took the stone from Digger and blew away the dust. He examined it closely, turning it this way and that. "Most of it is worn off. I can see 'place of contemplation, reflection and peace' but not much else."

J. J. looked at the others, determination blazing in his eyes. "We gotta find the other two pieces."

"Definitely." Digger agreed.

Genius nodded as he placed the stone back into Digger's bag.

The girls looked at Aaron. He was covered with dust and dirt, his shirt wearing Digger's footprints, and he didn't look happy. He brushed his hands through his hair, creating a cloud of dust. "Well, what the heck are we standing around for? We've got more stuff to find." He looked at J. J. "Which way do we go now?"

J. J. pointed down the hillside and the others hurried to pack up their things and start to pick their way through the rocky underbrush. J. J. hung back for a moment and looked up at the clear, blue morning sky. "Thanks for the help, Grandpa." He took two steps and then added, almost as an afterthought. "And Mr Butterfly."

Chapter Twenty-Three

Roberts had grown up on the edge of Sherwood Forest, so he was no stranger to traipsing through underbrush. Granted, it had been a few decades since then, but it came back easily. He did mourn the fact that his shoes would probably be ruined and he wasn't sure if even his dry cleaner would be able to fix the mess he was making of his suit, but once he had his treasure, he could buy a new suit and dress shoes, ones that would make these look cheap by comparison.

His voice was relatively even as he spoke. "If my calculations are correct, the clearing should be just ahead." Bruno grunted in response. The big man had been raised in numerous big cities and had very little patience with nature.

Roberts stopped as he reached the clearing and turned to watch his companions finish the climb up the wooded hill. Where he had stepped over branches, Bruno just bowled right through them, occasionally bending them out of his way before letting them snap back into place.

Hunter was right behind Bruno, huffing and puffing as he struggled to keep up. Roberts had a theory that if the young man had been wearing properly fitting clothing, the journey may have been a bit easier. It was difficult to hike when the waistband of one's trousers was around one's knees.

"This is a load of bull –"

Hunter was cut off mid-word as the branch Bruno had been holding snapped back and slapped Hunter across the face.

"Ouch!" Hunter rubbed at the red mark on his cheek. "You did that on purpose!"

Bruno grinned at Roberts as he entered the clearing.

"I'm gonna bust you in the mouth you foo!" Hunter then did the most foolish thing the boy had done yet. He dropped the last bite of his candy bar and charged at Bruno.

Roberts sighed as Bruno easily sidestepped the rush and snagged Hunter's collar before the boy killed himself. Roberts still needed to ensure that he'd found the other kids before Hunter was no longer needed for leverage. With an expression of pure glee, Bruno lifted Hunter into the air by the collar of his oversized shirt. As the boy flailed his arms in a feeble attempt to hit Bruno, Roberts was very strongly reminded of a puppy trying to act as if it were a vicious guard dog.

"Let me go you big oaf! A'ight! That's it! I'm gonna go buck wild on your mute butt! Let me go!"

Bruno's smile widened and Hunter froze, as if sensing that something was wrong. He looked down and instantly went pale as he saw that the clearing ended abruptly. The only thing that kept him from falling hundreds of feet to a rocky death was Bruno's grip on his shirt.

"I changed my mind! Don't let me go!" He reached up to grab Bruno's wrist but the big man shook him and he squealed, dropping his hands back to his sides.

Roberts peered over the edge and smiled as he saw the kids had survived the river. Based on their excited body language, he felt it safe to assume that they were working on their next clue.

That made things much easier for him. He turned to Hunter.

"And the children shall lead them."

"What?" Hunter's eyes were wide. "What does that mean?"

"My dear boy, you had to have known this moment would come sooner or later. I cannot believe that even you are thick enough to think that you would be allowed to return to your parents."

"What are you talking about?" Hunter's faux accent vanished along with his bravado.

"The boy with the map and his friends will lead Bruno and myself to the treasure. And, since we will have that, I will no longer need to concern myself with the money your father owes me," Roberts said. "Unfortunately for you, that means that I no longer need you as leverage against your father."

"I trusted you!" Tears began to stream down Hunter's face.

"It appears that we are both victims of broken trust, as I trusted your father not to lose all of my money." Roberts was unmoved by the tears. Had the boy faced his demise with dignity and courage, he might have had second thoughts about allowing Bruno to drop Hunter off the cliff. But, as it was, he would not be sorry to see the child go. He really was doing the world a favour. "Let me bestow on you a few words of wisdom regarding trust. Always base your trust on a person's actions, not their words, for words are easily spoken and forgotten. Action shows the true measure of a man." He paused a moment, then added. "If it is any consolation, you will be joined by your parents just as soon as Bruno and I return to the hotel with our treasure."

Roberts gave Bruno a nod.

"N-no! Please!"

Bruno let go.

Hunter screamed as he fell and Roberts closed his eyes, waiting for the inevitable end. With a muffled grunt, the scream stopped. Roberts opened his eyes, puzzled. It should have taken the boy much longer than that to reach the ground, and the final sound should have been more of a splat than a grunt. Bruno also looked confused, but Roberts wasn't sure if that was due to what had just happened or not. Too often, bewilderment was Bruno's go-to expression.

Roberts and Bruno approached the edge and looked down. There, hanging from a tree branch by his impossibly huge trousers, was Hunter.

"A'ight! That's what I'm talkin' 'bout!" Hunter whooped, throwing his hand in the air. For a moment, it appeared that the movement would finish what Bruno had started, but fate was on the boy's side and he remained where he was.

Bruno mumbled a series of curse words with which Roberts wholeheartedly agreed.

Hunter twisted his head up to look at Roberts and Bruno. "You had me goin' there, dawg! Whew!" He held out a hand. "Pull me up?"

Bruno growled and reached for his gun. Roberts held out a hand. "We've got more important things to do."

As they walked away, Roberts heard Hunter calling after them.

"A'ight, guys, this ain't funny no more! Help a brother out!"

Chapter Twenty-Four

Digger shifted the straps on his bag. The contents might have been protected from the water, but the straps had soaked up enough of the river to make the shoulders of his T-shirt uncomfortably damp. He wasn't going to complain though. He'd always prided himself as being the most in shape and athletic of his friends and, with Aaron there, his reputation was at stake. He did, however, suppress a sigh of relief as they reached the top of the hill to find an old dirt road. He was a soldier, not a mountain climber.

"Can we rest a bit?" Genius asked.

Genius was neither a soldier nor a mountain climber. He was the brains, true, but Digger had always felt a little sorry that Genius hadn't gotten any brawn.

"And let Dr Frankenstein and his monster find us? No thanks. We keep moving." Aaron immediately vetoed the request.

Suddenly, Digger stopped, images flashing through his mind.

A hand released its hold on a shirt.
Mouth wide open in horror, falling.
Jeans caught on a branch.
Chocolate.

"Did anyone hear that?" Karli stopped next to her brother.

"What's the matter?" Sandra asked. She grimaced as she

rubbed her knee.

"I thought I heard someone screaming," Karli said.

Digger started. Screaming? Like he'd just seen in his mind? What in the world was going on?

"I don't hear anything," Sandra said as she resumed walking.

Karli shrugged. "Probably just water in my ears."

Another picture flashed through Digger's head. This one of someone he recognized... kind of anyway. *Braids. Oversized clothes. A pudgy, frightened face.* As he hurried to catch up with the others, he asked, "Hey, do you guys think that kid's all right?"

Aaron glanced over his shoulder. "You mean Peanut Eminem?" He shook his head. "That kid is doomed."

"What are you talking about, Aaron?" Karli asked as she fell in step next to him.

Aaron's voice was grim. "Those two guys he was with, they're not playing a game. This is real."

A serious expression settled on the older boy's face and, for the first time, Digger thought that maybe this adventure hadn't been the best idea. Even when the men had been threatening the kid or when the arrows had been shooting at him, it had still seemed like some sort of game, like something Digger and his friends would've pretended behind their houses when they were kids, or played on one of their gaming systems. He'd played war and other various fighting games so often that the danger here hadn't really seemed that imminent until he saw Aaron – one of the cockiest guys he knew – show concern.

"I don't know how those guys found out about the map or the treasure," Aaron said. "But what I do know is that we'd better stay one step ahead of them, or we're all dead."

"Aaron's right." Genius expressed his agreement. "We need to find that treasure, if there is one, and fast. We may need it as leverage to save our own butts."

Any further discussion regarding leverage and death was put on hold as they rounded the bend and came upon a fork in the path. Without needing to be asked, Digger pulled the map from his bag. Genius came over and the two of them studied it together.

Genius ran his finger along a line. "According to the map, this used to be an old logging road, but the second part of it wasn't there when the map was made. The correct one should lead to a cabin of some sort."

"It looks like the road to the left is the correct one." Digger pointed. "That's the way the squiggly line goes."

"Great. We're following the squiggly line," Sandra said. "Any chance we can get something more definite?"

"Well, we're supposed to be heading west," Digger said.

"Okay, so how do we know which way is west?" Karli twisted her hair up behind her head like she always did when she was hot. Usually, she'd just tie it there with one of those mysterious things girls always seemed to have on their wrists or in their pockets, but this time it looked like she didn't have anything with her, so she let it go again and it tumbled over her shoulders like a wave of fire. When he was little, Digger had nightmares about his sister's head being on fire. He'd never told her that and never intended to either.

"I got it," Digger said as he dove into his bag one more time. After several minutes of searching, however, he came up empty. "Crap. I forgot my GPS unit."

"Great, Rambone. Now what?" Aaron sighed.

"Since the sun's rising over there," Genius said, pointing, "we can assume that west is in the direct opposite direction."

"Yeah, well, you know what they say about assuming, don't

you?" Aaron said. "I'm not heading into a forest I don't know without something that's going to keep us going the right direction when we can't see the sun."

"Um, this still works," J. J. said, pulling the compass out from under his shirt. He held the compass in his hand and let the needle adjust. "West is that way."

Digger pulled the pocket watch out and checked the time. "It's getting late, guys, and our parents are going to start wondering where we are."

"If Dad and Mom see we're not in the room, they're going to be pissed. And then when they realize we're not in the hotel, we're dead meat," J. J. said to his brother.

"Yeah, ours aren't going to be happy either," Karli said.

Digger nodded. He hated to think about what his dad would say if he found out that they'd abandoned their posts and fraternized with the enemy. Not to mention the fact that they were wandering around looking for a treasure that may or may not exist without having asked permission first.

"I think we'd better pick up the pace," Aaron said.

"What do you mean?" Genius asked, his voice filled with dread.

"We need to run it."

"All right," Digger yelled. "It's balls to the walls time, people!"

Aaron and J. J. started at an easy jog to build momentum. It was obvious Genius didn't want to do it, but he began to trot, resigned to his fate.

"Balls to what?" Sandra looked at Karli.

"It means 'go all out,'" Digger said. He checked the straps on his pack to make sure they were good and tight. The last thing he needed was to lose his duffel on the path. "So let's go, cupcakes!"

He took off running. His pace was a bit more brisk than was probably necessary, but he refused to let Aaron show him up. He didn't turn around, but he knew the girls must've started running too because he heard Karli call after him.

"If you ever call me a snack food again, you're going to need to run a lot faster than that to get away from me."

Digger picked up his pace. He'd once seen his sister beat up a playground bully twice her size because the boy had broken one of Digger's toys. The boy's mom had shown up on their doorstep to complain, but immediately left when tiny little Karli answered the door and the boy had started crying. He made a mental note to refrain from referring to his sister as any form of food. He had no desire to see if she'd make good on her threat.

***

A dirt-crusted hand shot up over the edge of the cliff and grabbed a handful of grass. Seconds later, a second hand followed. Pale, chubby arms strained as a groan sounded from below. Finally, a line of light brown cornrows appeared, slowly followed by a red and sweating face.

Hunter hovered at the edge for one frightening moment and then, with a last, desperate burst of energy, he heaved himself up onto the grass. He pushed back from the edge and flopped back onto the grass. He sucked in deep draughts of air as he waited for his heart to stop thundering in his chest.

He'd never been so scared in his life, not even when he'd first been kidnapped. He'd been so sheltered that the scariest thing that had ever happened to him before was being chased by an angry squirrel last summer. Then, in the last twenty-four hours, everything had changed. He grinned. It was official. He truly was living the thug life.

He'd almost gotten shanked.

He'd almost died like a hundred times.

He had street cred now.

"I's gots ta go on a diet, yo." He was still panting as he reached into his pocket and pulled out a chocolate bar. "Tomorrow."

He took a big bite. Yeah, he'd start working out tomorrow, get his body into shape for all the honeys who'd be checking him out now that he was legit. It was a hard life for a playa, he mused as he stared up at the sky.

***

Aaron and J. J. reached the clearing at the end of the path first, with Digger just a few steps behind. All three slowly turned, searching the trees for any glimpse of the cabin while the rest of their group caught up.

"So, where's the cabin?" Karli panted as she bent over and placed her hands on her knees.

Digger unfolded the map. J. J. and Aaron stood on either side, all three examining it as Genius walked over. He was still catching his breath as he looked at the spot where they were standing.

"I don't get it. It should be right –"

"What the heck is that?" Aaron interrupted.

"What?" Genius asked.

"That!" Aaron thrust his finger at the map, but stopped short of actually touching it.

"It's another symbol," Digger said. "How'd we miss that?"

The girls pushed their way between the boys, Sandra between Aaron and Genius, Karli between Aaron and her brother. Digger glanced at J. J. and rolled his eyes. J. J. gave a half-smile. Normally, the sibling behaviour would've been amusing, but at the moment, he was more than a little preoccupied by the possibility that their quest had come to an end.

"It looks like the letter U." Sandra looked where Aaron was pointing and gave her own assessment.

"No." J. J. shook his head, suddenly remembering something that he'd read. "It's a horseshoe."

"A horseshoe?" Aaron sounded sceptical. "How do you know that?"

"I saw one in the journal when I was going through it." J. J. rummaged in his own bag and withdrew the journal. He flipped through a couple of the pages and stopped, holding out the book so the others could see.

"There it is," Karli said.

"What's the journal say about it?" Aaron asked.

J. J. brought the journal back to himself and began to read. "'High above the bluff, a small dwelling for six, but more than enough. Find the second piece in the Ark's enclose, in the special room made for Ambrose.'"

"I bet there's a trail somewhere in these woods that leads to the bluff in that riddle," Digger said.

J. J. would've made a smart-aleck reply about Digger stating the obvious, but he'd just finished reading the next part of the passage. He hadn't remembered this part of it when he'd been reading before. He might have gotten distracted, or maybe just forgotten in the excitement of treasure hunting, but now that he'd seen it here, he couldn't ignore it.

Karli must have seen it written on his face, because she called him on it. "There's more to the riddle, isn't there?"

J. J. nodded, reluctant to share.

"Well?" Sandra looked at him expectantly.

"You're not gonna like this," J. J. said, trying to avoid actually having to reveal what he'd read.

"Dang it, J. J.," Aaron said, exasperated. "What's it say?"

J. J. hesitated and his brother glared at him. He knew that look. He either needed to read it himself, or Aaron was going to take the journal from him and he didn't know if he'd get it back. He took a deep breath and read the rest of the passage. "'When the woods go silent and the fog rolls in, the terror of Haunted Forest will begin. Be swift and don't look back, the ghosts of the slaughtered are on horseback. Seventy-five murdered scour the trees, searching for justice to set them free.'"

"What the heck does that mean?" Karli's usually fair face had paled even more.

"Haunted forest?" Genius shook his head. "Are you crazy? We're just going to merrily stroll through the freaking spook-infested woods? I could handle the attempted murder by the crazy Englishman and his ugly, mountainous sidekick. I survived the skydive into Skull Lake. I made it through the treacherous rapids in one piece and lived through the waterfall. But I draw the line at possibly being mangled by vengeful murdering ghosts!"

Digger attempted to be helpful. "The key word there is possibly."

"Read my lips. Heck no!" Genius set his bag on the ground. "N. O."

Sandra grabbed the front of Genius' shirt and, shocking everyone, planted her mouth on his. J. J.'s jaw dropped as Sandra kissed Genius. This wasn't some peck on the lips from one friend to another. This wasn't even a flirty bare brush of mouths designed to get someone interested. Even though Genius didn't seem to know what to do with his hands, this was a full-on, grown-up kiss, the kind that people used to measure every other kiss they ever had.

J. J. felt a momentary flash of jealousy, which was quickly replaced by admiration and grudging well-wishes to his friend. He wanted to look at his brother to see how Aaron was reacting, but he couldn't seem to stop staring. Besides, he had a feeling that Aaron really didn't care about Sandra, not with the way he looked at Karli.

"All right," Sandra said as she took a step back, a pleased smile on her face. "There's no such thing as ghosts, let alone bitter Village People ghosts. Now, we're all going to march through there, right?"

She turned on the heel of her sandals and marched past the gaping group toward the woods. After a moment, Aaron and Karli followed, amused grins on both of their faces. J. J. was pretty sure he actually heard his brother smother a laugh.

Digger looked at the still shell-shocked Genius and raised his fist. "Hooah!" He hurried off after the others.

"Way to go," J. J. said before leaving Genius still standing at the end of the road, the teen's mouth hanging open, a punch-drunk expression on his face.

Chapter Twenty-Five

Digger was pretty sure that forests weren't supposed to be this creepy, not unless they were the home of witches with candy houses or little green guys who talked funny. The further in the group went, the taller the trees got, the thicker the underbrush and the more densely interwoven the branches became. He wasn't about to admit it, but Digger didn't do so well in places like this. Underground tunnels with skeletons, he enjoyed, thought it was all good fun. A familiar wood with a hunting rifle was fine, but this type of forest was different. There was something about the way the light turned funny colours and how the shadows seemed to move all on their own. He'd gotten lost as a child in a forest like this and had hated them ever since.

"Where'd the sun go?" Karli asked.

Digger moved closer to his sister and hoped that it looked like he was in protective mode. She was right, though, it was getting dark fast. Too fast. They hadn't been walking *that* long.

Sandra grabbed Genius' wrist and held it close to her face, squinting at his watch in the rapidly dimming light. "That's weird," she said. "It's not even seven o'clock yet. Shouldn't it be getting lighter, not darker?"

Digger glanced at his sister, waiting for some snarky comment about stating the obvious, but it never came. He wasn't sure if it was because of Sandra kissing Genius rather than Aaron or if Karli was too freaked out by her surroundings, but either way, Karli didn't say anything.

"Looks like midnight, not morning," Aaron said.

Digger slowed along with the rest of the group and pulled his duffel bag over his shoulder. He rummaged in the bag and pulled out his tourch. He switched it on, pleased with the instant, strong light. He was still grinning when his light flickered and dimmed.

"Batteries going dead?" J. J. asked as they all stopped, unable to go any further without light.

"No way. K2 lithium ion battery, fully charged..." Digger's voice trailed off as a series of images flashed in front of his eyes, each accompanied by a growing sense of dread.

A field covered in bodies, grass stained with blood.

Trees creaked and groaned, moving without wind.

Once dead bodies rushed forward, pale with death but somehow still moving.

A flash of sharpened metal.

Digger shivered. "It's almost as if the darkness is absorbing the light. I don't like this."

All eyes turned toward him, eyebrows raised. Digger felt his face get hot. Yeah, that last bit had sounded a little... weird. Before Digger could get more embarrassed or try to figure out an excuse for his statement, a low rumble came from deeper inside the forest. Thoughts of headless horsemen and werewolves immediately came to mind, followed quickly by every deep woods horror film he'd ever seen.

"Do you hear that?" Genius asked, and even in the darkness,

Digger could see that his friend's face was pale.

As the rumble faded, an eerie silence fell on the forest. Digger hadn't realized just how much noise actually filled a place like this. There were no birds chirping, no small rodents in the underbrush. Even the mosquitoes that had been incessantly buzzing about from the moment they'd entered the woods were gone. Digger could hear the blood rushing in his ears, his heart pounding so loud he was certain that the others could hear it too. He strained his eyes, trying to see something, anything.

At first, he thought his eyes were playing tricks on him, the way they do when you try to look too long in the dark. He closed his eyes and opened them again, shook his head to clear it, but the thick fog rolling toward them just kept coming. It was surprisingly pearl-white in the dark of the forest, rolling around shapes that he could only assume were trees. From the fog, the rumble came again, this time louder and closer.

"Uh, guys." J. J. must have seen it too, but Digger didn't look at his friend, too caught up in what was happening right in front of him.

"Let's get outta here, now," Aaron said.

It was the fear in Aaron's voice that broke Digger's paralysis. "Go! Go! Go!" He grabbed Karli's shoulder and shoved her around.

When Digger turned, he could see light ahead. It seemed much further away than the treeline should have been, but it was there nonetheless. He started to run, J. J. falling in step beside him.

"Drums!"

Digger gave his friend a startled look, unsure if he'd heard correctly.

"Drums!" J. J. repeated.

This time Digger heard it too. The rumble. It wasn't thunder. It was the sound of drums. A sudden fear gripped him and he knew he should just run faster, but his ever-present curiosity was turning his head before he'd made the decision to look back. He saw J. J. doing the same.

Transparent flesh that managed to be pale, but not Caucasian at the same time. Angry, harsh features. Strange leather garments. Stripes of paint. He knew those faces, had seen them in his mind both in this form and in a more solid one. He had seen them on the day they'd been killed.

Both J. J. and Digger yelled at the same time.

"Keep going! Don't stop!"

"Faster! They're right behind us!"

"Who's behind us?" Karli called out behind her without pausing in her stride.

"Indians!" Digger and J. J. exclaimed in unison.

"Indians?" Sandra sounded close to panic. "You mean they're real?"

"We're gonna die!" Genius managed to speak between panting for breath. "We're all going to die! I died for love!"

"Shut up and keep running!" Aaron shouted.

What happened next was like something out of a movie, complete with slow motion. In front of him and to the left, Digger saw Sandra glance behind her. He didn't have to look to know what she saw and he didn't blame her for screaming. That was when she tripped.

***

This was bad. This was very, very, <u>very</u> bad. Genius had been sure they were all dead meat when they'd snuck out of their rooms and then again when they'd broken into the Butterfly House. His sense of doom had only increased when the two thugs and the strange dreadlocked kid showed up. When they'd gone through the fountain and into the creepy tunnel, he'd been sure he'd never again see the light of day. Then there was the skeleton with the tomahawk in its skull, the arrows, jumping into a sarcophagus then falling hundreds of feet. And, of course, the giant waterfall when he'd been fully prepared to meet his maker.

Now, Genius would have given anything to trade this moment in time for any of those other instances of certain death because at least then he wasn't being chased by Native American ghosts through a midnight-dark forest at seven in the morning.

He heard Sandra scream and automatically turned toward her. He liked to think that he would've done it even if she hadn't kissed him, but he honestly didn't know. But she had kissed him and that meant, when she was in trouble, he needed to go to the rescue. After all, wasn't that what heroes did?

Genius skidded to a stop as he saw Sandra fall. The ghost stalking her pulled a hatchet from his belt and Genius was sure it was all over. The other ghosts were still a few yards back, but closing in fast.

"Sandra!" he yelled, frozen in place. There was nothing he could do, no way for him to get there in time to get between Sandra and the tomahawk that was now spinning through the air.

Suddenly, there was a loud cracking sound and a branch fell from the tree Sandra had fallen against. Genius watched as it fell, not straight down, but at an angle, putting itself between Sandra and the hatchet. The ghostly object thudded into the branch with a surprisingly solid sound, leaving no doubt as to what it could do to human flesh. Sandra screamed again as the branch landed on her legs.

"Help!" The ghost was now only a few feet away and Sandra was struggling, desperately trying to get out from underneath the branch. "Genius, help me!"

"I'm coming, Sandra!" Genius' paralysis broke and he started to run toward her, knowing he'd never reach her in time. He heard the others shouting at him, but they'd been too far ahead for them to be able to reach her either. As the ghost reached her, the branch suddenly burst into flames.

Sandra's screams were no longer words, but sounds of pure fear. Genius tried to run faster even though he wasn't entirely sure what he was going to do when he got there. Fight a ghost? Pull a burning branch twice his size off Sandra? The ghost reached out and yanked its weapon from the wood, seemingly oblivious to the fire.

"Leave her alone!" Genius yelled without even knowing why he was doing it. He gestured with his hands, as if the ghost could be repelled that way. "Get away from her!"

The branch flew up into the air, through the ghost, and landed half a dozen feet away. Sandra scrambled backward, away from the outstretched hand. Genius grabbed her arm and pulled her to her feet.

"C'mon!"

"Did you see...?" Sandra stared, wide-eyed, at the branch as the fire flickered, dying.

"No time! Come on!" Genius grabbed her hand and tugged on it as the ghost turned toward them. Its companions were now only a few feet away and some of them had weapons too.

They ran after their friends who had turned around the moment they saw that Sandra was safe. The ghosts were close, too close, and the daylight too far away. Only Sandra's hand in his kept Genius from descending into complete panic mode. It was like something out of one of his nightmares. Something chasing him. Running in the darkness toward the light and knowing that he'd never reach it in time. Arms and legs pumping as fast as they could, all the while never moving.

Then, suddenly, they were free, bursting from the trees into the morning sunlight. They collided with the others, all of them falling into a heap on the ground and turning to see if their pursuers could cross that line from shadow to light. Between the trees, they could still make out the ghosts coming toward them. The one in the front raised its arm and flung its tomahawk, a look of pure rage on its face.

Genius wasn't ashamed to say that he was one of the group who yelled as the weapon tumbled toward them. There was a ghost hatchet flying through the air, headed straight for them, for crying out loud! Only an idiot wouldn't be afraid.

The cries of fear turned into ones of shock as the tomahawk passed from darkness into light... and instantly disintegrated.

***

"Holy crap!" Aaron said what all of them were thinking.

"Hey, jerk, you're on my hair." Karli smacked her brother's arm.

As they all scrambled to disentangle themselves, J. J. eyed the forest. The ghosts were gone, though the interior still seemed darker than it had before. It might have been just a trick of his imagination, thinking that the woods were still malevolent, but after what had just happened, he wasn't ready to take that chance.

"We made it." He sat down on the dew-damp grass next to his friend, not caring that his shorts were getting wet again. That was the least of his concerns at the moment.

"Yeah," Digger said. His face was unusually pale and he seemed to be trying to regain his usual swagger. "We looked death in the face, once again, and we defeated it. We rock!" He held up his hand and J. J. slapped it.

A familiar noise drew both boys' attention. Genius was sitting, arms wrapped around his knees, gasping for air. J. J. shook his head. Leave it to Genius to start hyperventilating after charging a ghost.

Sandra got up on her knees and put her arms around Genius' head, pulling it toward her so that the side of his face rested on her chest. J. J. suddenly wished that he was that face.

"Shh. Shh. It's okay. We made it. We're alive." She stroked his hair.

"We made it?" Genius asked.

"Yeah, and you saved my life." Sandra placed her cheek on the top of his head. "You're my hero."

Digger made a gagging noise and J. J. felt inclined to agree. Not because it was Genius and not him, but because that was just way too sappy. Not even Sandra's chest was worth that much saccharine.

"How did you get that branch off of me without burning yourself?" Sandra asked.

"What?" Genius straightened, his cheeks turning red as he realized everyone was staring at the two of them.

"That branch that was on my legs. It was on fire and you got it off of me but you're not burned." Sandra released him and sat down where she'd been kneeling, leaving not much space between the two of them.

"You kicked the branch away," Genius said.

J. J.'s stomach twisted. Something weird was going on and it had nothing to do with the ghosts in the woods. Something was actually happening to them. First Genius had moved that arrow and now that tree branch suddenly fell in the right place at the right time and then it was thrown away when neither person claimed to have done it. Not to mention the fact that it had been on fire and there hadn't been anything around to start it. Then there was the weird cracking sound when Roberts had let go of Sandra's leg, Digger's previous confession that he'd seen things, Aaron moving those stones and that lid, no matter how much he said the others had just loosened it and he had good leverage. And, of course, his own thing with the butterflies. Even taking out the whole 'ghosts' thing, this was not normal.

J. J. gathered his courage and spoke up. "Doesn't anyone else think we need to talk about what's happening to us?"

All eyes turned toward him, the expression on each face some form of incredulity.

"Are you kidding?" Aaron asked. "We almost got killed by ghosts. Ghosts, J. J.! I'm not really sure that needs much more discussion than 'let's get the heck out of here.'"

"I don't mean that." J. J. waved his hand toward the woods. "I mean with us. How we've been acting... different."

Digger visibly tensed.

"Come on, Aaron, you saw what just happened. How are you going to explain a tree branch bursting into flames out of the blue and then being thrown off when neither Genius nor Sandra says they did it?"

"How am I going to explain it?" Aaron asked. His voice rose

until he was almost shouting. "How? I don't know, J. J., maybe the same way I'd explain the fact that we were chased by ghosts out of a forest where it was night-time at seven o'clock in the morning."

"Aaron." Karli put a hand on his arm and his face tightened, but he stopped yelling.

"J. J., look, man, I understand you wanting to figure all this out," Digger said. "But don't you think it might be better to wait until, you know, we're not trapped between two armed thugs and a haunted forest?"

Reluctantly, J. J. nodded. Part of him wanted to argue that if they really had gotten some sort of strange powers, they could use them in the treasure hunt, but he knew that it would take more time to convince the others than they probably had before those two men and the kid found them.

"We need a way around that forest," Aaron said. He seemed calmer now that J. J. had let the whole 'weird' thing drop. "Everyone fan out and look around, but don't go back into the forest."

"Darn, there went my plan." Digger muttered so that only J. J. could hear him.

J. J. managed a weak smile as he moved away from the others to look. He needed a moment to think. Since the right side of the forest went straight up to the ocean, he wandered to the left where the edge of the woods tapered off as it reached a rocky cliff. Straight up, at least fifteen feet high, it didn't look like anything they could safely climb and there was no way of knowing exactly what was at the top. Just as J. J. was about to turn back around, he heard a familiar sound.

Psst.

He looked up, knowing what he was going to see. Sure

enough, a large monarch butterfly was hovering in the air just a few feet away.

Path.

J. J. watched as it flew a few feet closer to the rock wall and then back into the underbrush. He glanced behind him and saw that the others were all busy searching. No one was watching him. He pushed down some of the weeds at the edge and saw a faint trail weaving between the wall and the forest, a steady incline that looked like it would eventually lead to higher ground.

"Is it safe?" He kept his voice low, feeling foolish but also a little excited. Would it answer?

Safe. The butterfly bobbed in the air as if nodding its head. *Too much light.*

J. J. immediately understood what it meant. The ghosts couldn't come out in the sun. As long as the path was well-lit, they wouldn't be able to come out.

Hurry.

With that final warning, the butterfly flew up and over the rock wall and disappeared from sight. Before he could second guess himself, J. J. called over his shoulder. "Hey, I found something!"

Chapter Twenty-Six

The sun was halfway toward its zenith by the time the kids rounded the final bend and all of them were about ready to drop. The adventure had shifted from exciting to exhausting a while ago and even though J. J. still wanted to find the treasure, he was as ready for a break as the rest of them. What none of them had expected, however, was what was at the end of the trail.

Karli stopped dead in her tracks. "Whoa."

The others went just a step or two further before stopping as well, each face wearing similar expressions of wonder and surprise.

Aaron let out a low whistle.

"That's not a cabin," Digger said.

"That's what I call a house," Sandra said.

'House' wasn't the word that automatically came to mind, J. J. thought. 'Mansion' was more like it. Two stories high, it was easily as wide as two of their houses back home. White with black trim, it had an old, worn look though the grounds appeared to be cared for. The brush from the forest had been tamped down and the lawn rolling up to the house was neat and well-trimmed.

"I didn't think anyone lived up here," Genius said.

"They don't," Digger replied. "I've studied the island's schematics and they don't show anything up here. The eastern side of the island, aside from the south coast, is pretty much all woods."

"Whoever lives here has to have some way to contact the hotel, right?" Sandra asked.

"We're just going to give up?" J. J. looked at his brother.

"In case you haven't noticed, J. J., we're in a bit over our heads here." Aaron took a step forward. "And if nothing else, we have to tell the cops about those guys with that kid. I seriously doubt his parents let him go off with those two guys."

Aaron had a point, J. J. had to admit. As much as he wanted that treasure, it wasn't worth overlooking a kidnapping. He'd just have to figure out a way to convince the others to keep going after they'd called the police. Or, he supposed, if he had to, he could slip away and finish the search on his own.

"Is there someone on the porch?" Karli asked as they drew closer to the house.

J. J. squinted. He could just make out a rocking chair that looked like it had someone in it. "Maybe."

"Should we say something?" Sandra asked when they were only a few yards away.

"I don't know." Aaron shrugged. "I guess if he saw us, he'd yell, right?"

When they reached the steps, all eyes turned to Aaron, J. J. included. All of this may have been his idea, but Aaron was still the one the others looked to for leadership.

Aaron took a deep breath and stepped up onto the rickety wooden step. "Hey, mister."

There was no answer and Aaron went up another step. J. J. followed. Now that he was closer, there was something familiar about the figure in the chair.

"Digger, Genius, isn't that the old man from the Butterfly House?" he asked.

"You know this guy?" Aaron asked quietly as he took the last step needed to be on the porch.

"Maybe." Genius could have been answering either question. "I can't tell if it's him or not. He's not wearing a vest."

The group huddled behind Aaron as they inched forward.

"He looks dead," Digger said.

"Maybe the Indians got 'em." Aaron's expression clearly stated that he didn't want to keep moving.

"They can't come into the sun, Aaron," J. J. said.

"He's not dead," Sandra said.

Karli started to step around Aaron. "I think he's just slee–"

All of the kids jumped back, more than one letting out a squeak of surprise when the old man's eyes flew open. He sat up straight.

"Hello there. Didn't mean to startle you. I was just out enjoying the morning air and must've dozed off." He looked at J. J. "Jonathan, right?"

J. J. nodded. It was the guy from the Butterfly House. No matter how odd he'd been, J. J. hadn't felt threatened and that same sense of ease came over him now. He glanced up at Aaron. "We've met before. His name's Lloyd."

"Brought the whole gang, I see." Lloyd's eyes darted around to each of the others before coming back to rest on J. J.

J. J. nodded again. "Yes, sir." He wasn't sure why Lloyd was talking to him when it was obvious that Aaron was in charge, but he'd go along with it. "This is my brother Aaron and that's Michael's sister Karli and our friend Sandra. And, you remember Takumi."

"Yes indeed." Lloyd inclined his head toward Digger and Genius. "And it's very nice to meet the rest of you as well."

"Do you have a phone we could use to call the hotel?" Aaron

asked. "Our parents are going to be worried about us."

"I do have a line –" Lloyd began.

"And we need to call the police too," Karli added. "There's this kid who's in trouble."

"Oh, dear," Lloyd looked concerned. "As I was saying, I do have a line, but the rain last night must have damaged something because it's not working. I was planning on heading into town in a bit to let someone know that it needed to be fixed."

"Do you work here too?" Digger blurted out.

"Work here?" Lloyd considered the question as he tried to stand. He made two attempts before J. J. stepped forward and helped the older man to his feet. "Thank you, young man." Lloyd arched his back, breathing a sigh of relief when it gave an audible crack. "I suppose you could say I work here. I own it." He gestured. "It's mine."

Digger's eyes widened. "You could afford all of this from working at a place filled with bugs? You must've had one heck of a pension plan."

J. J. smirked as Karli elbowed her brother.

"Dig– Michael, don't be rude."

Digger gave his sister a puzzled look. "What'd I say?"

Lloyd, however, didn't seem to take offence at Digger's comment. "I volunteer at the Butterfly House. I find it a soothing place to be." He withdrew a pocket watch from his button-down shirt and flicked it open. "You kids are out and about rather early." He put the watch away. "Especially considering how far you would have had to travel just to get here. Not many people come out here." He looked at J. J. with shrewd, intelligent eyes. "And definitely not anyone from that direction."

J. J. looked at Aaron who seemed to be as much at a loss to

explain their presence as J. J. was.

"In fact, I'm willing to bet that you didn't just happen to wander to this side of the island," Lloyd continued. "I'll bet you're on a treasure hunt."

J. J.'s jaw dropped and he saw the others making similar faces. From behind him, he heard Sandra mutter. "Aw, crap. The old timer's on to us."

J. J. knew he had to cover and fast. "Why would you say that, Lloyd?"

"Real smooth, J. J.," Digger said.

A smile played around Lloyd's lips. "Jonathan Porter Hanks? Named after Lieutenant Porter Hanks, I believe." He thought for a moment. "He would be your great-great-great grandfather. Am I right?"

J. J. and Aaron exchanged startled glances. This was getting weirder by the moment.

"I started to suspect when I saw you and your two friends with that map," Lloyd said. "But when I got close enough to see you... well, you have his eyes, you know."

That was way too personal for Lloyd to be just some history buff, J. J. knew. "Did you know him?"

Lloyd laughed. "Heavens no. I may be old, but I'm not that ancient." He motioned for the kids to follow him. "Come inside. I have something to show you and then you can decide if you'd like me to take you into town... or if you would prefer to go somewhere else."

The inside wasn't anything like J. J. expected. Lloyd led them past a staircase that looked like it could have been in any home and into a living room. Or, J. J. guessed, a parlour if he remembered his history correctly. There was a large fireplace at one end of the room, unlit, of course, and rugs scattered around the hardwood floors. The furniture was older than what J. J. was used to, but was still in excellent condition. None of them were in perfect condition, but all had the slightly worn look that spoke of a family that liked to use them. The parts of the walls that weren't lined with bookcases were filled with pictures. Lloyd led the group to the fireplace where a large portrait hung.

"Judging by your appearances, I'm going to assume that you could all use something to eat and drink." Lloyd smiled at them. "Make yourselves at home. I'll be back in a few minutes."

"Make ourselves at home?" Sandra echoed. She leaned over to Karli. "I wish my house looked like this."

"I know, right?" For once, it seemed like Karli appreciated Sandra's presence.

"It is big," J. J. said.

Sandra chuckled as Karli gave a snort of derision.

"It's more than big," Sandra said. "Do you have any idea how much this is all worth? The furniture alone cost more than our houses back home."

"Really?" Digger cast a doubtful look at the closest chair's faded upholstery.

"Boys." Karli shook her head.

Genius spoke up. "Since it appears most of the wear is to the upholstery and not to the wood itself, most of these pieces could be sold for upwards of five to ten thousand dollars, more if they're refurbished with material from the same time period in which they were built."

Everyone stared at him and he flushed. "Remember how I was with my grandmother in Boise for a month last summer? We pretty much spent all of our time watching antique shows and auctions."

He looked at Sandra, a glum expression on his face. "I just lost man points, didn't I?"

"I don't think you had many of those to begin with." Digger quipped while Genius glared.

J. J. turned from his friends and found himself looking up at the massive picture above the fireplace. It appeared to be a family portrait of a man and his six children, only J. J. recognized the man but none of the children. The patriarch was also older here than J. J. had ever seen him. Still, J. J. would've recognized the man after whom he was named no matter the age. He'd seen the family's only picture of Porter hundreds of times, but it had been faded by time and the elements, leeching away a lot of detail. Those first few years after the war, the lieutenant had been branded a coward and deserter, considered by some even to be a traitor. No matter how it had hurt to hide it, the picture had been put away so as not to give the appearance of honouring what had been done. Only later generations had kept it out as merely a historical memento.

Lloyd was right, J. J. decided. He did have Porter's eyes; although it looked like the athletic soldier's build had gone to Aaron. The kids on either side of Porter looked like they could be anywhere from ten to eighteen and each one had the same nervous, pinched look that made J. J. think that they'd seen and heard a lot in their young lives. With their fair hair and light-coloured eyes, J. J. was fairly certain that he was looking at a set of six siblings, none of whom looked like Porter Hanks.

"I wasn't expecting visitors," Lloyd said as he came back into the room with a tray. "So you'll have to excuse the lack of variety." He set down the tray and J. J. saw toast and three different types of jam sitting next to a pitcher of what appeared to be iced tea.

J. J. motioned to the portrait. "That's him, isn't it? Porter

Hanks. My ancestor."

Lloyd nodded as he began to pour tea into the cups he'd set out. "That it is." He gestured toward the tray. "Please, help yourselves."

J. J. saw Digger and Genius exchange glances and then the boys dove in. The girls were next. Aaron and J. J. waited until the others had backed away from the tray to get their own food.

"You're all welcome to sit," Lloyd said. "I'm sure you've walked quite a bit. And don't worry about getting the furniture dirty. A little dirt never hurt anyone."

The girls glanced at Genius, as if remembering how much he'd said the furniture was worth, and then sat on the floor in front of the couch. The boys followed suit, all except for J. J. who perched on the hearth.

"So you have a picture of my however-many-greats-grandfather." J. J. tried to prompt the conversation.

"I do." Lloyd sank into the chair closest to the fireplace. "Now, I'm sure you and your brother have heard the story that Porter Hanks abandoned his troops during battle, that he was a coward."

J. J. and Aaron nodded, and J. J. leaned forward. He knew part of the story from Porter's journal, but he needed to hear from someone else that his ancestor wasn't a deserter.

Lloyd continued. "Truth is, his second in command knew that it was imperative that the lieutenant not be captured, so he sent Porter away. Hanks was wounded in the attack – an attack that came as a direct result of being betrayed by Officer Dousman, a spy for the British, mind you – but he still managed to get away." He gestured at the portrait. "He ended up here, in this clearing, and stumbled into the cabin where six siblings had been living for several years on their own. He took the kids under his wing, looked after them as if they were his own. Especially for the younger ones, he was the only father they'd ever known. Had that portrait done about two years after he found them, said he wanted to have something with all of them together."

"Why didn't he return home? Take the kids back with him and get his son?" Karli asked.

J. J. had wondered this himself. The personal entries had ended with a small passage saying a group of children from the island had gotten sick, and that Porter now had an idea of where he would hide his part of the treasure. Everything after that had been the clues to finding it.

"Because the army would've shot him," Digger answered. Everyone turned their attention toward him. "No matter what the circumstances were, in the eyes of the military, Lieutenant Hanks was a deserter and would be sentenced to death if he was caught."

"That's right," Lloyd said. "He knew that his son was safe, being raised by Porter's own sister, and that was enough. Porter changed the way he looked and let the people on the island think he was the children's biological father. He spent most of his time up here and no one thought to question who he really was. If he returned to the mainland, questions would be asked and he would be found out."

Lloyd pushed himself up out of his seat and pointed to the smallest of the children, a serious-looking boy with haphazard curls. The kids got to their feet and crowded around, food and drink forgotten.

"That little fella there is my great-grandfather Ambrose."

"Ambrose?" J. J. looked at Digger and Genius.

"From the riddle," Genius said.

Digger shook his head. "Wow. Even when we're not looking

for clues, we find them."

"He's cute," Sandra said. She ignored the surprised look from Genius and pointed at the oldest boy, a handsome young man with a charming smile. "Who was he and does he have any living and available grandchildren?"

"That was Samuel." Lloyd's smile faded. "He and the four others died shortly after this portrait was completed. Tuberculosis. Only Ambrose and Porter survived, and it was a miracle they did, especially back then."

"That's so sad," Karli said.

J. J. didn't say so, but he agreed with the sentiment. To lose your parents when you were young was hard enough, but to then lose all of your brothers and sisters too... it was awful. He shot a sideways glance at Aaron. As much as his brother annoyed him, losing Aaron would be horrible.

"It was," Lloyd said. "But it was a different time back then. They didn't have the medicine to cure things like TB or other diseases that we don't think anything of nowadays."

"So, if there wasn't medicine, how did Ambrose and Porter survive?" Sandra asked.

J. J. was pretty sure he was the only one watching the old man's face, which made him the only one who saw the shadow pass across Lloyd's eyes. The hesitation could have been written off as emotion if J. J. hadn't seen that slight change in expression.

"Porter always said that he was immune. None of his family had gotten sick when TB had gone through his town as a kid. As for Ambrose, well, no one really knows how he managed to survive. He did get sick at first, that much I know, but he recovered even though he'd always been the weakest of the kids." Lloyd shrugged. "They say the Lord works in mysterious ways."

Lloyd was hiding something. J. J. was sure of it.

"So, what do you know about this buried treasure?" Aaron finally asked the question that had been on all of the kids' minds since arriving.

"Come with me." Lloyd turned and began to walk back the way they'd come.

"Where's he taking us?" Digger whispered to J. J. as they followed Lloyd to the staircase.

J. J. shrugged. The only thing he was sure of was that Lloyd knew something, both about the treasure as well as something else. J. J. wasn't sure why, but he suspected that the other thing had something to do with all of the weird stuff that was going on with him and his friends. Before the day was over, he intended to have answers.

The hallway Lloyd led them down was as immaculately clean as the rest of the house, but had more of an unused air about it. As they passed door after door, J. J. wondered when the last time was anyone had been up here except to clean. When Lloyd finally stopped, they were at the far end of the corridor, the area lit only by the morning light coming in from a small, high window.

Lloyd pushed open the door and walked inside. The kids hesitated at the door for a moment before J. J. summoned up the courage to enter first.

"Wow." He stared as he walked further into the room. Behind him, he could hear his friends making similar comments as they took in the cluttered study. The walls were covered with pictures, charts, maps and newspaper clippings. The bookcases were stuffed with books, some of which looked older than Lloyd, and the desk was buried under a mountain of books and papers.

"It's like stepping back in time," Karli said as she examined the bookshelf closest to her.

"It's got that old person smell." Sandra's attempt at being quiet didn't work as her voice easily carried.

The corner of Lloyd's mouth tipped up at her comment, but he didn't respond to it, focusing instead on something else entirely. "My family has lived on this island for generations. We've survived off of riches that had been left to us by Ambrose."

"His part of the treasure," J. J. said.

Lloyd nodded and J. J. heard the others moving closer. Here, with the sun streaming in through a large window, with the dark of the forest and the two thugs behind them, the hunt for the treasure once again seemed exciting rather than dangerous. Even the thoughts of the dreadlocked boy didn't seem to be as urgent as they had just a short while ago. Surely the two men wouldn't hurt Hunter. After all, they hadn't so far.

"The treasure was equally divided between my great-grandfather and yours." Lloyd walked over to the desk. "Now, this desk was left to me by my grandfather and it had been left to him by Ambrose."

"That looks just like the one in our basement," J. J. said to Aaron. He turned back to Lloyd. "It had been left to our dad."

"I suspect Porter and Ambrose had matching ones specially made," Lloyd said. He opened a drawer and removed a leather-bound book that looked virtually identical to the one currently in J. J.'s backpack. "I found this in a secret compartment."

J. J. tried very hard to keep his eyes on Lloyd and ignore the stares he could feel coming from the rest of the group.

Lloyd continued, either oblivious to or ignoring the kids' reactions. J. J. suspected the latter. The old man was sharper than he'd originally given him credit for. "This journal has instructions on how to avoid the elaborate booby traps that had been constructed by Porter Hanks. Traps designed to deter thieves from finding his portion of the treasure. The portion that he never spent, wanting instead to leave it all to his son."

"So why didn't you try to find this treasure and give it to Porter's descendants?" Aaron asked. The suspicion in his voice was clear. "Or, for that matter, why didn't your father or grandfather?"

"Oh, we've all had our go at it. Myself included. After Porter Hanks died without disclosing where he'd hidden the treasure, we all tried to find it. Searched this island high and low for years, but without the map, this journal was of no use. It was just another piece to an incomplete puzzle." Lloyd looked at J. J., as if sizing him up and J. J. tried not to squirm. When Lloyd held out the book, J. J. could hardly believe it. "This rightfully belongs to you and your brother, the descendants of the son Porter Hanks never got to see grow up. I know that's what he would have wanted."

J. J. took the journal carefully, aware of how much more delicate it was than the one he had, having been perused for nearly two centuries while the other had remained hidden. Lloyd watched as J. J. leafed through the pages, neither one saying a word.

It was Genius who broke the silence. "Lloyd, on the map, and in the riddle that led us here, it talked about a small cabin, but this place is enormous. Is there another building on the property? Something smaller that could have at one time been a cabin?"

"There was once," Lloyd said slowly. "Right where you're standing. My father tore down the cabin and built this house in its place."

J. J. closed the journal, his shoulders slumping in defeat. He could feel the others' disappointment in how their adventure had ended, maybe even at him for bringing them along for it. He crossed to the window and looked outside. The sun was still shining, the view still spectacular. He wasn't sure why he'd expected to find it any less than so, somehow without colour and sad now that their hopes had been dashed.

"Well, that's it then," he said to his friends. "It's over. The room for Ambrose has been destroyed."

"And the second piece of the Ostracon with it," Digger said.

"The room for Ambrose?" Lloyd asked.

J. J. turned to look at the old man, sure he heard amusement in the question. When he saw Lloyd grinning, the hope that had been crushed just seconds before leaped up inside of him.

"Come with me." Lloyd exited the study with a speed that surprised all of them. He hurried down the hallway and back down the steps as the kids followed. J. J. tucked the journal into his bag as he walked, feeling a certain satisfaction as the two journals rested against each other.

"Any idea what the old man's thinking?" Aaron slowed his pace to fall in step beside J. J. as they descended the stairs.

"Not a clue," J. J. said as Lloyd opened the front door and went outside.

"So he could be completely senile and take us down some imaginary rabbit hole to talk to a stoner caterpillar." Digger joined the conversation. When J. J. gave him a look, Digger added. "What? My sister made me watch that stupid movie at least a hundred times. Something was bound to stick."

"Or he could be leading us into the shed where he kills all of his visitors and stores their bodies to eat later," Sandra said.

J. J. raised his eyebrows. "Seriously? You take a look at that old man and you think serial killer and cannibal?"

"What?" Sandra shrugged. "Weirder things have happened.

214

And, I might add, weirder things have happened to us in the past twenty-four hours."

"She has a point." Genius added his two cents' worth.

"He's not a serial killer cannibal," J. J. said.

"But he might be senile." Digger looked at Aaron who shrugged.

"I guess that is a possibility," Aaron said.

J. J. didn't bother to respond as they'd caught up to Lloyd who was standing next to a small, wood-framed boathouse. The old man was still grinning as he threw open the double doors. Inside the building was a small boat that looked like it had seen better days and a tangle of fishing equipment piled in one corner.

"My father didn't have the heart to bulldoze this place. He told me more than once that it was his grandfather's 'special' room." Lloyd led the kids inside.

"Doesn't look too special to me," Sandra said.

"Also doesn't look like a place to butcher my visitors, does it?" Lloyd laughed as Sandra's face turned red. "I may be getting up in years, but my hearing's as good as ever... when I'm awake at least." His expression softened. "No offence taken. You don't know me and it's always better to be too cautious."

"Did your father ever say why this was Ambrose's favourite room?" J. J. was eager to get back on track. They were running out of time. He could feel it.

"He said that Ambrose loved it." Lloyd thought hard. "And, once, he told me that these walls were made from the same exact wood as Noah's Ark itself." He chuckled. "Maybe there is a bit of crazy running through my blood."

"That's it!" J. J. exclaimed.

"Spread out!" Genius gestured wildly. "Search every inch of

these walls!"

"What's going on?" Lloyd asked as the kids scattered, running their hands over the walls and searching the corners of the shed.

J. J. explained as he tilted his head back to look up at the ceiling. "The riddle said that the second piece of the key could be found within the Ark's enclose."

Understanding lit up Lloyd's eyes. He moved to an empty space of wall and began to examine it.

"What exactly are we looking for?" Karli asked as she ran her fingers alongside the threshold.

"Everything and anything." Digger stood on his tiptoes to peer on top of a shelf.

Karli glared at her brother. "Well that narrows it down."

J. J. ignored the sibling banter and walked over to where Aaron was thumping his fists against the wall. "What are you doing?"

"Looking for a secret compartment," Aaron said. "They do it on TV all of the time."

"That is actually a good method to use," Genius said from Aaron's other side. "The sound quality differs between a solid object and a hollow one."

The side of Aaron's fist hit a plank with a thunk and a knot in the wood fell backward into the wall.

"Guys, over here!" J. J. called as he crossed to Aaron's side. A small hole less than three inches in diameter had appeared in the plank. "Can you see what's in there?"

"No." Aaron shook his head. "But I heard that knot hit something." He looked at J. J. and then at Karli. Taking a deep breath, Aaron stuck two of his fingers and his thumb into the hole and began to feel around. After a minute, he withdrew his hand, a small, dusty vial clasped between his fingers. "Got it!" He beamed.

"Great," Sandra said. "So, what is it?"

Chapter Twenty-Seven

Roberts stood at the edge of the cliff, his eyes narrowed as he searched for some clue as to where the children had gone. Bruno was standing at his side, a doubtful expression on his not-so-smart face. Up until an hour or so ago, they'd been right on the kids' trail. Then, the cliff had gone one way and the path the kids were taking went the other. He'd considered climbing down and following them then, but the sides of the rock wall were a little too steep for comfort. If he'd been ten years younger...

Bruno grunted and gestured toward the forest and Roberts was inclined to agree. They weren't dumb enough to try to go back and the only other option was straight ahead. There was a small chance that in the half-mile since the cliff had curved away and back again, something had happened, but that wasn't what Roberts' gut was telling him.

He frowned as he studied the treeline. Something about that forest didn't seem right. In his profession, he'd learned to listen to his instincts, and right now, they were telling him to stay as far away from that unnatural darkness as possible.

"Gusts," Bruno mumbled.

Normally, Roberts would have scoffed at the claim of ghosts and cited numerous scientific studies to support his convictions. He would have been condescending as he mocked Bruno's uneducated superstitions. Instead, he said nothing. He didn't believe in ghosts, but if he had, those woods would be exactly where he knew they would live... or whatever it was that ghosts did.

"I wonder," he mused aloud. "If our little friends went into the woods, how many of them would come out."

Bruno held up his hand, his thumb and fingers forming an unmistakable zero.

"Unless," Roberts' sharp eyes caught something. "Unless they find a different way." He pointed. "I believe that's a path."

As they walked along the top of the cliff, carefully following the trail that ran along the forest's border, a plan began to form in Roberts' mind. The kids obviously had the advantage when it came to finding things and following the map, as well as a knack for surviving crazy situations. What they didn't have was a way to carry the treasure once they found it. When the cliff had originally cut away, Roberts and Bruno had followed it and found themselves at the outskirts of a nice little development. A development that had carriages. Once he and Bruno found the kids and figured out where they were going, a quick side trip would get them transportation – well, more or less – and they'd have the upper hand. Between Bruno and Roberts' own weapons, taking the treasure from the kids would be no more difficult than taking candy from the proverbial baby.

There was no way this could fail.

Chapter Twenty-Eight

Lloyd and the kids cleared off the top of the desk, leaving the books and papers shoved into corners in haphazard stacks that leaned precariously. Once the space was clear, Aaron carefully opened the vial and peered inside. J. J. could barely stand still. He wanted to know what was in there, but it had been Aaron's find so it was Aaron's to reveal.

"It looks like a piece of rock," Aaron said. He tipped the vial and shook its contents out onto the desk.

"Limestone," Genius said as he studied the pale stone.

"No pictures this time." Aaron gently turned it over. "Just what looks like a serial number."

"Serial number? On a piece of limestone from 1827? I don't think so." Genius shook his head.

Aaron turned the rock so that the others could see it better. J. J. leaned closer and read aloud, "N 45:8511."

"If that's not a serial number, what is it?" Aaron asked.

"Genius is right," Digger said. "It's not a serial number. It's coordinates." He dug into his bag and pulled out the map.

Aaron scooped up the rock as Digger and J. J. spread the map out across the desk. Lloyd set a paperweight on one end while Karli placed a book on the other, holding the map flat as Digger began to explain his theory.

"I knew there was something different about this map. It's topographic."

"For those of us who don't talk like Christopher Columbus, what does that mean?" Sandra asked.

"Topographical maps are characterized by quantitative..." Genius began. His explanation faded away when Sandra glared at him. "Sorry."

"Basically, it's designed to show not just places and rivers and stuff like that, but also the land formations," Digger said, simplifying things, much to J. J.'s relief. He didn't want to have to ask Genius to dumb things down for him. Digger continued. "Back in the day, the military used these types of maps to assist in planning for battle and for defensive emplacements." He pointed. "See? Latitude and longitude readings."

The hope that J. J. had been feeling fell. "But we don't have a GPS unit to track them."

Lloyd snorted. "Kids and their technology." He opened a drawer and pulled out two metal things that J. J. had a vague recollection of seeing somewhere before, though he couldn't remember where or what they were. "Not all is lost. You can use these."

"Chopsticks?" Sandra asked.

"No," Genius said. "They're compasses. Like we use in school for geometry."

"Or like people used to use before technology started doing it all for us," Lloyd added.

"I suck at geometry." Aaron sighed.

J. J. had to agree. His brother did suck at geometry.

"Look, we can use this to triangulate the coordinates." Genius

220

picked up one of the compasses.

"How?" Karli asked as she picked up the other one.

"Easy," Genius said.

J. J. refrained from telling his friend that not everyone found this type of thing easy. Sometimes Genius being a genius came in handy. Other times, it was just annoying. J. J. waited to see which of those times this was going to be.

"Distances can be measured on a map using the spikes at the end of the compasses." Genius put the point onto the map as Lloyd smiled and nodded, seemingly impressed by the young man's knowledge. "If the hinge is set in such a way that the distance between the spikes on the map represents a certain distance in reality, and by measuring how many times the compasses fit between two points on the map, the distance between those two points can be calculated."

Sandra and Karli shared a look that said they understand as much of that as J. J. had, which was to say pretty much nothing. Aaron was trying to look like he had a clue what Genius was talking about even though J. J. knew that wasn't the case, and Digger hadn't even looked up from the map to acknowledge the exposition.

"Really, it's simple." Genius looked pleased with himself.

"You mean we can locate the treasure now?" J. J. asked the only question that any of the kids really cared about.

Genius ran his hand through his hair. "Not exactly."

"But you just said it was simple," Sandra said.

To everyone's surprise, Digger spoke up, "We only have one of the coordinates." There was silence for a moment and then he looked up. At the expressions on their faces, Digger shrugged and said, "I may not have understood half of what Genius just said, but

I know maps and we only have half of what we need."

Lloyd agreed. "He's right. You'll need both latitude and longitude to pinpoint its exact whereabouts."

Aaron sighed. "And how do we find the other coordinate?"

J. J. knew that the others weren't going to like his answer. "By finding the last piece of the Ostracon."

The girls groaned and Aaron closed his eyes. Only Genius and Digger appeared unconcerned, more interested in the map than what J. J. was saying.

"I understand the need to keep the treasure hidden," Aaron said. "But would it have killed Porter to make it just a little easier to get all of the pieces together?"

Lloyd pointed to a symbol on the map and everyone leaned forward for a better view. Lloyd's finger was resting just in front of a pentagram with the letters S, A, L, V and S inscribed at each point.

The old man frowned in concentration. "I've seen this before."

"It's the only symbol left on the map that we haven't figured out," J. J. said.

"Where'd you see it, Lloyd?" Genius asked.

"I don't know." Lloyd straightened and walked over to the window, a thoughtful expression on his face.

"J. J., check your ancestor's journal," Digger said.

J. J. pulled the journal from his bag, slightly embarrassed that he hadn't thought of it. He began flipping through the pages, scanning for that same symbol. About two thirds of the way through, something caught his eye and he flipped back.

"Here it is!" J. J. began to read. "The darkness and turmoil have taken their toll, a day of reckoning for a faithful soul. Bone-chilling cries and bellowing calls, children's tears that seep through walls."

"This is going to suck, I just know it," Sandra grumbled.

J. J. didn't respond and kept reading. "'No medicine to cure the pestilence scourge, only a dark, cool place and hopes to emerge. A burrowed passage in a desperate quest, that leads to surrender and final rest.'"

"Yeah, it's gonna suck," Sandra said.

"What's a borrowed passage?" Aaron asked.

"'Burrowed,' not 'borrowed,'" Karli said. "Basically, underground."

"Like that stupid tunnel under the Butterfly House," Aaron said. "Great."

"We need that third part, Aaron," J. J. said. "Without it, we'll never find the treasure."

"Yeah, yeah. I'm just not looking forward to it." Aaron looked toward Lloyd. "So where do we start?"

The old man slowly turned. "I remember where I've seen that symbol before."

Chapter Twenty-Nine

The sun was almost directly overhead, the sky a clear, beautiful blue. The temperature was just right, not too hot and not too cold. Under any other circumstances, Sandra would have been enjoying the day. Unfortunately, these weren't other circumstances. These were the crazy circumstances that she'd been dealing with ever since she'd agreed to go with Aaron and Karli after the three boys. The only positive thing she could say about the past twenty-four hours was that she'd discovered that Genius' nickname applied to kissing as much as it did to school stuff.

She squeezed her eyes shut as the wagon she was in took a sharp turn around some trees. Her stomach churned and she was starting to regret the two pieces of toast she'd eaten earlier.

"When the rich old man offered to give us a ride, I was thinking more along the lines of a Bentley." Sandra had to raise her voice to be heard over the horse's hooves and the creaking wagon wheels.

"No cars on the island, miss," Lloyd called over his shoulder.

Drat that man's hearing. Sandra dropped her voice as she added, "Right, because that would just make things too easy."

"Woohoo!" Digger let out a whoop. "Now this is what I'm talkin' about! Just like in the Wild West."

Sandra's eyes flew open and she scowled. She had a sudden urge to strangle Digger, just to see if he'd find that particular adventure just as exciting as the rest of it. Even as her hand was reaching toward him, Genius took it. His cheeks were red, as if he was embarrassed by his own boldness, but he held tight. Sandra managed a weak grin and settled back against him, wincing at the jars from each bump, but feeling a bit better. He really was cute when he was embarrassed which, let's face it, was often. She wasn't sure how she felt about this little development, but for right now, she was content to let it play out.

Suddenly, the wagon lurched to a stop, throwing all of the kids forward. Digger tumbled off the side of the wagon, landing on J. J., and Sandra fell against Genius. Their faces were only an inch from each other and Sandra heard her heart pounding in her ears as adrenaline raced through her body. Then she saw Genius' eyes widen and realized that his hands were pinned between them in a slightly awkward place.

"Hey!"

Aaron yelled and Sandra jumped back, feeling the heat rising to her cheeks. Genius scrambled into a sitting position, his face bright red. Both had their mouths open, ready to make some excuse about what had just happened. Then they looked at Aaron and realized that he wasn't talking to them at all. In fact, none of the others were looking at them, their attention was focused on the path ahead. Sandra and Genius climbed to their feet and peered over Lloyd's shoulder.

"Snoopy Diddy's alive, what d'you know." Aaron sounded amused.

Sandra really couldn't blame him. Standing in the middle of the path was the pale, chubby boy she'd last seen in the Butterfly

House. Had his name been Harold? Harmon? She was pretty sure it had started with an 'H'. He looked decidedly worse for wear. If anything, he even looked worse than any of them did. His face and clothes were covered with dirt and what Sandra sincerely hoped was chocolate.

"Come on." Aaron held out a hand. "Get in. We're heading back to civilization and you look like you could use a ride."

He looked like he could use a bath more than a ride, Sandra thought as the boy plopped down into the wagon. She sniffed distastefully at her own clothes and grimaced. Then again, they could all use a shower after what they'd been through. That was the second thing she was going to do when she got back. The first thing she was going to do, treasure or no treasure, was thump J. J. Hanks on the head for getting them into this in the first place.

***

The kid seemed in surprisingly high spirits considering he'd spent the previous night and this morning with two guys who were like something out of a gangster movie, or at least the British approximation of one. Karli wasn't sure if that meant she should be impressed or a little concerned that the boy wasn't quite right in the head.

"Are you all right?" she asked him.

"No!" He shook his head, little flecks of dirt flying from his hair. "I'm starving."

Lloyd turned around, holding out a napkin that held a couple of pieces of toast slathered with orange marmalade. The boy snatched the food eagerly, but his face fell when he saw what he was being offered.

"Really, Pops? Dry bread with some orange crap on it? You don't got no snack cakes or sumptin' like dat?"

Lloyd ignored the question and asked one of his own, "What's your name, son?"

"Hunter." He took a bite of the toast and made a pleased face. When he spoke again, it was around a mouthful of food. "Hunter Dousman."

Lloyd's eyes widened and he looked at J. J. and Aaron who wore similar expressions. Karli felt like she'd missed something.

"Did you say, 'Dousman'?" J. J. asked.

"Yeah. What of it?" Hunter tried to sound indignant, but just managed to be petulant.

"I don't get it," Karli whispered to Aaron. The name sounded familiar, but she couldn't quite place it.

"Um, Dousman was the name of the man who betrayed Lieutenant Hanks and his men."

"Right." Now she remembered. Lloyd had mentioned that name when he'd been talking about J. J. and Aaron's ancestor.

Hunter continued talking around bites of toast, oblivious to what was going on around him. For someone who had been disappointed in the fare provided, he sure was putting it away, Karli observed.

"I don't go by dat name in my profession. My peeps call me Original-One."

"Those men that you were with, Roberts and Bruno," Karli prompted.

"Yeah, dat was whack!" Hunter jumped at the new topic. "They kept me tied up forever. No food. No water. Thought I was gonna die."

Genius leaned forward. "How'd you get away?"

"Let me break it down to y'all." Hunter gestured, sending bits of toast and jam flying. "The big guy was buggin', right? He grabbed my threads and was gonna drop me off the side of a cliff."

Karli clapped her hand over her mouth and Digger looked vaguely ill. That was understandable, Karli thought. As strange as Hunter was, the idea of someone being willing to drop him off a cliff was sickening.

"But he was just plain busta! So I went all buck wild on him, clockin' him left and right. Wanted to bust a cap in his a..." Hunter glanced at Karli and Sandra. "Um, bust a cap in him. But I didn't want no beef with the fuzz."

"Geez." Sarcasm practically dripped from Sandra's voice.

"Wow." Aaron crossed his arms, scepticism in every word. "And all of this while your hands were tied behind your back and weak from hunger and thirst."

Hunter started to glare at Aaron and then seemed to realize just how much bigger Aaron was than him. He decided to finish his story instead. "B-but then the old geezer..." Hunter glanced at Lloyd. "No offence."

"Oh, none taken." Lloyd seemed to be entertained by Hunter rather than annoyed.

"Yous a cool dude, pops, stoppin' an all." Hunter shoved the last corner of toast into his mouth and chomped it a few times before continuing. "Anyway, the old dude, thinkin' he's all hardcore and stuff, catches me blind and takes his cane and swings it at my head –"

"Wow."

Karli was pretty sure J. J.'s comment was focused more on the complete lack of believability of Hunter's story than any sort of awe, but Hunter apparently didn't get it.

"Ya feelin' me, yo? So I grab hold of the cane, rip it outta his hand and wave it like a mad fool. 'Course they's scared when Original-One gots a weapon and they done bolted."

As Aaron turned, Karli became aware of a noise from behind them and twisted to see what was going on. At first, the trees kept her from seeing anything more than movement, then she caught a glimpse of a horse and a carriage barrelling toward them.

"Apparently they've gotten over their fear of you, Lil' Heavy," Aaron said, "because here they come!"

J. J. turned to Lloyd. "We need to go, now. Those are some bad men and they want the treasure!"

A determined look came over Lloyd's face. "Hang on!" He snapped the reins. "Hyah! Hyah!" The wagon jumped forward, throwing the kids back as the chase began.

Chapter Thirty

The carriage bounced over rocks and branches, throwing Roberts from one side of the carriage to the other until he was certain he would be covered with bruises if he wasn't thrown out first. If he had the treasure, he didn't think he'd mind, but at the moment, he was not pleased with his situation. He braced himself and stood, gripping tightly to the back of the driver's seat.

The big man was handling the horses with surprising skill considering Roberts didn't think Bruno had even seen a horse in the flesh until today. Still, Roberts wasn't entirely confident that they'd reach their destination in one piece, though, admittedly, that was due to the way the carriage was shaking rather than a reflection of Bruno's driving.

Roberts caught a glimpse of a wagon up ahead. "Faster! They're right in front of us! Let's get this over and done with!"
Bruno grunted and snapped the reins again, urging the horses to move faster. It was time to put an end to all of this.

***

Aaron was seriously regretting having gone after his little brother the night before. If he'd had just let the boys go on their own, they wouldn't have been able to get the fountain open and none of this would have happened. They'd all be on that stupid scavenger hunt with their parents and he'd be thinking about whether he liked Karli more than Sandra, rather than being jostled in the back of a wagon while being chased by two lunatics in a carriage. It was like the worst chase scene ever.

"Hold on!" Lloyd called over his shoulder. "I'm going to go for the shortcut between Fort Holmes and Skull Cave."

"Did he just say Skull Cave?" Genius asked.

"No more skulls!" Sandra clung to Genius' arm. "I don't want to see any more skulls!"

Aaron couldn't blame her for that sentiment. He'd seen more than enough skeletons to last him a lifetime. Right now, however, he was more concerned with becoming a skeleton for someone else to stumble on in a decade or so.

The wagon hit something, throwing everyone up into the air. Almost like something from a movie or a nightmare, Aaron watched as Digger and J. J. flew toward the back of the wagon. He heard Karli's scream, his own brother's yell, but it was all just background noise. He leaped forward, reaching toward the two boys with no other thought than to grab them.

The moment his hands closed around their wrists, one in each hand, he planted his feet and hoped that he had enough leverage to keep from going over as well. As his feet came up against the edge of the wagon, he pulled back, thinking that he might be able to get both boys high enough that they could hold on to the edge until Genius and the girls could help Aaron pull them in. Instead, Aaron found himself staggering backward as J. J. and Digger came flying up over the back of the wagon and landed in a heap on the floor. Aaron sat down hard, eyes wide.

"How...? How did you do that?" J. J. gasped.

Aaron shook his head, at a loss for an explanation that made any real sense. He grasped for something and came up with the only thing that he could think of. "Um, adrenaline?"

Before J. J. could start on another one of his tangents about how they all had something strange going on with them, Lloyd shouted over his shoulder.

"All right, kids, you ready for some fancy driving?"

Aaron's eyes locked with Karli's and he could see his own worry reflected there. He couldn't hear her over the noise of the wagon, but he could read the single word she said. "Fancy?"

Lloyd let out a whoop that said he was enjoying the thrill of the chase far more than his passengers. "Your cars can't do this!"

The kids clung to one another and the sides of the wagon as Lloyd urged the horses forward. They bobbed and wove, squeezing through places that Aaron was certain the wagon had no business going and flying over dips with more air beneath their wheels than he was comfortable with. More than once, he felt the wagon begin to tip, riding on two wheels as Lloyd took turns far too sharply. Still, Aaron couldn't help but listen for the warning shot he was sure would come at some point, the yell that would tell them that they'd been caught. But as the minutes passed, their pursuers made no move.

He had to know. If the crazy British guy and the large mute man were going to kill them all, Aaron wanted to know how long he had. He grabbed onto the side with a tighter grip and raised his head until he could see over the back of the wagon.

There was no sign of the carriage tailing them. He sat back down, feeling a faint ray of hope. They might just survive this after all. And when they did, he was going to kill his brother.

***

Genius was pretty sure that they were all going to die in a wagon crash before they reached wherever it was that the old man was taking them. He was also fairly certain that at least one person in the wagon was going to end up wearing the toast and iced tea they'd consumed back at the house. The likelihood of that person being him was increasing with each passing minute. He was in the process of figuring out how he could best avoid throwing up on Sandra when the wagon turned sharply and the ride suddenly became smooth.

"Almost there," Lloyd said as the kids struggled into sitting or kneeling positions.

Genius got onto his knees and leaned over the side of the wagon, waiting for his stomach to either calm down or completely rebel. His eyes told him what the rest of him had already deduced. They were no longer on a poor excuse for a path through the woods. Instead, they were on a regular road. And they weren't the only ones, either. Several other carriages were making their way down either side of the street, though none moving at as brisk a pace as what Lloyd was still using. That was probably a good idea, Genius thought. Roberts and Bruno didn't seem like the type to care much about making a scene in public.

The wagon hit a small bump and Genius groaned. If he vomited all over himself or Sandra, he would never forgive J. J. Then again, he reasoned, if they hadn't gone on this little adventure, Sandra might not have kissed him, so he supposed, technically, he owed J. J. a thank you for that. Maybe the two cancelled each other out.

Lloyd eased the wagon to a stop and hopped down off the driver's bench, surprisingly spry for such an old man. The kids climbed out of the wagon, all of them slightly green and wobbly on their legs.

"Where are we?" Sandra asked, looking around.

"'Mission House,'" J. J. read the sign above the old-looking two-storey building.

"That doesn't really help," Sandra said. Genius was inclined to agree.

"Missionaries built this place," Lloyd explained. "It was initially designed as a school to convert Native American students to the standards of the New England style of living."

Lloyd looked around and then motioned for the kids to follow him. They moved through the underbrush at the back of the building and ended up at a door almost completely hidden by the vegetation. Lloyd reached into his pocket and pulled out an ancient-looking key. Genius put his hand over his trouser pocket where his own key was safely zipped inside. The two looked very similar and Genius wasn't sure what that meant. It would definitely be something to think about in more depth... maybe when the possibility of bodily harm or death wasn't quite so imminent.

"This area's off limits to the public," Lloyd said as he pushed open the door.

"And you have a key?" J. J. asked.

Lloyd smiled. "There are perks to having spent my entire life on the island. Now, let's get inside before our friends show up again."

Genius wholeheartedly agreed and followed the others into the Mission House.

***

They were almost back where they'd started, J. J. realized as he looked around before following Lloyd into the Mission House. The original Butterfly House was just a bit further west of here. Which meant the authorities would be on the lookout for whoever had broken in the night before. J. J.'s stomach flipped. He could only imagine how badly Roberts and Bruno had messed things up. As he stepped through an interior doorway into a small, empty room, he wondered how long it would be until the cops showed up here. It wasn't like the island was that big. He just hoped his cellmate was in for counterfeiting or something like that. He wasn't looking forward to prison.

"What happened to the school?" Genius asked as they passed through a second empty room. It was as dim and shadowed as the first, only the faintest of light coming through the windows.

"What?" Lloyd asked.

"You said that the Mission House was 'initially designed as a school.' So, what happened? What made it stop being a school?"

Lloyd stopped as they reached what had been the kitchen. Ancient appliances stood against either wall, and a large window above the sink let in enough light for the kids to see that Lloyd's expression had changed. He no longer looked like the excited adventurer he had been when they'd been in the wagon being chased. He seemed older, somehow, and sad.

"Back when... when the children started getting sick and it was identified as TB... they were quarantined." Lloyd used his key again to open a door.

A damp, earthy smell floated up from the darkness below and J. J. was reminded of how this entire adventure had started with him on some stairs, looking down into darkness, terrified that he would feel a spider crawling on him any moment. Spiders were the least of his concerns now, even if he still didn't like them.

Only the first few steps were visible until Lloyd took a torch from his pocket and waited for the kids to retrieve theirs. Carefully, with Lloyd leading the way, they descended into the cellar. Once they reached the bottom of the staircase, the kids stayed huddled together while Lloyd ventured further into the cellar, his light moving across the earthen walls as if searching for something.

"While the quarantine stopped the spread of the disease, it did nothing to help the ones already sick," Lloyd spoke without prompting. "So the quarantine was moved down here."

"They locked sick kids in the cellar?" Genius sounded as horrified as J. J. felt.

"Why?" J. J. asked.

"No medicines to cure 'em and, back then, some people thought that a cool, damp place would help 'em." Lloyd's words were matter-of-fact but J. J. could see the emotion in the old man's eyes, even in the dim light. "But it didn't."

"This place became their prison," Digger said slowly, looking around at the small, dark room.

"That's awful," Sandra said, true sympathy on her face.

"It's horrible!" Karli agreed. "How could people be so cruel?"

"They didn't know any better," Lloyd said. "They thought this was the kids' best chance to survive. As for locking them in, they had to do it. Some of those kids were too young to understand that if they left, they could infect the entire island. And, in part, the lock was for the parents too. If they caught it from their kid and went back to their healthy families, we could've lost so much more."

A silence fell over the group and J. J. knew that each one of them was thinking about what had happened here all those years ago. He couldn't imagine what it would have been like, to be sick, to know that you were probably going to die in this cold, wet place, away from your family, surrounded only by other children who were waiting for the same thing. The only thing that would have been worse, he thought, was if one or more of those kids were your siblings. And J. J. had a very bad feeling that this was where Lloyd's story ended up.

Hunter broke the silence as he covered his mouth with his arm. "Yo, dats some wicked stink.'"

"Wow, that's insensitive." Karli shook her head and took a step away from Hunter.

Aaron looked down at the younger boy. "Are you serious with this whole Vanilla Ice thing?"

Hunter looked puzzled. "Who's 'Nilla Ice? Some wannabe gangsta tryin' to steal my flava?"

"Forget it," Aaron said. "You're an idiot."

Before Hunter was able to get too offended by Aaron's insult, Lloyd called from the far corner of the cellar. "Found it!"

The kids hurried over and crowded around the old man. He pointed to an old wood-burning furnace, shining his torch on the cast-iron door. Scratched there, faint but still visible, was a pentagram with the letters S, A, L, V and S.

"Simon, Alexander, Lucy, Victor and Sarah." Lloyd ran his fingers over each of the letters as he softly spoke the names.

"They were Ambrose's brothers and sisters, weren't they?" Karli asked.

Lloyd nodded.

As the old man's fingers passed over the centre of the pentagram, J. J. saw it. "There it is! The last piece!" Despite how eager he was to get the final piece to the puzzle, to find the treasure, to bring this adventure to an end, he waited for Lloyd to finish his nostalgic moment and step aside.

J. J. wiped some debris off of the centre. "There's coordinates on here too." He glanced over his shoulder at Genius. "W - 84:61812."

"Digger, the map," Genius said.

As Genius spread the map out on the floor and began to make his calculations, J. J. straightened. He'd caught a glimpse of something behind the furnace. He circled it, carefully stepping over the uneven floor. There, tucked in a corner so that it blended in with the shadows, was an opening. It was narrow, almost too small for Aaron to get through without turning sideways.

"This is it, guys. This is the entrance."

"Yeah, but to where?" Aaron asked, shaking his head.

"Hell?" Genius suggested from where he was making the final calculations.

Hunter gasped and Aaron shot the boy a disgusted look. "Seriously, J. J., how do we know this isn't going to take us to some new booby-trapped tomb or underground river with a waterfall waiting to kill us?"

"It's going to take us to the treasure," J. J. said emphatically. "I know it."

"As much as I really don't want to go into another creepy tunnel," Genius spoke up. "I have to agree with J. J. According to my calculations, we're almost there." He rolled the map back up and handed it to Digger.

"All right," Digger said, "let's go."

Sandra sighed. "I was afraid you were going to say that."

"Digger," J. J. said. "You lead the way."

Digger gave his friend a wry grin. "I was afraid you were going to say that." He moved past the others to join J. J. behind the furnace. "Hooah!" His voice echoed down the tunnel as he slipped into the opening.

Genius went next with Sandra right behind him, followed by Hunter, then Karli and, finally Aaron. J. J. turned to Lloyd. "Go ahead. I'll be right behind you. I want to go last so I can keep an eye out for those guys following us."

Lloyd shook his head. "No. This is your adventure. Not mine." He smiled. "That chase back there was more than enough excitement for this old man, so here is where I will say good-bye."

"Are you sure?" J. J. asked.

Lloyd nodded.

"Thank you," J. J. said. "For everything."

"No, thank you," Lloyd said. "It's time that the Hanks family received their due. Your great-great-great-grandfather would have been proud."

J. J. smiled and started toward the passage. He hesitated. This might be the only chance he got to ask Lloyd the question that had been hovering at the edge of his mind since this adventure began, the one that the others didn't want to discuss. He'd started piecing together bits of information Lloyd had given and had a theory. While not ideal, now might be the only time he had to test it. He walked back over to Lloyd.

"Can I ask you something?"

"Of course." Lloyd's face was blank.

J. J. had been wondering how to approach the topic and had finally decided on the right way to lead into what he really wanted to know. "You said before that Porter's second-in-command had been insistent that Porter not be captured. I understand the danger of a commanding officer being taken by the enemy, but it seemed a bit pre-emptive on Corporal Burke's part. Unless, of course, there was some other reason that Burke knew of why Porter couldn't be captured."

"That's not really a question, J. J.," Lloyd said. "But I suppose I know what you're really asking." His eyes narrowed and he looked at J. J. with an intensity that made J. J. squirm. "Understand that this is legend, speculation based on stories that my grandfather told my father and myself before he passed."

J. J. nodded as he tried to contain his excitement. This was it, he was sure. He was finally going to get some answers.

"According to my grandfather, Porter Hanks had the ability to imbue certain objects with qualities that could be transferred to certain people that possessed those objects." Lloyd chose each word with deliberate care. "My grandfather said that Porter gave a talisman to each child and linked its powers with certain aspects of that child's character so that the talisman couldn't be used by just anyone, but only by those who possessed the same qualities."

"Did he happen to say what these talismans were or where they were?" J. J. stuffed his hands into his pockets to keep himself from grabbing the compass hanging around his neck.

"He said that after his brothers and sisters died, the talismans disappeared. He always assumed that Porter had taken them for some reason and hidden them away."

"Why would he do that?" J. J. asked.

"Ambrose believed it was out of guilt. You see, the object Ambrose claimed that he had been given was the very bullet that had been dug out of Porter's side that day he found the kids. My grandfather claimed that it was this bullet that had healed him when the others had died. Ambrose thought that Porter always blamed himself for not protecting all of the children that way." Lloyd gave J. J. a searching look. "Now, if they did exist, I suspect that Porter may have had a different purpose behind hiding those talismans. Someone with that ability... perhaps Porter could see something coming, something that his descendants and their friends would need his talismans to defeat." He smiled and shrugged. "But that may be merely the musings of an old man." He gestured toward the passage. "Best hurry up before they think that something happened to you."

J. J. nodded. "Thank you, Lloyd."

"I'll see you on the other side," Lloyd said.

J. J. hurried back to the entrance and slid inside, hurrying along to catch up with the others.

Chapter Thirty-One

Digger kept the pace slow despite his desire to just be done. His training made him put one foot in front of the other and focus on getting to the end of the tunnel safely. The passage was rough, wider in some places, narrow enough in others that they had to shuffle sideways.

"Unbelievable," Genius said from behind Digger. "Those sick kids must have dug this tunnel to escape."

"Could you imagine, barely being able to breathe when you're just sitting or lying down and then forcing yourself to dig with whatever you happened to find here in the cellar?"

Digger could hear the sympathy in Karli's voice and, for once, didn't feel the need to make fun of her because of it. What she said painted an awful picture.

"Oh, please don't let there be any more dead bodies down here." Sandra's words drew Digger's attention and he looked back at her. "Skulls with hatchets, skeletons in the water. What's next? Mangled corpses?"

A white-faced Hunter grabbed Sandra's arm and Digger's eyebrows shot up. That was bold.

"Hands off, not-so-slim." Sandra's fear evaporated in annoyance. "Unless, of course, you want to lose it."

Hunter's hand disappeared and Digger smirked.

Aaron's voice came out of the shadows. "Thought you were

supposed to be a hardcore gangsta, Cream Puff Sonny."

"You buggin'. I ain't scared. I'm a straight-up thug." Hunter's final statement was punctuated by a high-pitched squeak, followed by Aaron's laughter. "Yous a punk bit... jerk."

Digger shook his head and turned his attention forward again. He squinted into the darkness and flashed his light ahead. "Hey," he called over his shoulder. "Looks like it opens up in a couple of feet."

As Digger stepped through into the open space, his jaw dropped. "Holy..."

**

J. J. heard his friend yell out and picked up the pace. He hadn't meant to get so far behind. As he got closer, he heard Karli speak.

"Did you find the treasure?"

"No." Digger's response sounded as if it was coming from a much larger area. "I found something better."

Better? J. J. was just a few steps behind his brother and followed Aaron into what looked like a bigger space. As soon as he entered the room, he understood Digger's reaction. Natural light streamed down through several openings high up on the walls, giving them all plenty of light to see by.

The passage had led them into an eighteenth-century underground bunker. The room, however, wasn't really what was impressive. Rather, it was the contents of the bunker that had Digger so enthused. The far side of the area was packed with muskets, bayonets, a sixteen-gun brig and a dozen barrels that J. J. believed were filled with gunpowder.

"I don't understand why you're all excited," Aaron said. "All I see is a bunch of rusty junk."

"Are you crazy?" Digger exclaimed. "Do you have any idea how much I can get for this stuff on eBay?"

"I like the way yous thinkin'," Hunter said. "It's all 'bout the Benjamins. Am I right?"

"Oh, shut up!" Sandra snapped.

Karli glanced back at J. J., a sad expression on her face. "Didn't the riddle say something about a final resting place?"

"Some of the kids must not have escaped," Aaron said as he looked around.

"None of them did." Genius' voice was sombre.

"According to Porter's journal, the outbreak on the island infected more than two dozen people, half of that children," J. J. spoke up. "He didn't go into a lot of detail and I thought, at the time, that he wasn't affected by it. Now, I guess he didn't talk about it because he was too close to it."

"With at least a dozen kids down here, how do you know none of them made it?" Sandra asked, her tone saying that she wasn't entirely sure she wanted to know the answer.

Genius pointed to the walls. "Limestone. Soldiers could've dug this out easily enough, but it is way too hard for kids, especially sick ones. There was no way out."

"So they died in here?" Karli asked.

"In here or they went back out and died in the cellar," Genius said.

"There's sun in here," J. J. said softly. "They would have stayed in here until the end."

"Which means their bodies are in here," Aaron said.

Hunter gulped, but the others didn't react with the horror J. J. had thought they would. Somehow, thinking of these skeletons was sad rather than creepy. Without a word, the kids spread out, searching the bunker. After several minutes, Karli found something.

"There are rocks placed by the wall over here." Her voice was soft. "Three of them."

J. J. saw Aaron walk over to Karli and slip his arm around her shoulders. Genius took Sandra's hand as they and Digger joined the other two. All of the excitement and fear of the past twelve hours had vanished, leaving a solemn sort of sadness. J. J. started to go over to the others when something caught his eye. The limestone along one section of the wall had cracked as tree roots had pushed their way down. Tangled in the roots were five muskets, each one looking as if they'd been stuck into the dirt floor, as if marking five locations.

J. J. knelt down, reaching out to run his fingers over each one. "I found them, Grandpa," he whispered. "Over here." He raised his voice, but didn't look away.

"But there's grave markers here," Digger said.

"Those are the other kids. Maybe ones who didn't have families to bury them out there." J. J. stood, suddenly certain that he knew what had happened. "Porter would've taken the others back, let their families bury them. But the ones without families, he would've wanted them together, with the people they'd spent their last minutes with."

"There are five muskets here," Aaron said.

J. J. nodded. "His family." He remembered Lloyd's words about Porter feeling guilty about not saving them all and how Porter had cared about the kids as if they were his own. Everything clicked into place. "He chose this place because he wanted to bury the treasure with them. He wanted them to know how much he loved them, and he wanted his son to find them. To know about

245

them. To know that he had brothers and sisters, even if not by blood."

"Dang, J. J." Aaron looked down at him. "When did you get all insightful?"

J. J. gave his brother a half-smile, knowing no one was going to like what he was going to say next. "You guys are going to hate me for this, I know, but I can't do it. I can't dig up these graves for money."

"Dude, it's not just money," Hunter said. "It's treasure money! Yous could get some serious bling wit it."

"Shut up, Dousman," Aaron said, not even looking at the boy. "Come on, J. J. Think of everything we've been through to get this treasure."

"I can't do it either," Karli said. "It isn't right."

"You're really going to give up all that because you don't want to dig up a couple of centuries-old skeletons?" Digger said. "Didn't you see Lloyd's house? That was bought with just a part of that treasure."

"J. J.," Aaron put his hand on his brother's shoulder. "If we don't get this, we're going to lose everything."

J. J. shook his head. "No we won't. We might lose the house and we might have to move, but we'll still have each other. All of us." J. J. suddenly felt like the older brother. "We'll have our family. Don't you see, that's what Porter was saying by putting the money here. Family is what matters."

"I can't believe I'm saying this," Aaron began, "but, okay. I'm with you, little brother."

The brothers turned to the others.

"It's your family's treasure," Digger said reluctantly. "I'll go with whatever you say."

"Me too," Genius said.

Sandra sighed. "All right, but someone is going to pay for my manicure and dry cleaning when we get back."

"I do have to say one thing, though," Aaron said. "J. J., no more chick moments. You sounded like a girl."

Karli punched Aaron's shoulder and he laughed. J. J. grinned, feeling like a huge weight had been lifted from his shoulders. Now he couldn't wait to talk to them about what else he and Lloyd had discussed. They wouldn't actually be coming out of this completely empty-handed.

"Well, well," a familiar voice said from the passageway, "isn't this just heartwarming."

The kids turned, Aaron automatically stepping in front of the rest, his arms out slightly as if to protect the others.

Roberts made a show of clapping. "Isn't this whole thing just touching, Bruno? I feel as if we've been here before."

Bruno grunted as he laughed.

To no one's surprise, Hunter had something to say. "Well, if it ain't tongue-tied and twisted."

Bruno growled and pulled out his gun.

"Shut up, you idiot," J. J. hissed. Things were bad enough without Hunter running his mouth. They didn't need him to make things worse.

"Huh. Aren't you just the fat cat with nine lives." Roberts gave Hunter an amused look. "I didn't think you had it in you to get off of that branch."

"Who *are* you people?" Karli asked.

"My dear child, who I am matters not in the least," Roberts said. "What does matter is that you hand over that map before someone gets hurt."

"The map?" Hunter asked. "What do you need the map for? The treasure's right–"

The air sudden rushed from Hunter's lungs as J. J. slammed his elbow into the boy's side.

Hunter glared at J. J. "What'd you do dat for, fool?"

"As always, Hunter, you have proven yourself to be a great help," Roberts said.

"Oh." Understanding dawned on the boy's dirty face. "Oops."

"Now that everything is out in the open, shall we get to work?" Roberts rubbed his hands together. "Since Bruno and I have been working extraordinarily hard to keep up with you, I think the least you can do is finish the job for us."

"What're you talking about?" Sandra asked.

"Dig."

"With what?" Aaron sounded like he was trying to stall.

"Perhaps I wasn't clear," Roberts said. "I wasn't merely making a suggestion. I don't care what you use, but you will dig up that treasure for me."

"Not a chance, dirtbag," Karli said.

"I'm with her." Sandra surprised them all with her response. "I've been shot at with an arrow, fell through a coffin into a lake with skulls in it, been chased by ghosts and ruined my 100 dollar manicure. You both can bite me."

The big man moved much more quickly than J. J. would've guessed. He grabbed Sandra's arm and yanked her out from behind Aaron, starting to pull her toward Roberts, maybe to use as leverage, J. J. didn't know. And they didn't get a chance to find out.

A loud crack echoed through the bunker and Bruno let out an unmistakable yelp of pain. He shook his hand and growled. As the big man raised his fist, Genius took a step forward, clenching his fists. J. J.'s eye widened as he saw the rocks against the far wall rise several inches off the ground. Based on the gasps behind him, the others had seen the same thing.

Before anyone could act, there was a very distinctive clicking sound followed by another familiar voice. "I don't know where you boys had the misfortune of growing up, but in my day and age, we treated ladies much better."

All eyes turned toward the passage. Lloyd stood there, an ancient musket in his hand and a serious expression on his face. J. J. had never been so happy to see someone in his life.

"Put the gun on the ground," Lloyd said. Bruno scowled but did as he was told, using his foot to move it away from him. "Kids, come this way and go behind me to get back through the tunnel."

J. J. kept his eyes on Roberts and Bruno as the others began to make their way toward the passage, but he didn't move. He wasn't going anywhere until the rest were safe. He'd gotten them all into this and he'd make sure they all got out of it.

Inexplicably, Roberts smiled. "Dear sir, I'm afraid that your weapon is even older than you are and I suspect that you are bluffing. And even if you intended to use it, I do not believe that it will work."

Everyone froze. J. J. could see it on the old man's face. Roberts was right. The gun was useless.

Then, everything happened at once. Lloyd reached behind him to shove Sandra back into the passage. Bruno threw himself to the ground, reaching for his gun, and Roberts watched. As Bruno's hand closed around the gun, Lloyd swung down the butt of his gun, connecting with the back of the big man's skull. A flare of hope ran through J. J. as Bruno crumpled to the ground. That hope turned to horror as the gun fired.

The round hit high up on the wall and ricocheted down. J. J. and Lloyd dove toward the tunnel even as the round went straight into one of the barrels, scraping over one of the metal rings. J. J. saw the spark and then there was an earth-shattering explosion and the world became dust and darkness.

Chapter Thirty-Two

J. J.'s ears were ringing, the other sounds muffled behind them. He coughed, breathed in more dust and coughed again. He could feel little rocks raining down on him. His skin and tongue felt gritty, but he was alive and didn't seem to be hurt, so he wasn't going to complain. He pushed himself up and looked around. He'd landed half in the bunker, half in the tunnel. Both sides were full of dust and debris, dark shapes that could've been rocks or people.

From the other side of the bunker near the tunnel entry way, J. J. heard his brother.

"Everybody okay?"

The words sounded a little off, but J. J. could tell that his hearing was slowly returning to normal.

"I'm okay," Sandra said from inside the tunnel, her voice rough. She choked, coughed, and spoke again. "Genius? Karli?"

"J. J.?" Aaron called.

"Here," J. J. said. As he continued to look around, his eyes fell on a pair of legs right next to him. His gaze moved a little higher and he made out the distinct shape of a body. His fingers bumped against his torch as he started to move and he gripped the handle tightly as he inched closer. As the light fell on the dusty, silver-white hair, J. J. reached out, his heart in his throat at the idea that

Lloyd might be dead.

"Lloyd?"

A groan sent a wave of relief through J. J., a feeling that was compounded as he heard Digger and Genius announcing that they were okay. Lloyd rolled over. Other than a few scrapes and cuts, he appeared to be uninjured.

J. J. stood and held out a hand. As he pulled Lloyd to his feet, Digger and Genius appeared, followed by a dishevelled Sandra. From the opposite side of the mouth of the tunnel, Aaron emerged, his face pale.

"Where's Karli?" He asked.

"I thought she was with you," Sandra said.

"Where was she last?" Genius asked.

"She was right in front of me. We were going around the other side trying to stay out of the big guy's line of fire," Aaron said.

"Karli?" Digger shouted, panic in his eyes. "Karli?"

"Over here!" Karli's voice came from behind a large chunk of ceiling. J. J. could hear the pain in her voice. "My leg's trapped."

"We're gonna get you out of there," Aaron said. He crossed to the rock and bent his knees, his fingers searching for a handhold along the bottom.

J. J. watched Digger and Genius exchange glances. This rock was, for lack of a better word, a boulder, and far bigger than the sarcophagus lid that they'd moved earlier. Still, J. J. thought, he believed that something had happened to each of them, something that may make it possible for Aaron to do the impossible.

"Come on," J. J. said. He positioned himself at the edge of the rock and the others did the same.

"Ready?" Aaron asked. "Lift!"

J. J. pulled with all of his might and knew that his friends were doing the same. A look to the side revealed Aaron's muscles flexing and moving, his face red. Then, J. J. saw his brother's arms ripple and Aaron's eyes closed.

Suddenly, the rock gave, practically flying in the air as it tumbled back and away from Karli. J. J. saw Genius' shock at what they'd done and knew that his friend's scientific mind was hard at work trying to figure out what had just happened.

"Karli." Aaron's voice drew J. J.'s attention back.

J. J. winced as he saw Karli's leg, unable to believe she was still conscious. He was no doctor, but this was bad. Three pieces of bone stuck out of her leg, one above the knee, two below. Her ankle was twisted at an angle that made J. J.'s stomach turn and he was pretty sure that part of her foot was smashed. He looked away and saw his friends do the same. The sunlight streaming in from the newly made hole in the ceiling just made things look that much worse.

"We need to get help," Aaron said from where he was kneeling next to Karli. He looked up at Lloyd. "We need a doctor."

"Aaron." Karli grabbed at Aaron's arm, her eyes wide and full of something other than just pain.

J. J. really didn't want to see the injury again, but he looked nonetheless, sure that something was happening that he would want to see. He and the others stared as Karli's bones and flesh shifted. Beneath the blood and dirt, J. J. could see the torn muscles and skin knitting back together.

"What the heck?" Sandra said what the others were thinking.

"There may have been some truth to Ambrose's stories after all," J. J. said to Lloyd.

"J. J., you kept saying that something was happening to us," Aaron said. "What's going on?"

"Remember those objects I found in the desk along with the journal and the map?"

The others nodded, but J. J. didn't get the chance to explain.

"A'ight, who's messin' wit Original-One?"

Hunter stumbled over to the group. As he came close enough for the others to see him clearly, a large purple bump of his forehead became visible under the dirt.

"Ouch," Digger said. "You okay there, peanut?"

"Peanut?" Hunter shook his head and winced. "You best respect." He looked at Sandra. "Where am I? Who are yous crazy lookin' fools?"

Genius chuckled. "He lost his memory."

"That reminds me," J. J. said. "Where are Roberts and Bruno?"

The others shrugged and Aaron motioned toward the rest of the rock-littered room. "Somewhere under there, and I don't really feeling like looking for them."

J. J. tended to agree. Somehow, having a gun pointed at him made him feel less inclined to go searching for either of the men.

"Hello?" A voice came from up above.

The kids looked up and saw something move.

"Hey!" Aaron yelled.

"Help us!" Karli cried.

"We're down here!" Sandra shouted.

A young man wearing an eighteenth-century soldier's uniform appeared. "Hello?"

"Stewart?" Lloyd asked. "Stewart Matheson?"

"Mr Lloyd? Is that you?" The kid bent over, squinting to see.

"Stewart, we're going to need you to get the police and some ambulances," Lloyd said.

"Yes, sir!" Stewart snapped off a salute and disappeared.

"Was he – was he wearing a uniform?" Karli asked.

"Stewart's a re-enactor," Lloyd said. "Nice kid."

"Is he single?" Sandra asked. She winked at Genius. "I do love a man in uniform."

Chapter Thirty-Three

J. J. was pretty sure that a grounding was in his future, but at the moment, his parents were just so thankful to see he and Aaron alive and unhurt that there was no mention of the fact that they'd snuck out in the middle of the night without permission. His friends' parents seemed to be having the same reaction. Even the normally straight-laced Hiroto Kumai had hugged his very surprised son. Sandra would probably be the only one to get off without any real punishment.

As Lloyd finished talking to the police, the paramedics loaded Bruno and Roberts into two separate ambulances, each one accompanied by an officer. Both men had been buried under the rubble, but the medics were confident that they would make a full recovery and be entirely capable of standing trial for their crimes. Hunter was sitting by the other ambulance receiving a more thorough examination than the other kids, who'd all been cleared with just minor cuts and bruises. His mother was hovering over him, much to his annoyance, and kept interjecting her two cents into her husband's interview with the cops. J. J. tried to hear what they were saying, curious as to how they fitted into the picture, but wasn't able to get anything and he had a feeling that his parents wouldn't appreciate him trying to sneak away again.

"Mr and Mrs Hanks?"

J. J. turned away from the Dousmans as Lloyd extended his hand, first to Jonathan and then to Gabriella.

"You have a fine set of boys here." Lloyd smiled at J. J. and then at Aaron. "As I was telling the police, they and their friends demonstrated an extraordinary amount of courage in the face of overwhelming odds."

"We don't understand," Jonathan said. "Just who were those men and how did everyone end up here?"

"There are some pieces that the police are still trying to fill in," Lloyd said. "But what they do know is that Mr Roberts was an investor in Melvin Dousman's company that went under a few weeks ago. Roberts apparently hired the other man to help him collect. When Dousman didn't have the money, Roberts went after the son who, apparently, had heard these kids talking about a treasure. Since young Hunter is suffering from memory loss, the exact details aren't known, but it appears that Hunter and his kidnappers chased the kids halfway across the island."

J. J. felt Aaron go very still behind him. It sounded like Lloyd was completely glossing over the fact that it had been them who had broken into the Butterfly House first and then all of them who had snuck into the Mission House, although it had been Lloyd who'd let them in with his key.

"The kids ended up at my place." Lloyd gestured in the general direction of his house. "And when they told me about the guys following them, I decided to help. My phone wasn't working so we came here so I could call the police. The two men caught up with us, so I told the kids to hide. One of the men shot into an old barrel of gunpowder that exploded. And that's pretty much it, I believe." He looked at J. J. for confirmation.

J. J. nodded. "Yeah, that's basically what happened."

"I'm just so thankful you two are okay." Gabriella pulled J. J. into another hug. She looked over his head at Lloyd. "Thank you so much for helping my boys."

"Of course, ma'am," Lloyd said. He looked down at J. J. "You kids are welcome to come see me any time you're on the island."

"What a nice old man," Gabriella said as Lloyd walked away.

"He is," J. J. agreed.

"I'm going to go check with the officers to see if we can take the boys back to the hotel, let them get cleaned up," Jonathan said.

A thought suddenly occurred to J. J. and he took a step back. "Mom, did all of you guys miss out on the geo-caching because of us?" He sighed. There went any chance they had of not losing their house. "I'm sorry."

"Sorry?" Gabriella shook her head. "J. J., none of us cared about this stupid contest. We cared about finding all of you."

Jonathan returned. "I don't know what kind of pull that old guy has, but the police are going to pretty much use his statement and that of the Dousmans. Apparently, those two thugs are wanted back on the mainland for murder and there's enough evidence to put them away without needing anything from the kids."

"Why don't you go tell the others and the boys and I will head for the carriage," Gabriella said. "I'm sure all the kids want a shower, food, and a nap."

"That does sound really good," J. J. said.

Gabriella started toward one of the carriages that were parked in front of the Mission House.

"You know, J. J.," Aaron said as he fell in step beside his brother. "You really surprised me during this whole thing. I didn't think you had it in you." He ruffled J. J.'s hair. "I guess you're not a total butt-wipe after all."

J. J. grinned. "And you really did a good job of taking care of everyone and leading." He reached up and tousled Aaron's hair. "I guess you're not a total idiot after all."

Chapter Thirty-Four

"Your parents seriously put a GPS tracker on your phone?" Karli asked Aaron.

"Yep." Aaron looked down at the cell phones in the middle of Sandra's bed. "And if they text or call, J. J. and I have to answer right away."

"Or?" Sandra asked, reaching out to touch Aaron's arm.

"Or we won't be leaving our parents' sides until we go to college," J. J. said. He leaned back in the plush chair, putting his feet up on the footstool. As much as he'd enjoyed having an adventure – well, enjoyed the parts that hadn't involved having his life threatened – there was something to be said for clean clothes, good food and a three-hour nap in a soft bed. "What about you guys?"

"When we get back, Digger and I are grounded for a month." Karli sighed. "Though it'll probably be more like two weeks as long as we don't do anything crazy again."

"Sounds like you guys got off easy," Genius said, frowning. He was sitting in the other chair, trying to look like he wasn't watching Sandra flirting with Aaron. It was hard to tell if she was doing it out of habit, because she wanted Genius to be jealous, or because they'd returned to the 'real world' and she'd decided to forget about

Genius along with everything that had happened.

"Genius?" J. J. asked.

"You think a GPS in your phone or being grounded is bad?" Genius stuck out his leg and pulled up his pants to reveal a black strip around his ankle. The little black box attached to it was blinking green. "If I go more than 200 feet from either of my parents, it beeps."

"Good thing we all came here then," J. J. said. "The rest of our rooms are too far away."

"What about you, Sandra?" Karli asked, her voice tight as her eyes followed Sandra's fingers on Aaron's forearm. "What's going to happen to you?"

"Oh." Sandra actually seemed embarrassed and she took her hand off Aaron's arm. "My mom's taking me shopping for new clothes and a manicure."

For a moment, everyone stared at her and then Karli burst out laughing, earning a dirty look from her friend. "You've got to be kidding me!"

Sandra had a half-smile on her lips that J. J. thought looked rather sad. "I think my mom thinks if she punishes me, I'll just tell her that I want to go live with my dad." She shrugged and her old confidence returned. "And it's not like I'm going to pass up the chance to add to my wardrobe. Besides, my nails were completely ruined."

"It could have been worse," Karli said.

"Yeah, like you could be in the hospital with a really messed up leg," J. J. said. He'd decided it was time to talk about the proverbial elephant in the room. Everything else that had happened, the others could explain away, but they'd all seen Karli's leg.

Karli flushed.

"All right, J. J., out with it," Aaron said. He shifted as if trying to figure out which girl he wanted to sit closer to before giving up and leaning back against the headboard. "You've been wanting to say something for a while now."

Now that the time was here, J. J. wasn't entirely sure where to begin. "Remember when I first asked if weird stuff was happening?" Judging by the uncomfortable expressions on everyone's faces, they did. "Well, when we were in the cellar and I stayed back a bit to talk to Lloyd. I'd had an idea about why that corporal was so insistent that Porter Hanks not be captured. Part of it could've been because he was the highest ranking soldier, but leaving a post when the battle had just begun didn't sit right with me."

"He has a point," Digger said from where he was sitting on the floor.

"So I asked Lloyd if there was another reason Porter needed to avoid being captured and he told me that his grandfather had told him stories about Porter Hanks."

"Stories like what?" Genius asked.

"Ambrose told Lloyd that Porter had the ability to give certain objects powers that could be used by people who had the talismans." It sounded silly when he just came out and said it like that, but J. J. didn't falter. "But not just any people, only ones who were similar to the ones the talismans were created for."

"What in the world are you talking about?" Aaron asked.

"Ambrose told Lloyd that the reason he survived the TB epidemic is because Porter gave him a talisman that allowed him to heal. He said Porter made one for each of the kids. Six talismans, six powers. And the one with the ability to heal was the bullet Porter had been shot with when Corporal Burke sent him away."

"A bullet?" Karli's eyes widened and J. J. knew that she'd just put two and two together. She dug into her pocket and then held out her hand, a bullet resting in her palm. "J. J., is this the bullet?"

"I think so." J. J. looked around at the disbelieving faces. "Come on, guys, you can't tell me that you haven't noticed those weird things? None of you saw the rocks in the bunker start hovering in the air when Genius got pissed at Bruno for hurting Sandra?"

Genius' face turned red and he pointedly kept his eyes away from Sandra. "You can't seriously think that I moved them with my mind. Telekinesis is science fiction, J. J., not real."

"So you weren't thinking of how you wanted to hit Bruno?" J. J. asked. "Or before, in the forest, when Sandra was trapped under that burning branch, you weren't thinking about how to get it off of her? And you didn't want those arrows not to hit you?" He turned to Sandra. "And no one else heard those loud cracks, like when someone gets shocked by electricity, not once but twice when those guys were grabbing you? First at the Butterfly House and then in the bunker?"

Sandra shook her head. "You're crazy, J. J. It was just –"

"Just what?" he asked. "And how did that branch catch on fire? It had to have been damp from the rain, which means it would've been almost impossible to get going with a lighter. Then it went out rather than spreading to the leaves on the ground?"

"What, you think I'm some sort of fire-starter or electrically-charged person?" Sandra folded her arms over her chest, as if she didn't want to touch anyone.

"Sure, Sandra," Aaron said. "We can call you Sparky."

"Bite me." She scowled at Aaron but her pink-tinged cheeks said she really didn't mind.

"Aaron, care to explain how you picked up that boulder on Karli's leg?"

"We were all lifting," Aaron said.

"Guys, why are you arguing about this?" Karli asked. "We saw ghosts this morning. *Ghosts*. And you all saw my leg heal. There's no logical explanation for either of those things. How can you not think that J. J.'s right?"

Silence greeted her question and J. J. let it hang. It was a lot to wrap their heads around, he knew. Suddenly, Digger's entire body stiffened and his eyes went wide, not looking at anything in particular.

"Digger?" Karli climbed off of the bed and knelt at her brother's side. She grabbed his arm, but he didn't acknowledge her. "Digger?"

Just as suddenly as it had happened, it stopped. Digger blinked. "We need to go back."

"What?" J. J. asked as the others crowded around Digger.

"Remember how I said before that I thought I saw something that had happened before it actually did?" Digger asked. The others nodded. "Well, I just had another one of those... whatever you want to call them, and we need to go back to where that tree is. The one that had its roots down in the bunker."

"Are you saying that you had a *vision* of the future?" Karli asked.

"I guess so." Digger ran his hand over his short hair. "Not really crazier than a severely broken leg healing in minutes, is it?"

"I guess not," Karli said.

"All right then." Digger's face was pale, but he seemed fine otherwise. "I'm not really sure what's going to happen there, but I know that we need to be there when it does."

Chapter Thirty-Five

J. J. was acutely aware of his parents, as well as the parents of his friends, standing behind him, waiting. It had taken quite a bit of convincing to get all of them out here and now J. J. wasn't even sure why they were there, only that Digger had said that they needed to be.

When he'd gone to his parents and told them that he needed to go back to the bunker but hadn't been able to provide a concrete reason why, they'd tried to talk him out of it. It wasn't until Aaron had chimed in, saying that he too wanted to go that Jonathan and Gabriella had relented. Sandra hadn't really needed to do much to convince Marsha, and Karli had simply told her parents that she'd lost the necklace she'd been wearing, a present from her late grandmother. J. J. had to admire that one. He'd never considered saying that he'd left something there. Genius had been the one who'd had the hardest time talking his parents into coming, but that didn't surprise anyone. Only after he'd told his father that the other families were all going to support their kids did Hiroto relent.

So, twenty minutes after Digger's statement, all four families were gathered at the bunker, standing just outside the police tape. The workers inside the tape barely paid them any attention after initially cautioning them that they needed to stay back. According to Digger, they wouldn't need to cross the tape, only stand near the tree.

After nearly five minutes of waiting where nothing happened, Digger leaned down and whispered in J. J.'s ear. "I don't understand. I thought something was supposed to happen. There was a butterfly and all of us hugging and cheering... I just don't get it."

J. J. shrugged. "It's okay. We're still trying to figure all these things out."

Psst.

J. J.'s head jerked up and he saw a large monarch butterfly hovering overhead.

"That's it!" Digger exclaimed. "That's what I saw!"

The butterfly dropped down in front of J. J.

Show your hand.

Automatically, he put out his hand. He saw something shiny fall and then, a moment later, something cool landed in his palm. He waited until the butterfly fluttered away before he looked down. J. J. stared, unable to speak.

"Is that what I think it is?" Digger asked.

J. J. nodded mutely. He held up the gold coin for the others to see.

"Dude, did a butterfly just give you a gold coin?" Aaron asked.

Psst.

J. J. turned around, fully expecting to see the butterfly again. Instead, perched on the side of the tree were two giant woodpeckers.

"Hey, that's what I saw on the trail," Genius said.

"J. J., Aaron, I don't understand." Gabriella walked over to them. "Why are you guys looking at some birds in a tree?"

As the woodpeckers began to drum on the tree, the rest of the parents approached.

"Karli, shouldn't you be looking for your necklace?" Beverly asked.

Before Karli could come up with another lie – or perhaps tell the truth this time – something bounced out of the newly created hole in the tree. Aaron's hand shot out and caught it before it hit the ground.

"Is that a gold coin?" Jonathan asked as Aaron opened his hand.

J. J.'s eyebrows shot up as he realized what had happened. "Porter's treasure! It's in the tree!"

Ignoring the questions and surprised expressions of their parents, Aaron boosted J. J. up into the tree. J. J. crawled across the branch, waiting for the woodpeckers to either fly away or attack, though he was hoping for the former.

Shiny.

J. J. stopped, his mouth falling open. Had the bird just talked to him?

Shiny inside.

Okay, yes, the bird had just talked to him. So, apparently the compass let him communicate with more than just butterflies.

"Can I see in there?" He kept his voice low, hoping no one below would be able to hear him.

Yes.

As J. J. grew closer, the birds hopped up to the branch above the hole. Part of him knew that it was crazy to take his eyes off of the woodpeckers, but he told himself to trust in his grandfather's abilities and peered inside. It took his eyes a moment to adjust, but once they did, he let out a whoop of excitement.

"It's here! The treasure is here!" J. J. stuck his arm into the tree, all thoughts of crazy animals vanishing as he began to pull out handfuls of gold and jewels, sending them down in showers over the others. He heard the exclamations coming from below as the treasure fell, but didn't stop to try to hear exactly what they were saying. He just kept digging until he emptied the entire wooden chest onto the ground below, then dropped down.

The instant his feet were on the ground, his mother grabbed him in a hug as the other kids and their parents scrambled to pick up everything. There was a lot they would need to do, he knew. They'd have to prove their right to the treasure in its entirety and not just a finder's fee. Lloyd, he knew, would help with that. He and his parents would have to figure out how much to give to the other families because even though it belonged to the Hanks family through inheritance, J. J. knew he'd never have found it without his friends. But all of that was a small price to pay for what they'd gained. They wouldn't be moving.

***

It was the Fourth of July and officially J. J.'s favourite holiday. His family stood together on the Grand Hotel porch, mingling with their neighbours as fireworks exploded in the sky. Gone was the former animosity and competitiveness that had always been present in other gatherings. The Hanks family had made it known that the other three families would receive a portion of the treasure and, though the details hadn't been worked out yet, the offer had been graciously accepted by all. Even with paying off their debts and giving the others a percentage of the treasure, the Hanks family had more than enough to make their lives comfortable. Things weren't perfect, J. J. knew, but they were close. He still had questions about the talismans and what these new powers would mean for him and his friends, but he was confident they would be able to get through whatever came their way, as long as they were together.

He looked around at each one, grinning as he saw Genius trying to strike up a conversation with Sandra. The blonde stood between Aaron and Genius, dividing her attention between the two. Karli was on Aaron's other side, looking annoyed at Sandra once more. Digger had found himself a spot standing on the base of one of the pillars – which J. J. was pretty sure wasn't allowed – and was cheering for the loudest fireworks.

J. J. moved away from the group and peered up at the sky. He'd never really thought much about the man after whom he was named, not really in any depth anyway. In the last forty-eight hours, however, he'd come to not only appreciate Lieutenant Porter Hanks, but to think of him with fondness.

"Happy Independence Day, great-great-great-grandpa," J. J. said as he saluted the sky. No matter what happened next, he would face it head on and with the strength that came from being Jonathan Porter Hanks.

CPSIA information can be obtained
at www.ICGtesting.com
Printed in the USA
BVHW030404160219
540451BV00002B/185/P